Avast, Ye Airships!

Edited by
Rie Sheridan Rose

Avast, Ye Airships!

edited by Rie Sheridan Rose

Copyright © 2015

Synopsis

In a daring history that never was, pirates roam the skies instead of the seas. Fantastical airships sail the clouds on both sides of the law. Within these pages, you will find stories of pirates and their prey with a few more pragmatic airships thrown in. With stories ranging from Victorian skies to an alien invasion, there is something for everyone in these eighteen tales of derring-do!

Table of Contents

Editor's Note

Ahoy, mates! Welcome aboard. Here there be pirates. When it was suggested that Mocha Memoirs should do a Steampunk Airship Pirates anthology and that I should edit it, I had absolutely no idea what was involved. I'd been in a lot of anthologies, but never worked the other side of the boat, as it were. It's been a wild ride. We started taking submissions in May of 2014 and ended in December. We had dozens of stories, but I think we picked the best. There are proper pirates, would-be pirates, retiring pirates. There are British pirates, Ottoman pirates, and Confederate pirates. There are pirates with pistols, with swords, with buzzards! There is romance. There is adventure. There is even an alien invasion—with a living airship. In short, I think there is something for everyone within these pages. I hope you agree.

Rie Sheridan Rose
February 2015

Come and Be a Pirate

Leave behind the law and lawyers,
When you leave behind the land—
For the law that rules a pirate
Is you take whate'er you can.

So you want to be a pirate?
Well, repeat after me—
I'll pillage, whore, and plunder
And live the life that's free.

Little boys who listened
When their Mamas said they should
They ain't the kind o' pirates
That will do me any good.

I want a crew that's ruthless
Cutthroats, thieves and ghouls.
'Cause we don't hold tea-parties,
And we don't live by the rules.

We sail upon the heavens,
In an airship tried and true
It's a whole new world of treasure
That we'll find before we're through.

So, if you want to be a pirate
Come on down to the ship.
We need a dozen sailors
To replace those lost last trip!

Rie Sheridan Rose
lyrics from *Dragons vs Pirates*
for Marc Gunn

Beneath the Brass

Stephen Blake

This Journal is the property of Miss Alice Reynolds, and this is my record of the things that are occurring around me.

Thursday 13th April 1878

The doctors, in their wisdom, have allowed me to keep this journal. It was the young doctor, Dr. Wilson, who convinced the others. He thinks jotting down my thoughts might be more helpful than the ice baths and drugs. I'm all for a diary over an induced seizure any day.

I don't know where to start. I know there is nothing wrong with me. I'm a healthy woman of twenty-two years. My parents passed away, and—although my elder brother promised to care for me—here I find myself. In this asylum.

Of course, when I tell people that my brother's love went beyond that of a sibling—when I try to tell people what happened to me—I know that I play into his hands and re-affirm to everyone that I'm disturbed and delusional.

I know I should lie. I just can't do it. I am the one wronged and yet it is I who am being punished.

One of the orderlies decided he knew what I needed to put me right. He's not been seen for a while. Seems a rusty spoon and his scrotum did not mix; no matter how hard I pushed.

No man will touch me again.

The doctors did note my mood had improved. I told them the orderly's new sweet singing voice had cheered my heart. He was squeaky before the incident, but it soothes me to pretend I made him speak so.

Friday 14th April 1878

I'm writing this down here because I can scarcely believe what has happened.

Late last night, this strange metallic creature kicked my door in. I can only describe him as some sort of automaton; brass-like in appearance, but amongst the clockwork mechanisms was a human being.

When I read this back later I will probably think myself mad, for as I stepped beyond my cell I saw numerous amalgams of men and machine each with the visage of a pirate.

One of them spoke to me. He introduced himself as Frank. He was bare-chested, other than a bandolier over his shoulder, various sheathed blades and a couple of pistols. From the waist down, he was machine—merged with a chair with wheels. Steam chugged from this part of him as he whirred around. He explained that they were a liberation force and offered a simple choice; stay at the asylum or leave with his group.

Without hesitation I asked to leave. My fellow patients and I formed a queue, whereby we were briefly questioned as to our ailments. It seems that those with severe mental health issues were promised transport to a facility guaranteeing safety, security, and genuine care. The rest, including those with physical disabilities, were asked if they wanted to join the crew. One man, who could not stand without crutches, asked if he would have to have a machine fitted to his body. The answer given was staggering.

He was told this: "You can have aids if you choose, or if you need them, but we are asking if you wish to contribute what you can, with or without them. All we offer in return is shelter, food, respect and dignity."

Well, the man sobbed his heart out. He replied that "respect and dignity" was all his heart and soul desired, and that he would gladly abstain from food and shelter for some small semblance of dignity.

When they came to me, they eyed me suspiciously. Thankfully, they agreed that I was not in the least bit mad and I confirmed I was physically able. They offered me escape and a new identity. It seems a couple amongst their ranks took exception to helping me until Frank intervened.

He told me as we left that many of the crew harbored resentment to able-bodied people because of how badly they had been treated. I've seen enough with my own eyes to understand this and feel no resentment toward them.

I asked Frank what he had said that made them accept me. He told me that he had reminded his comrades that not all wounds or scars are visible but that they exist all the same.

Saturday 15th April 1878

Yesterday's escape was nothing short of astonishing. Behind the asylum, I was amazed to see airships of various descriptions. Each was a ship of sorts hanging beneath a trio of balloons. One was for the poor souls who were being taken to a place of healing. Their vessel appeared to be enclosed, looking like a whale with numerous portholes. Each window showed a face peering out. I could not meet their gaze.

Another was like a large galleon. The front of the vessel opened to allow us to walk or be carried aboard. Before boarding, I looked right to see the final vessel. It was similar to the one I was boarding except the "pirates" (I'm not sure if that is the right or wrong way to describe them) were using that one as a cargo ship. I believe they were stocking up on medication, various pieces of metal and other bounties the crew had liberated.

We were blindfolded for the duration of the night-time flight. I will not lie, I did not like it one bit. Still, I did as they asked. My face felt the cool breeze and I concentrated on finding my flying legs.

I'm proud to say that I did not throw up. Judging by the retching noises around me, others were not so fortunate. The swaying of the ship under its balloons was a strange sensation, but one I must say I enjoyed and felt quite at home in.

I find myself this morning in a room with fifteen other women. The lodgings are sparse, but the cots are comfortable and the bread they've given us, delicious.

I'm promised a meeting with their leader tomorrow. Captain Hawk is his name. I'm really not sure what to say or ask for.

Sunday 16th April 1878

I actually got more than a few hours of sleep last night. To be sure, the nightmares were still there, but when I woke I felt safe. It's reassuring to know the threat is only in my dreams and that the waking world is a little less threatening.

Daylight leaves my "rescuers'" appearance no less startling. The sun offers them a shine to their metal accompaniments. Some take a break from their aids; their limbs look sore where metal and strapping have rubbed on flesh. I note that many could not get around without the aid of these mechanisms. Once you get past the unusualness of it all, you have to appreciate how marvelously inventive they are and how many of these folk are renewed and able to take on this world.

I'll update again in a bit, when I've seen the Captain.

I'm not sure what to write. I'm at a complete loss for words. I've met an extraordinary man. Well, to begin with, they took me to the highest point at our location. I realize now that we are on an island. A small outcrop really, with accommodations built into the landscape; but mostly there are numerous docking points for airships.

It was to the uppermost docking point that I was taken, where I boarded a small vessel. It had the appearance of a Viking longship, but with lodgings at the stern and all manner of technological devices located throughout the deck.

I was shown aboard and then left alone, so that I might have my meeting with Captain Hawk. I called out, "Hello!" but no one answered. It was then I heard something akin to a small locomotive. I turned to see this automaton, garbed as a pirate, stride towards me.

I must admit, his fierce visage, along with his near seven foot bearing, caused me to step back a couple of paces.

As he came close, he removed his hat, swept it down before him, and bowed low. He—it—had a flamboyant air about him.

He wore a beautiful blue velvet tunic. The brass buttons were so highly polished that they distracted from his grim gray metallic face.

The greatest shock came when he spoke. I can only describe his speech as stilted. Every word had a pause between them, in the way a foreigner tries to seek the correct word to use next.

He asked for my name, if I was well, and if I required anything. It took me a while to decipher his questions, since his speech seemed muffled, like a voice from within a fog.

I found myself speaking to him like he was a simpleton, pausing between words, just as he did when speaking to me.

As we conversed I looked again at him and saw, now, cables or piping, leading from him to the covered area at the stern of the ship. I moved to walk past the Captain, but he blocked my path, stating merely that the area was "off limits."

I cannot lie, my interest was piqued. I've never been good with "off limits" or "not allowed." I managed a pirouette or two and unbalanced my host briefly, before dashing past him.

When I entered the covered area, I found a handsome man, with long dark hair. He sat in a contraption—I'd call it a chair, but there was so much more to it. It seemed to have pipes, wiring, and all sorts of other components running from it. Cocooned within the seat was this man. I circled him, and surmised by the stillness of his body that he was paralyzed, from the neck down, possibly more.

His body appeared languid, thin; his features were strong, but it was his eyes...his eyes were fiercely determined—they radiated a life-force the likes of which I've never met.

His pirate avatar joined us, and I saw now that a series of blinks—which appeared to be monitored by a light that shone on his face—enabled the automaton to speak and move.

It was like a code of some sort. I found myself hearing the stilted speech coming from my prone host and I looked at him intently as he spoke.

We talked then, for what I thought was a short while, until a French gentleman interrupted and advised us that it had actually been hours. The dimming light outside confirmed this. Apologies were made on both sides. I'm slightly shocked to say I asked if I might return and talk with the Captain again. I am delighted to say he agreed.

The Frenchman escorted me back to my quarters. I learnt from him that he, and a few others, were behind the technology I saw around me. It was he who had used phonaughtograms to record words which the Captain then played back to me to mimic speech. He also explained that the person bristling with ideas, and by far the most inventive mind on the ship, was our good Captain.

It's late. I've written here much more than I intended. The other women in the dormitory would like me to put out the light, so I shall sign off for today. I cannot wait until tomorrow.

Sunday 23rd April

Um, well, I've not written for a week. I don't know where the time has gone. I just seem to sit and talk with the Captain each day. He assures me that he is pleased with the company. He is the first man who has ever appreciated my opinion on matters without metaphorically patting me on the head like a good little girl.

The man's spirit is a tempest of strength and intelligence.

I think I may be falling in love with him. He tempers his inner passion with a gentleness that renders me breathless around him.

I'm being silly. Or not. I'm confused. I've never felt this way before, especially about a man, especially after what happened with my brother. That's the strange thing though. I've not dwelled on the past at all. I've not thought about my brother, about revenge. These last few days, I've lived and loved the present, and maybe I'm a little hopeful for the future.

Tuesday 25th April

A shocking thing has happened. A number of the pirate airships had been out rescuing others from asylums, as they did me, and they returned last night with supplies and others rescued, waiting for re-homing, etc.

I was part of the group that welcomed the new arrivals. I was shocked to see that one of the people who walked off the ship was Arnell—the orderly I had had problems with.

My first reaction was to question why he was here. It seems he claimed to another he was permanently physically injured following a brutal attack. Upon seeing me, he named me as the attacker—and accused me of being a spy for the police as well.

These are good people here, generally speaking, but they do not always question things, so a large number immediately believed the effeminate-speaking idiot, and tried to detain me.

Some of the Captain's allies quickly surrounded me and prevented a lynching.

Arnell, a couple of guards, and I went up to see Captain Hawk. The automated, more intimidating, version of him I should add.

Somehow, the Captain already knew what had occurred. The mechanical pirate quickly strode toward Arnell and lifted him high into the air. A piston-driven arm flipped my nemesis upside down like a child might throw around a rag doll. Holding him by the ankle, he dangled him over the side of the ship.

Arnell firstly wet himself, and then, fumbling in his pockets, produced some sort of pistol. Before any of us knew what was happening, a flare was sent up high into the air. Arnell had obviously tried to signal someone.

The Captain, dropped him with one hand, and caught him with the other. Seemingly Arnell thought his work was done in locating us, and promptly spilt the beans that he was here on behalf of a gentleman who sought us, and not on behalf of the Bow Street Runners or such like.

He stared hard at me. I'm proud to say I met that stare, held it, and forced him to look away. The Captain noted this and queried how we knew each other. I, rather embarrassed, told the tale of the rusty spoon. I was not embarrassed for my actions, it must be understood, but rather for my vulnerability. It was odd talking to the machine and not the man, but such is the technology that the automaton held my gaze and tilted its head to one side, seemingly reflecting the real man's concern for me. At least that is how I interpreted it.

This moment between us seemed to have loosened the grip he had on Arnell, who swung himself free of the Captain and lunged at me.

I had never seen a man killed. Good or bad, death by sabre is not quick and despite sometimes thinking of hurting others, I see now that it is not for me. Arnell represented much of what I hated in men—but in that moment I knew pity for him.

I cradled his head as he spluttered and gurgled blood.

It seems he too had an epiphany in that moment. Perhaps knowing he was about to be judged on how he lived his mortal life had an effect on him. I'll never know. I only know he said two things. One, he asked my forgiveness. For the first time in my life, and with the support of the good Captain, I gave it. Secondly, he revealed it was not the Captain and his pirate crew this mysterious person sought, it was me.

Wednesday 26th April

Last night's developments, the terrible loss of life, and the anticipation that someone may arrive any moment looking for me has left my nerves wrecked.

Did anyone see his flare? Who is interested in me? Why?

All I want to do is be with the Captain, but early this morning his airship sailed off. I don't know where he's gone. I'm worried about him.

Thursday 27th April

Right, I understand the whole "absence makes the heart grow fonder" adage. I do understand it. I don't like it though. There is an emptiness within me. He needs to come back. I need him back. I wonder if he feels the same way? I don't care. To know him, to be with him is enough. I just want him to come back to me.

Friday 28th April

Captain Hawk has returned. His automated self held a meeting with his most trusted advisors. Knowing that the real man was tucked away from that gathering I went to him and—propriety be damned—I hugged him for what seemed an age.

I looked into his eyes and I knew he felt just as I did. Tears welled in both of us. Tears of joy.

No news can dampen my happiness at his return, but the information brought back has come close. The person seeking me is my brother. The Captain has called in favors and gathered intelligence. It seems my brother fears what I may say in public about him. We have learnt he has gone into politics and is concerned how I may tarnish his reputation amongst fellow ministers and the public at large.

The outcome of the meeting is that the rescues from the asylums will temporarily halt whilst we move location.

I understand now that we are in the English Channel, not far from the Isle of Wight. It seems arrangements have been in place to move to another location for some time anyway. I very nearly wrote down where, but I think I'll not do that on the chance someone else may one day read this. We do good work, good secret work, and keeping it secret allows it to continue.

The plan is to leave the day after tomorrow.

Sunday 30th April

Moving day.

The most vulnerable left yesterday. Today, the last of us set off with the remainder of the supplies. I travel on the Captain's ship, the *Argonaut*.

We had to delay leaving for a short while, as a terrible storm made it unsafe to set off.

By early evening, the winds had died down and the lashing rain had eased. The ropes were untied and the final three ships crept from their harbors and swept into the clouds.

We did not see our attackers. We heard them. The boom of cannon fire pierced the silent skies.

I stayed close to the Captain and watched as he expertly guided his airship around to meet the assailants.

There appeared to be only one vessel, larger than ours—slower moving, but infinitely more muscular in appearance.

Our ship weaved its way against the wind. As we came alongside the enemy, we fired three harpoons into their hull. With ropes attached, winches dragged our vessel next to theirs until metal and wood groaned as the two hulls met.

Rather than being taken by surprise, our foes hungrily leapt aboard. That was their first mistake. If they had looked to their feet they would have seen the metal mesh all along the decking. A flash of light confirmed the electric current running through it. The smell of singed flesh, and the sight of hopping men confirmed that the first invaders were barefoot, and they quick-stepped back to their own ship.

Three men, obviously different, obviously in charge, arrived on board. Their boots insulated them from the effects of the electrified deck. The Captain's avatar engaged them. He held two sabres, and launched into a fluid, purposeful volley of attacks.

The three men seemed unperturbed by the sight before them. They surrounded the automaton and engaged him with pistols and swords.

Feints, thrusts and parries seemed to go on for an age. I was careful not to distract the Captain, allowing him to concentrate on his maneuvers. I was soon aware that the battle was being drawn out. I could see in the distance the other vessels from our fleet had already gotten away. I whispered this fact to the Captain.

Immediately, out on deck, his avatar's attack became fiercer, as he sought to end the fight. He crossed his arms against his chest, and then, swinging both arms apart in a broad outward slash of his blades, he took out two of the aggressors. They were not dead, but injured enough to stop fighting.

A new attacker seemed to arrive from nowhere with an axe. The automaton leapt forward to avoid his hacking stroke, realizing too late that it was the cables linking it to the Captain that were the true target.

Our metal protector stopped in his tracks. His connection to the Captain severed, he stood still now, no different to an empty suit of armor in a museum.

The axe man returned to his ship. The unwounded gentleman who had been engaged in the sword fight stepped into the accommodation where the Captain and I waited.

As he pulled back the curtain and removed his hat, I saw that it was my brother. I had thought long about what I might say or do, but in his presence I found myself both silent and frozen with fear.

He smiled at me and moved closer. The smell of him made a thousand bad memories flood back into my mind. Still I was immobile.

He did not speak as he drew a small dagger and moved toward my Captain. I threw myself atop my love and held him, whilst I waited for the blade to pierce my body. I looked deep into those beautiful eyes. There was no need for words between us.

He blinked frantically, as if trying to speak to me. I realize now that he was still operating systems.

I briefly heard my brother scream. I only know that I found myself cocooned within a pod with the Captain, ejected from the airship. Wings, of a sort, unfolded from each side of us and we silently rode the wind's breath.

As I looked back, I saw the *Argonaut* explode. The blast would have killed all on board. The remains of the airship fell toward the sea, dragging what was left of the harpooned enemy ship down with it.

I cried for the death of my brother. Cried for the kind boy I'd once known, not the cruel man he had become.

Our pod glided like a bird, until we eventually—with even a little grace—splashed into the dark waters below.

I believe my Captain had it planned all along. Why else would he have my journal with him, if not that I might carry on writing here?

Monday 1st May

We were rescued by our own people a few hours after we splashed down. At no time did I fear drowning or death. I simply held my love in my arms and gazed into his eyes.

We've arrived at our new location and it is stunning. There are facilities to help people, facilities to help people help themselves.

My Captain has a new automaton to use. This one is just as fierce—it even has an eye-patch. I think I may be the wrong person to judge how intimidating he appears. I feel a strong affection for the splendid contraption.

I wondered what was going on, since he sent the machine back to the engineers for several hours. Our French comrade, Edouard, later told me that the Captain had asked for its vocabulary to be enhanced. It seems there were certain words he had never expected to utter.

Tuesday 2nd May

My love and I are aboard our new airship, en route to a church.

Those new words he wanted added to the automaton went like this, "I love you. Will you marry me?"

My heart feels like it is going to explode with joy.

I'm finished with this journal now. It covers a portion of my life, a chapter if you will, that has now ended. I don't need it any longer. I'm going to throw it overboard in a moment.

If you read this, neither of us need your pity or care for your judgments. We simply are two souls that were meant to be together and we need no other approval.

Adieu.

Maiden Voyage

Jeffrey Cook & Katherine Perkins

All indications were that Emily's career was really going somewhere. The invitation to perform aboard the *Sky-Dancer*—the newest, biggest, and most luxurious airship of its kind—on its inaugural voyage had come as a surprise. It also made the trip from Milan to Paris for an upcoming engagement a lot easier. Getting paid to make the journey, instead of paying for it, was a significant bonus.

The launch had been made with no small amount of fanfare. The ship's creators had spared no expense in building the luxury cruiser itself, nor in promoting it. There was music and speeches, and the bottle of champagne that had been broken over the hull at the christening would have cost a year of Emily's pay when she worked with the traveling show. And there was the program billing in shiny embossed letters: *Performances by Emily Carew, the Living Doll!*

During the first afternoon, Emily had the opportunity to work with her tiny support corps of dancers—while reveling in the fact she had a support corps of dancers. After years of dancing her own variations on *'L'espièglerie de Swanhilde'* for people who didn't know who Swanhilde was, she now had more options, more production opportunity. While none of the wind-up toy costumes were quite as authentic as the Living Doll's, with the leg braces that allowed her to continue to walk and dance after her accident and the fine threads of copper that had replaced a good portion of her hair, the costumes were still elaborate, and good imitations. The girls were also pretty good imitators, able to keep up as a background to Emily, even if they didn't quite mimic the mechanical as well. Despite the all-too-brief chance to rehearse, they were picking up her routines and moves well.

Luca rested against the side of the ship. That most of the rich guests aboard the ship avoided her suited her fine. She'd done all right for herself and Emily, working mercenary assignments as they traveled, ever since she bought out her dancer's contract from the show to which medical bills had indentured her. This, however, was a different level of fancy entirely. Even without her cavalryman's cuirass, and wearing fancy gentleman's clothing instead of her usual canvas trousers, Luca didn't feel like she belonged, and the feeling was obviously mutual. The heavy scarring across her face, and the dark leather eye-patch secured directly to her skull certainly didn't help matters any. Still, Emily had been insistent with the recruiters: either Luca had a staff berth on the luxury ship, or Emily wouldn't be dancing for them. Luca had even offered to join the ship's security detail for the voyage, but the recruiter took one look at her and politely declined.

The security guards that she had seen were, in fact, mostly quite a bit prettier than she. They were all armed, at least, but she wasn't sure she'd call it well armed. The pistols were reasonably imposing, but she was pretty certain, based on the decor, that most of those ceremonial swords had never been out of their sheaths.

The security men were universally polite and approachable, in their freshly cleaned uniforms, but she wouldn't swear to the military backgrounds of most of them. While she wasn't permitted to carry them, she made sure she knew precisely where her own old cavalry sword and guns were being stored, just in case.

The time came at last for Emily's first performance aboard the airship. She waited calmly behind the curtains, already rising *en pointe* with a hiss of valves, as she preferred to be ready before the show began, not as the curtains were opening, and to never show audiences real signs that she was anything but what her title suggested. Taking their cue from her, the rest of the dancers took their positions several seconds before the red curtains parted.

Luca had initially been poised to argue with the people handling the seating. Emily was her girl, after all. She thought better of it, for risk of disrupting the show, and managed to settle herself without too much rancor over their efforts to make her as invisible as possible at the back of the room.

The curtains opened, with Emily turning gracefully on her toes, spinning clockwise in contrast to the array of other made-up dolls, twirling counter-clockwise all about her. The graceful dancers became significantly less-so, however, when the ship lurched, then briefly tilted sideways, scattering dancers and audience alike.

Luca managed to grab onto the doorway, keeping herself upright as things devolved into chaos. As the ship righted itself, she raced out the door, heading above decks to see what was causing the problem. The top deck was even more chaotic.

Security was fighting a desperate battle, firing across the gap between themselves and a lighter, faster craft, attached to the *Sky-Dancer* by boarding hooks, with the first of the airship pirates braving the gaps to engage the luxury liner's forces in melee. Though she had to admit that the blue-clad security forces were holding their own better than she'd have given them credit for, it didn't look like they were going to last long. Similarly, she was pretty sure she wasn't going to last very long in a firefight wearing a gentleman's suit and no weapons, so she raced for the cargo hold.

Two security officers ran into the theater room, closing and barring the doors, guns out. They spoke rapidly with the captain, who had attended the show, and now appeared half-panicked. The rest of the ship's officers weren't looking much more composed. Emily scanned the room for Luca, but even though her companion tended to stand out, she saw no signs of her. If there was a problem that had the officers so worked up, she kind of preferred it that way, trusting that, if there was trouble, they were better off with Luca out in it, instead of barricaded in the room.. She made her way over to the small group of officers, and no one objected as she listened to the news.

"They'll kill us all," the captain was whispering loudly, as she arrived.

"Who?" she demanded, looking to the security officers, not the captain.

"Pirates," one answered.

"Pirates? In this day and age?" she asked.

"We'd thought them cleared out some time ago, but obviously they were either laying low, or some got missed. We'd never have launched, or at least would have hired on more security if we'd have thought there was any chance of this," he answered.

Emily frowned. "Your security's understaffed?"

"Well, you see..." started the captain, before the security officer answered.

"More security on hand means less room for guests."

"Wonderful," Emily said with a sigh. "But they won't kill the people here if we handle this right."

The others looked at her quizzically. "Miss Carew," the captain said. "These people are more than capable of murdering hundreds for a few of the place settings, much less for the whole ship!"

Emily laughed. "I've seen the guest list. If some of these people are killed, their families—if not their whole countries—will pay a fortune to hunt down the murderers. Or they'd pay at least the same to get them back alive. Their ransoms are worth far more than the ship, and a few highly placed hostages will be more useful than things they can't fence without leaving a trail. Trust me, just stay calm, and we'll be all right."

The captain looked at her dubiously. "You know a lot about pirates."

She looked back at him evenly. "I danced for the first passengers of the Orient Express. You may have heard what happened there. I have some experience."

She didn't bother mentioning that the 'young man' she traveled with was an ex-soldier turned mercenary. She didn't think that would help much. Regardless, the pair of security guards took her suggestions, working to calm everyone down.

Luca reached the cargo hold where they'd placed her weapons. While normally there was some type of watch posted here, whoever it was had obviously gone to investigate the disturbance. The door was securely locked, but the fourth time she put her shoulder into it, the hinges gave way, giving her access to the room. Luca frantically searched for her things, eventually finding the steamer trunk she shared with Emily, though she had to unbury it. By the time she'd uncovered it and collected her guns and the well-used cavalry saber, she heard voices in the hallway.

The doors to the theater held for a time. Eventually, however, someone on the other side shot out the lock, almost starting a new panic in the room. A tall, white-bearded man in mix-and-match finery entered first, followed by a few less opulently-dressed members of his pirate crew. Though the two security guards had their guns readied, apparently, Emily's suggestions had gotten their attention enough that they surrendered at once instead of firing and sacrificing themselves against the significant number of pirates.

"Where's the captain of this ship?" the pirate leader demanded. "He'll show himself and turn over control of this ship, or we'll see if we can't find a plank for some of this lot to walk." He grinned like he'd just made a great joke, showing off a mouth as mismatched as his wardrobe, with a blend of teeth, gold, and gaps. The crew took the cue, laughing along.

"I...I'm the captain," the Sky-Dancer's skipper offered. "We surrender. You don't need to kill anyone. Let's just talk about this. I'm sure...I'm sure that the people here would offer up quite a substantial reward if you just let us go."

"And how would we go about collecting that?" the pirate responded. "We can negotiate later, when you all start writing home and we figure out who might be worth what."

Three pirates noticed the broken-down cargo door, and entered the room cautiously. Luca cursed herself for not finding some better way in and ducked down behind the steamer trunk.

She didn't dare open fire, for fear of drawing more attention, so she left her gun at her belt and waited, listening to the voices as they coordinated their search of the room. As soon as two of them were close by, with the third working on the opposite side of the room, she stood and attacked.

She took the first entirely by surprise, nearly taking his head off with the swing. The second didn't have time to shout before she was on him as well, cutting him down as he dropped the case he had in hand and fumbled for his weapon. She was lucky with the third, too busy listening to himself complain while rifling through valuables to have heard the bodies drop. She cut him down as he was pocketing some jewelry. She dragged the bodies out of sight and checked the hall, starting her way upward again.

"Captain," Emily began, speaking with quiet poise to the lead pirate, even as the other pirates were starting to survey both the crowd, and the dancers, as if they were ready to get on to the plundering. "You say there'll be plenty of time later. It won't do you any good to have these people panicking. Why don't you give them a show of good faith? Let things settle down while your people go through the passenger list, and maybe you can get through this whole affair without having to kill any of these gentlemen when they try to be a hero. Some of them are worth a lot to someone."

"What did you have in mind?" the pirate captain replied, surprised at this conversation with a showgirl dressed like a wind-up doll.

"We were just starting a performance. Maybe your command crew would like front-row seats? It would be an easy way to keep control of things for a while, and you seem like the type of man who can appreciate a good show."

Luca killed two more pirates on her way out of the cargo area, hiding the bodies in the bays they'd forced open, while she mentally ran through her list. To have any hope, they'd need to do take control of the *Sky-Dancer* back, do something about the pirate ship, and then deal

34

with the rest of the pirates. It was a tall order, but the alternatives weren't good.

She was pretty sure they weren't going to just execute the passengers, but having some of the politicians and old war heroes that were aboard taken prisoner was still a disaster, especially when enemies might pay as much or more than family for many of them, whether to try to steal secrets, or for public executions.

Arriving cautiously on the upper decks, she was surprised at how quiet it was. A bit of scouting revealed a pair of pirates guarding the boarding ropes, still secured to the back of the ship, while the Sky-Dancer's master was by the wheel, explaining the quirks of handling the massive ship to another brigand.

A handful of other pirates moved about the decks, mostly guarding the ship's normal crew. Two realizations hit her at once. First, they needed the normal crew working, and thus probably didn't have enough crew for both ships. Second, she heard music filtering up from somewhere below. The same music she'd heard starting before the pirates began boarding.

"Good girl, Emily," she whispered.

It was a fairly new *polonaise* by Tchaikovsky. The line of dancers showcased straight lines of legs in brisk clockwork steps. The choreography was proceeding just like they'd rehearsed. Emily was sure that later, she wouldn't be able to thank the girls and the musicians enough. It was probably their first time performing in an obviously life-threatening situation.

Freeing most of the crew members proved fairly easy. All it took was a finger to her lips, and they'd looked away. Once she launched her assault on the pirates guarding the work crews, the men had joined in, turning on their guards and making quick and quiet work of it. They followed her commands to put on the dead pirates' clothing to better blend in and be able to assist her.

The *Sky-Dancer's* captain was a different matter entirely. Luca was tempted to throw the man overboard herself when his expression and hesitation nearly gave her away before she could kill even the first of the pirates near him. Thankfully, the men she'd freed had been able to get close enough to help, and the captain—and control of the ship with him—was freed without an alarm going up, though it was a near thing. Even once the pirates were dead, he at first resisted Luca's orders to put on one of their uniforms and continue piloting the ship.

"You're going to get us all killed. The dancer said—" he began.

"The dancer said whatever was necessary to address the exact moment she was talking. She knows me. She was buying time. Even if everyone lives, a lot of you won't want to when the pirates are done with you," Luca insisted. "Now, go get dressed. I need you to fly the ship, or tell me who can."

When she'd finished that particular fight, she spoke to the other crewmen, and got verification that there were more pirates in the engineering room, but they shouldn't be able to hear much of what was happening elsewhere. Most of the pirate ship's officers and a few of the crew had gone below decks some time before, as discussion spread of dancing girls. Luca thought back to some of Emily's practice sessions, and tried to guess at just how much or how little time she had.

As the music reached the height of its playfulness, Emily threw herself into a long sequence of quick *tacquetée* steps and sudden leaps, moving in erratic orbits amidst the other dancers, playing up the clockwork aesthetic for all it was worth. Sometimes, this Tchaikovsky fellow's music seemed just made for her. Emily thought he really ought to consider specializing in toy dancers.

Luca managed to get fairly close to the guards at the back of the ship, but they were on alert, and there was no way to get around them. Finally, she just trusted in engine noise and the music, along with having cleared the deck for the time being, and charged. The first got a shot off, but it went wide. Luca's shoulder crashed into him, and he tumbled over the back rail, screaming all the way down. She managed to bring her sword around, chopping down the other man as he fired his gun. Another miss, thanks to her quick reactions, but close enough to leave her ears ringing.

The Living Doll and her toy *corps de ballet* resumed their contrasting turns as the music returned to its earlier strains, slowly coming literally full circle. Between her gradually more staggered pirouettes, Emily counted pirates. The men in ragtag uniforms seemed more relaxed than the rest of the audience. Understandable, considering who had the weapons. The pseudo-mechanical woman was 'winding down,' but her mind was racing.

Luca inched across the boarding ropes, moving hand over hand along a rope from the underside. It was more difficult, and far more dangerous, than crawling over the top. Luca reasoned, however, that it was not as dangerous as being seen. She pulled herself up onto the pirate ship, noting the handful of men moving about the decks, and guessed she'd been right about not having enough of them to crew both ships. They still far outnumbered her, however, so she had to find a way to disable the ship quickly and for good.

Sneaking past a few of the pirates, she made her way to their engine room, killing one man along the way. The door was unlocked, but she drew attention right away. A shout went up from one of the engineers, and half a dozen men came toward her at once, while she heard footsteps from above as well.

She managed to get one shot off before they were on her, then she was on the defensive, readying her sword and backing up to a wall. The one saving grace was that no one seemed to have guns. Of course, she reasoned, that made a certain amount of sense, given the coal-fed steam engines. An accident with gunfire could be a disaster for the whole ship.

There was polite applause from the tense crowd—and very impolite applause from the pirates, complete with lewd suggestions—as the music ended and the dancers stilled like spent clockworks, then took their bows.

"Well," Emily announced, turning to the snaggle-toothed pirate captain. "The gentlemen could see a bit more if we did an encore—if you think that's a good idea, sir."

"I did like all the parts with the kicking," the pirate said. "Let's have a bit more of that."

Emily's painted smile widened brightly. "That's a perfect idea, sir."

After a quick word with the other dancers, she called to the musicians, "A quadrille, gentlemen. Any quadrille, but skip to the finale."

A good, loud encore quickly started up.

Luca had dropped three of the engineers by the time reinforcements arrived. In turn, she'd taken a couple of nasty cuts and one bad bruise from attacks with their various tools.

Having heard more people coming, she'd fought her way nearer to the engine, managing to acquire a shovel along the way. As better-armed pirates moved in, she whirled about, attacking anyone who dared get too close with saber in one hand and shovel in the other. While the latter was somewhat more unwieldy, she had to admit, it made a pleasant sound ringing off the skull of a pirate. She knocked over one of the bins of coal after setting her feet, making their footing far more precarious.

With slightly more room—but only slightly—she swung her sword wide to back them off, causing one of the men to trip, and stuck her shovel into the red hot engine, then swung that about as well, flinging burning coals at the attackers and around the room. When half of the people fighting her quickly shifted their attention to trying to put out the embers before fires started, she collected another shovel full of coal, and weaved away from the attackers, kicking over another bin, and tossing the hot cinders into the debris, starting new fires. The blaze was growing rapidly as she fought her way past the last people paying her any mind and raced out of the engine room, pulling the door shut behind her.

Emily was proud of her fellow dancers. There were no protests of "but it wasn't supposed to be that sort of job" and not a single "I'm not that kind of girl." Emily told them to alternate high kicks and *battements* and follow her lead, and each of them was doing her best, with all the energy of a music hall. Their more respectable clientele would no doubt survive watching a cancan line. At least they would if this gave Luca even a little more cover.

Luca reached the boarding ropes. With the fires having spread beyond the engine room, no one was paying her any attention at all. She sawed through most of the ropes to make sure the pirate ship wouldn't take the *Sky-Dancer* down with it.

Even if they saved the pirate ship, it wasn't going to be in any shape to pursue. She didn't think she had time to make her way across, and then cut it loose, especially since word had to get out about the fire sooner or later.

When she was down to one final rope, she grabbed it as tightly as she could, stepped over the rails, and cut it.

She barely had time to sheathe her sword and grab the rope with both hands before she was pulled off of the pirate ship and out into open air, swinging across the gap. She was grateful for her gloves and their extra grip, managing to barely hold on when the rope went taut. After wincing a moment, she verified that—despite her initial impressions—her shoulders were still in their sockets.

Luca started climbing.

Two pirates burst into the room where the performance was taking place, just as the encore had been drawn out as far as it could go. They attracted quite a lot of attention, particularly from the pirate captain, as they raced up, and shared their news with him in hushed tones.

"What?!" he bellowed, before shouting to his first mate, "Guard these lot, I'll see what's going on." He gestured to three of his men. "You're with me, the rest of you, stay here."

Nervous glances were cast around the room at this new development.

Emily stepped up to the front of the stage. "Everyone is doing well. Just stay calm a little longer. I'm sure everything will be all right."

Luca pulled herself up over the rails. Everything ached after the fight, and especially after the climb. All she wanted to do was lay there and catch her breath, but shouts from further along the ship spurred her back into action. She cut down the first very surprised pirate who reached her position, all his attention on the burning vessel. The second grabbed her sword arm before she could recover and swing again. He held on as two other pirates approached, one of them an older man with a limp. From his manner of dress and the commands he was shouting, Luca guessed the older man might be their captain. Rather than trying to pull free, Luca grabbed her closest opponent's belt and fell backwards, managing to wrench her arm—and sword—away from him as he pitched over the rails.

Just as she was getting to her feet, she had to dive out of the way again, and a shot tore up the wood of the deck where she'd just been standing. The older man's first shot grazed her leg, and his second bloodied her face when the near miss kicked up a hail of splinters from her hiding place. The pair continued to approach, with the occasional shot ringing out to keep her pinned down.

"I don't know who you are, but you're a dead man!" the pirate captain shouted between gunshots.

Emily helped settle the crowd from the stage, while the pirates prowled the room uneasily. With the Captain and his accompaniment gone, Emily counted only eight remaining. Two of those stepped outside the door to await their captain's return. Three took positions around the room to keep an eye on the crowd, while the first mate and two others stepped up to the front of the stage to address the prisoners. With most fearful eyes on him, Emily managed to catch the gaze of one of the security officers who'd first alerted them to the threat. She thought there was a slight nod.

"Show's over, folks," the first mate began. "I don't know what kind of trouble is up out there, but don't think we won't—"

He never got the next words out, as Emily kicked him in the back of the head with one copper-and-brass-reinforced leg. There was a ringing of metal off bone, and the man dropped. Two of the other dancers, having gotten used to watching Emily and taking their cues from her, launched themselves off the stage to tackle one of the other pirates. The security officer was up and wrestling for a gun with a brigand who'd ended up near him. The rest of the room erupted into chaos, as Emily lashed out at the next nearest target.

Hearing the pair closing in, Luca steeled herself, took a deep breath, and emerged from cover, taking her shot while she could and firing at the nearest voice. The surprised pirate dropped, clutching at his stomach.

The older man in mis-matched finery turned his gun on Luca. She managed to close the gap enough to knock the shot aside, but still felt a burn along one arm where the shot grazed her. Her cut caused him to drop the gun and stagger back, but he drew a blade of his own, facing off with her. Even as the two crossed blades, she saw small melees breaking out about the deck of the ship as more of the pirates made three discoveries. First, they were leaving their ship further and further behind. Second, their ship was burning. Third, not all the apparent pirates on deck were what they appeared. The *Sky-Dancer*'s crew might not have been as well-armed, but now they had numbers on the pirates.

As the fighting jostled the *Sky-Dancer*'s captain at the wheel, the ship rocked and jolted. Luca and her opponent both nearly lost their feet a couple of times. She had to admit, the pirate leader was clearly well-trained with the blade. Likewise, he showed no hesitation in continually trying to maneuver himself to take advantage of her blind side. While even before the eye-patch, she'd only ever been an average shot, when she held her sword, few people lasted long enough to try to make use of the blind spot. Even without the handicap, she wasn't sure she would have been his better. With it, she was continually forced backwards, fighting defensively, until he had her back against the rail.

Emily dropped another pirate with a kick, as he was trying to regain his feet. She noticed the other security officer and a few of the former hostages joining in the fight, trying to overwhelm the remaining pirates with numbers. Had they not turned their back on her, had they not split their numbers, or had the ship not pitched and taken almost everyone off their feet, giving people a chance to overwhelm the armed men, she wasn't at all sure they'd have done as well. There were wounded, especially from the effort to take down the sentries who'd stationed themselves just outside the room.

Emily herself had taken a shot, and had the deep dent in one of her leg braces to prove it. She couldn't help musing that she'd have just been crippled, if not for her expensive augmentations from having already been so.

As the last skirmishes settled, Emily set herself to organizing the room. The security officers and anyone else who felt they had something to offer—and could borrow armaments from the defeated pirate guards—were sent above decks or set to guarding the doors.

Everyone with any kind of medical knowledge was asked to get to work helping the injured, while anyone who fell into neither category was asked to either help those of the wounded who could move to get up on stage, out of the way, or to simply stay out of the way themselves.

Luca parried attack after attack, desperately fighting off the pirate captain's efforts to run her through, or drive her back over the rail. She had already almost lost her balance half a dozen times and nearly pitched overboard. Fatigue was settling in after all of her efforts, and her hand was starting to go numb from the numerous impacts of the swords. He was still trying to maneuver to her blind side, attacking from his position of strength.

"I give you credit, sir," the pirate captain taunted. "I don't know what unit you were with, but you were obviously a soldier, and you've fought like an officer and a gentleman. It's over, though."

Luca parried his next attack and pressed back. She wasn't going to last long, matching him strength for strength, especially in her current state, but she held on for the moment. "Thanks," she responded, the comment inspiring a last ditch idea.

She snapped her head forward, smashing the captain's nose with her forehead. He staggered, almost losing his balance. A moment later, he did lose his head after dropping his guard while trying to stay on his feet. "I suspect you're the only person on board who thought I was a gentle anything."

Later on, Emily was sure, there would be speeches praising the people who helped fight off the pirate attack. Those who died would be named, and called heroes. She had a sneaking suspicion that neither she nor the other dancing girls would get much credit, which suited her fine.

Luca, on the other hand, had graciously accepted the position of head of security for the remainder of the trip, and the pay to go with it. She was pretty sure that there would be a bit of extra pay, to assure the company wouldn't end up having to praise the scarred mercenary in front of any genteel crowds. That also avoided any awkward questions, of course.

"All set for Paris?" Luca asked, near the end of the journey, with France in sight.

"After this trip? I can't wait. Maybe you'll finally get to see me perform this time." Emily answered, holding Luca's hand as they admired the view of the French countryside rolling below.

"Wouldn't miss it."

Colonel Gurthwait & the Black Hydra

Robert McGough

A pair of elderly men, so alike in looks that they could have been brothers, sat in the trophy room of the Rodania Blade and Barrel Club. Pipe-smoke threaded through their thick mustaches as the two slowly leafed through the day's broadsheet. *The Lundgrin High Herald* was one of the more sensationalist presses, having made its way on the coverage of the "Haymarket Horror." It was a favorite of the club however, having given rather favorable coverage to some of its members in their exploits in the art of hunting.

The high-backed armchairs the two sat in were so overstuffed as to nearly engulf the men, creating tiny forts of privacy. Too old now to go out and hunt themselves, they relied on their past deeds to ensure their continued membership. That, and the sizable wealth they had accumulated over a life-time of wandering the forgotten places of the world—a wealth they used to sponsor other up-and-coming young hunters.

"Says here the Black Hydra took another merchant ship," said Arthur White, around the stem of his ivory pipe.

Howard Jennings nodded. "Heard they raised the bounty. Two thousand crown royals."

A pair of eyes, beneath incredibly bushy eyebrows that had only recently grown back, began trying to furtively peek over Jennings' chair.

White winked discreetly at his old friend. "Someone will get a knighthood out of this one, I'm sure."

A twinkle of laughter sparkled in Jennings' stark blue eyes. "Oh, quite right. Surely a knighthood."

If the men heard the muffled squeak of barely repressed excitement that emanated from behind the chair, they tactfully ignored it.

White continued. "Third ship in a month. All in the Port St-Lucie sky-lanes. Shouldn't be too hard to find, I expect."

When the sound of quickly receding footsteps reached their ears, they glanced around the backs of their chairs to see Colonel Gurthwait quickly making for the door. Chuckling to themselves, they resumed thumbing through their papers.

"Think we should tell him?" asked Jennings.

White laughed. "Oh I am sure he'll figure it out. I mean, surely the man will do at least a *little* research before heading out."

Wind whistling through his thick sideburns, Colonel Gurthwait scanned the skyline with his glass, hoping to catch sight of the beast before it caught sight of them. The sky was far from clear, half filled with thick, gray clouds that looked to bring a storm sooner rather than later. The captain of the *Lady's Favor*, a dour dwarf named Sergei, did his best to keep them wide of the storm clouds, though it was proving to be a losing battle.

With a sigh, the hunter folded up his umbrella and started climbing down from the crow's nest, taking care to make sure the sun shield did not catch in the ropes.

Several crewmen were already in the rigging, readying the ship for the coming storm, scurrying up and down the ropes with a grace and ease that made the Colonel quite jealous. With another melodramatic sigh, he jumped down the last couple of feet, landing beside the squat dwarf captain who was looking up at him expectantly.

After one last wistful look to the rapidly nearing cloud banks, he faced the dwarf. "Let's call it a day, Sergei. I doubt it'll be out in weather like this."

"*Da*," replied the captain, his voice thick with a Rus accent.

The dwarf was less than pleased to be racing around the Port St-Lucie sky-lanes for weeks on what he considered to be a wild goose chase, but having taken the Colonel's money, was obliged to do so, no matter how strange the man's requests had been. Stomping off, he began bellowing orders to the half dozen crewmen nearest to him.

The wind was picking up, and Gurthwait felt the first few raindrops begin pattering around him. Voicing a curse under his breath, he began heading for his cabin under the protection of his umbrella. He was almost to the gangway leading down when a particularly fierce gust of wind snatched the umbrella from his hand, whipping it towards the starboard side. With a cry, he dashed after it, coming within a scant few inches with the tips of his fingers before it sailed over the railing, out into the sky sea.

As if taunting him, it bobbed and swirled just out of reach for a moment, and then sailed off in the eddying torrent of the winds. He watched as it disappeared into the gray clouds that engulfed the ship on all sides now and pounded the oaken railing with a tight fist. He stared after it in the forlorn hope that it might suddenly reappear thanks to the vagaries of luck, but it was not to be.

As the rain began coming down harder, he started to turn and head below decks, resigned to the fate of future dreadful sunburns, when a flicker of movement caught his eye. Whipping his head around, he could see a speck of inky blackness started to emerge from the gray of the clouds. As the spot grew, excitement began boiling up within the hunter.

An evil looking black head parted the clouds. Clearly reptilian in nature, it had two long sweeping horns that curved back over its broad skull. A half moment later, two more heads, one to either side of—and identical to—the first, roiled out of the clouds. Gurthwait cried out in joy and excitement, his quarry at last at hand.

That cry became strangled as the trio of heads were not all that came from the gray. Instead of the sinuous body of a hydra connected to the heads, there was the prow of a massive skyship.

Gurthwait's eyes widened as he realized that the black hydra was, in fact, the *Black Hydra*—a ship, not a creature. A ship flying an ominous flag.

Cursing himself for a fool, he ran for the prow, shouting all the way, "Pirates to starboard!"

Around him, a crew which had been moving with practiced purpose, erupted into a whirlwind of activity. Sergei dove for the wheel, taking it from the helmsman, and screaming orders at the top of his lungs. The first mate, Jurgen, a heavily muscled man, began passing out cutlasses from the weapons' locker.

The *Lady's Favor* was normally only lightly-armed, with but a pair of cannon to either side. Gurthwait, however, had paid to have a trio of harpoon guns put on each side to aid him in his hunt, as well as having hired crewmen to use them, so the ship was better prepared for a pirate attack than it might have been otherwise. Seeing the dozen or so cannon bristling from the sides of the *Black Hydra*, the hunter knew they were still massively outgunned.

Reaching the prow, he ran towards a tarp-covered contraption, rain stinging his face all the while. Snatching the covering off, he revealed his pride and joy, his Sorin-Graph Tri-barrel hunting rifle mounted to a sturdy, swiveling tripod. The gleam of steel meeting tenderly polished oak brought a spark to his eye as he slid behind it, matching butt to shoulder.

The pirate vessel had come on too quickly to escape, so flight turned to fight as Sergei ordered men to the guns. The captain had to struggle to be heard over the wind and rain, which was threatening to turn into a full-blown storm at any moment. Beside him, Andreaus, the ship's bladejack, leaned into the wind with a sword in each hand, grinning with mad-eyed anticipation.

The ships closed, each angling to try to gain the better firing position. Gurthwait could see the enemy ship run out its guns, readying to fire, their nine port side guns far outstripping his ship's two. Swearing, he took sight down the barrel.

The deck of the *Black Hydra* was surprisingly empty—likely because most of the crew was below deck manning the cannons. A half dozen bladejacks stood along the railing, chanting some haunting war-song that only faintly managed to reach his ears. Beyond that, he could only see what looked to be the helmsman, captain, and a few men in the sails. An evil slit of a grin split his face as he pulled the trigger.

The mouth of the topmost barrel erupted in flame. A massive .700 grain bullet went spiraling across the gulf that separated the two ships. The one drop of rain that touched it in its flight instantly vaporized into steam, so hot was its passing. With a thunderous crash, it drove through the pirate ship's wheel, shattering the top half of it into a rain of splinters, then carried through into the helmsmen, sending him flying backwards.

With no hand on the shattered wheel, the *Black Hydra* tilted frightfully. Several of the bladejacks tumbled backwards, while one man fell screaming from the rigging. The captain, a gaunt orc, took a sword from his belt, and stabbing it into the wheel hub, began trying to right the ship.

Sergei struck during the chaos. The order to fire came through the storm, overpowering even the rumbling thunder. The two cannons launched their loads into the side of the pirate ship. One ball struck a cannon bay, destroying it, while the second tore a huge swathe of rigging down.

Gurthwait ratcheted his rifle, causing the barrels to rotate. Taking aim at the orc captain, he eased the trigger just as a flash of lightning split the air between the ships. Half blinded, his shot went wide, instead cutting down a nearby bladejack. Cursing furiously, he ratcheted in the third barrel.

The enemy ship had righted itself. The ships were close enough now for the harpoon guns to fire, which they did. Two more pirates dropped, but in return, the pirate captain at last called the order to fire.

Eight balls launched themselves into the *Lady's Favor*. In a heartbeat, the well-ordered ship disintegrated into a whirlwind of wood splinters and hot lead. The screams of broken crewmen reached the hunter's ears even though he was practically deafened due to the cannon fire. Both starboard cannons and two of the harpoon launchers were completely destroyed. Gurthwait knew they were done for, their only hope being to spin the ship, which would give the pirates time to launch volley after volley into them.

The force of the blasts had knocked him away from his own gun. Stepping back into it, he sighted down the barrel once more. He began seeking the enemy captain, hoping to sever the head of the snake attacking them.

As he panned across the pirate ship's side, his keen eyes crossed the hole blasted by their earlier cannon shot. Within it, he could see a pair of men rolling a barrel towards the cannons. Knowing it could only be gunpowder, he fired.

A massive explosion ripped through the center of the Hydra. Bits of ship, men, and cannons burst outwards, leaving a flaming hole in its side. It was quickly joined by a trio of additional explosions as other powder kegs caught. The deck buckled and the ship threatened to split in half. Its mast—leaning precariously forward—began to topple over.

The few pirates left raced around to try to put out the fires before they could spread to the main powder store, but it was a futile effort. With a deafening crack, the Hydra burst in half in a hail of fiery death. So close were the ships that bits of flaming debris rained down on the *Lady's Favor*, sizzling under the torrents of rain pouring down.

The crewmen cheered, even as they raced around to put out what fires resisted the storm's force.

In the trophy room of the Rodania Blade and Barrel Club, there are all manner of fearsome creatures mounted on its walls. There is only one ship's figurehead, however, and it dominates the northernmost corner of the room. Beneath it is a brass plate that reads:

The *Black Hydra*

Hunted and Slain by

Sir Reginald Gurthwait

It is the only trophy of a non-living creature in the club. The fight to include it was fierce—causing no less than four members to tender their resignations in disgust. Its inclusion won out, however, mostly thanks to the rather sheepish defense from a pair of shamefaced old hunters who forevermore swore off practical jokes.
They even paid for the mounting.

Captain Wexford's Dilemma

Ogarita

Captain Wexford leaned her head against the frame of a viewport that spanned half the bulkhead of her cabin and tried to draw comfort from the bucolic scene below. Sunlight sparkled on the slow-moving River Wye, and the rooftops of Little Tingeford peeked above a thick canopy of elms and oaks. Almost directly below, the stones of a small, ancient church glowed in the afternoon sunlight. Much of its surrounding churchyard lay shadowed by the massive gas-filled balloon of Her Majesty's Airship *Boadicea* and its almost equally large steel gondola. The deck plate under Wexford's feet pulsated almost imperceptibly, a reminder the engines were in good operating order, if doing nothing more critical right now than keeping the ship aloft in what she devoutly hoped was a temporary mooring.

Beside her desk, a sound-powered phone hung in a leather holster attached to the bulkhead. A voice whispered for several seconds. Wexford couldn't make out the words, but then, she didn't particularly want to.

The ship swung slightly, and a metal mooring mast, almost as high as the ship's balloon, slid into view. Wexford's eyes traveled the length of the stout metal cables that ran from airship to mast then down to the mast's four massive legs. Three were anchored in a field, where cows grazed peacefully in the shadow of the airship above. The last leg lay just outside the stone wall of a small churchyard.

Next to this leg lay a thick, coiled metal cable that, five days earlier, had been lowered from the *Boadicea.*

Wexford regarded the cable with loathing.

It was intended to be attached to a tractor near the base of the mast, whose power would help the Deck crew pull the ship to a regulation-safe position closer to the ground. Instead, the tip of the cable had impaled itself in a corner of the churchyard.

A sailor on the ground had immediately scurried over the stone wall; the First Lieutenant had reported to Wexford that no graves or stones had been damaged. Extraction of the cable tip, however, would take several hours, and as the day had been coming to a close, Wexford had acceded to the First Lieutenant's request that this effort be left to the following day.

Far more important—or so it had seemed at the time—were tests the Chief Engineer was running on the steam plant while *Boadicea* awaited an open berth in the Royal Navy Airship Yard, where she was scheduled to spend the next six months in overhaul.

Wexford had dashed off a note of apology to the vicar of St. Michael's, Little Tingeford then dismissed the incident from her mind.

Until just after midnight, when the voices began. Things had gone downhill quickly over the ensuing week.

Knuckles rapped on the open door of her quarters, and a barrel-chested man with a shiny head appeared. The unhappy expression of the *Boadicea*'s command master chief boded no good.

Wexford suppressed another sigh.

"Yes, Barrowman?"

"Cap'n, just wanted you t'know Miss Soaring Dove of the Autumn's left the ship. One of the bosons took 'er down the slide."

Something suspiciously like a chuckle emanated from the sound-powered phone.

"Any results?" said Wexford.

Barrowman heaved a gusty sigh. A strong stink of cigarettes and sardines filled Wexford's nostrils.

"No, ma'am. She—Miss Soaring Dove, that is—says as how the ship's well and truly cursed, and nothin' can undo it. Which is to say everything's as mucked up now as it was this morning. And yesterday. And the day before that, and—"

Wexford held up a hand.

Another voice whispered from the phone. Wexford restrained an impulse to rip it from its holster and throw it out the viewport.

"Who's next?"

Barrowman pulled a crumpled piece of paper from a pocket. "At thirteen-hundred the Reverend Gerald Addington will come onboard. Commander Goss is on the quarterdeck t' meet him. Then, at fifteen-fifteen, we've got Mr. Joyous Able Goodbody."

"Who's he?"

"Voodoo, ma'am. He comes recommended by young Shalakins, down in Engineering, whose mum belongs to Goodbody's congregation. Apparently he's highly thought of there."

Wexford's lips twisted. For three days now a parade of men and women representing a dizzying array of religions had tramped up the gangplank clutching carpetbags and promising relief from the lunacy that had infected the ship via that cursed cable.

Bells rang. Chants echoed down passageways. Leaping, whirling dance shook the deck plates. A shaman had thrown off his robes and attempted to embrace the chadburn in an indecent manner, claiming the machine the source of the infestation. The sacrifice of a chicken on the mess deck had caused two seamen to vomit noisily over the rail, and several hundred candles on the quarterdeck, lit by a hopeful high priest, had reduced the Safety Officer to hysterical warnings about the sensitive hydrogen within *Boadicea*'s enormous rigid balloon.

It all amounted, Wexford reflected, to an undignified hustling of assorted rabbits' feet on and off the ship. And every one had proved as effective as one might expect from rubbing vermin fur against modern machinery.

The Britannia Royal Naval College had provided her with an outstanding education in the mechanics of airships, navigation, battle tactics and strategy, and in all these areas she had excelled. Alas, not one of the College's great minds had thought to impart advice on how to grapple with an invasion of—Wexford hated even to think the word—the dead. More precisely, the voices of the dead that had taken advantage of a damnably errant cable.

"Has the incense been blown out of the berthing areas?"

"Should be finished late this afternoon. Doc says the two asthma attacks should improve by tomorrow."

"And the sage-and-cow-dung mixture the witch doctor spread about?"

"Every knee knocker and porthole's been scrubbed. Smell's still a bit strong, though, especially near the bridge. Um..."

"Yes?"

"A few of the lads—Methodists mostly—have asked to be excused from Mr. Goodbody's voodoo ritual. They got Religious Views on the subject."

"I didn't hear any complaints about Miss Berkeley's séance yesterday, and surely Methodists have views about Spiritualism?"

"Yes, ma'am, but...well, I mean, did you see her, Captain? She could've conjured ten devils for all they cared, as long as she smiled them pearly whites and jiggled her, uh..." Barrowman coughed.

Wexford turned back to the porthole. The *Boadicea* had moored here after an eight-month underway, awaiting an open berth at the Royal Navy's Airship Yards, a few miles distant. Rather than fuming at this delay, Wexford had actually looked forward to a few quiet days before the ship became caught up in the clamor and dirt and upheaval of a yard period. Half the crew had been sent on leave as soon as the ship had moored, and she had hoped those still aboard could enjoy a relaxed schedule.

Another rap sounded on the door, and a slender man with an oversized mustache hovered on the threshold at respectful attention.

Wexford eyed her executive officer. "Yes, Goss?"

"The Reverend Addington is in the chapel, ma'am, donning his vestments. Quite a few sailors have showed up for the... *event*." Goss's voice dripped with disapproval. "They should be ready for you shortly."

An involuntary smile tugged at Wexford's mouth. "Commander, an exorcism, while unusual, is a perfectly respectable ritual within the Church of England."

"It's unseemly, ma'am, if you'll allow me the liberty of saying so. All of this is damned embarrassing, especially the Chervil incident yesterday." Goss didn't handle the inexplicable happily.

"Has anyone come to claim Mr. Chervil's body?" asked Wexford.

"His son will be here this evening," said Goss.

The late Mr. Chervil had been among the first to answer Wexford's desperate pleas for spiritual assistance in ridding the ship of the disembodied invaders. And, while his fate had been sad, his last words had provided some insight into the *Boadicea*'s dilemma before expiring.

In plunging deep into the churchyard, it seemed, the errant cable had acted as a sort of telegraph wire, providing the departed of St. Michael's, Little Tingeford, an opportunity to abandon what should have been their final resting places and stampede upward...not to Heaven, alas, but to what they seemed to believe was an even more agreeable outlet: Wexford's ship.

Barrowman sighed. "A pleasant man, Mr. Chervil. I thought he was getting somewheres, communing with them crazy voices. Shame his heart took bad like that."

Muffled laughter erupted from the phone.

The voices were now entrenched in their new home. Communication between the ship's various departments and decks, which hitherto had been swift and simple via the sound-powered phones, was interrupted by voices expressing views that ranged from flowers to fornication.

The Chief Engineer had reported that one particularly cranky voice continually berated his people about paint and a minor boiler valve repair. Attempts to call up steam using the bridge chadburn were thwarted when that normally reliable piece of equipment abruptly and unaccountably ceased to function, and the phones were taken over by an ongoing, vituperative conversation between three vicars, each of whose interpretation of St. Paul's epistle to the Hebrews apparently maddened the other two.

Worse followed.

Everything else having failed, Wexford finally yielded to pleas from her staff and appealed to religious authorities for a solution. Admitting this move to the Admiralty had ranked as the worst day of her career...until she discovered that, with the mysterious wings embarrassing news seems always to possess, word of *Boadicea*'s troubles had flown throughout the fleet.

The airship *Excelsior*'s commanding officer, whom *Boadicea* had bested two years running for the Battle Effectiveness pennant, sent the first message: *Regret to hear of your spirited problems. Hope you're not laid out by it all.*

Spooky, wrote the captain of the *Princess Royal*. He had held a grudge against Wexford since their midshipman days, when a liberty-port incident in Rangoon found him—after a night of revelry—chained to a statue of the Buddha in the Golden Temple, wearing only a feathered boa and a sign that read "Spank Me." *Sins caught up with you at last?*

Barrowman coughed. "Er, any more word from the Admiralty, ma'am?"

"Admiral Clemens sent a message this morning. I have twenty-four hours to work out the situation or—" Wexford turned back to the viewport, "—I shall be relieved."

Barrowman's jaw dropped. "But...that's not right, captain! Not right at all!"

Goss's face turned pink. "Everyone knows this isn't your fault, Captain. Those jackasses at the Airship Yard, *they're* the ones who fouled up the schedule and forced us to moor here. They're the ones who ought to be held responsible for siting the blasted mooring mast next to a churchyard. That you should be relieved is outrageous!"

Wexford shrugged. "It all ends up on my shoulders. You know that. Complaining won't do us—or me—any good."

The sound-powered phone chittered softly.

"What are they talking about now, do you suppose?" said Wexford.

"Last I checked," said Goss, "some old goat was complaining about the valve inspection again. Apparently it's not up to his standards."

"And Mrs. Pendleton-Shirt is being very sharp with some of the lads today," said Barrowman. "Petty Officer Lappstrop got a bit impatient at not being able to communicate with the bridge and said something a bit, er, *strong* over the phone. Mrs. P's threatened to find Lappstrop's grandmother and tell her what a rascal he is. Gave him quite a turn, as his gran's buried up Yorkshire way."

Wexford rubbed her face with a weary hand. "So, there's nothing more we can try?"

Barrowman and Goss exchanged glances.

"There's something," said Barrowman. "The Chief Engineer suggested it this morning."

Goss snorted. "Another preposterous idea, Captain, I assure you."

"More preposterous than being invaded by the dead?"

"Very close, ma'am."

"Mebbe," said Barrowman. "But at this point, doing somethin's better than floppin' over dead. Right, Cap'n?"

"You could have found a happier metaphor, Master Chief." Wexford pushed away from the viewport. "Let's go see the Chief Engineer."

"Young Sherman's got an idea worth hearing, Captain." With a grimy handkerchief, the Chief Engineer dabbed ineffectually at smears of grease on his face and hands. "Talented boiler tech, she is. More to the point, she's from Little Tingeford."

He gestured at a slender figure behind him, whose skin and coveralls were so filthy that only the eyes and a glimpse of pearly teeth revealed Sherman wasn't an animated pillar of grunge.

A series of wolf whistles emanated from a sound-powered phone dangling on a nearby bulkhead.

Something inside Wexford snapped. She seized the phone and held the mouthpiece close.

"GET OUT OF HERE, YOU BASTARDS! Before I dig up your bodies and feed them to the first dogs I can find!"

A startled silence fell.

Then, from the phone, several voices snickered.

"It's no good, Captain," said Goss. "It just amuses them."

Wexford dropped the phone as if it was a venomous snake. "If the vicar's exorcism doesn't work, perhaps we should—"

"Ma'am?" said a soft voice. "I-I think my granddad might be able to help. He was a...a sort of a sailor."

Wexford had forgotten about Sherman.

"Oh? He knows about phone circuits?"

"N-no, ma'am."

"Does he serve on an airship?"

"No, ma'am."

"Then what good is he in this circumstance?"

"He's dead."

Wexford stared.

"Fifteen years now," nodded Sherman. She fell in bashful silence.

The Chief Engineer nudged her. "Out with it, lass. The captain needs to know all."

"All what?" Wexford prompted.

"He's buried down below," said the Chief Engineer.

"You mean he's...he's one of *them*?"

"Oh, no, ma'am. At least, I've not heard his voice. Anyway, I don't think this lot would've invited him along. You see, he's not *exactly* in the churchyard because he, um..."

"Get on with it!"

"He c-couldn't be buried there because he was an—" Sherman blushed, "—atheist." She whispered the last word. "The vicar and the vestry folks, they said he'd foul holy ground."

An atheist? Few people cared to admit to that particular religious dissension. The Church of England wielded considerable power in the empire, and a self-proclaimed atheist in a family's midst constituted a serious social embarrassment.

But then, even in the finest houses in England there lurked men and women who flouted church and societal conventions. Wexford's own great-uncle Hartley, a younger son, had taken Holy Orders after attending Oxford and been established in a snug living in Herefordshire. Several years later his portrait was hastily removed from the Yellow Sitting Room and hung in the water closet of the third-best guest bedroom after it was discovered his blessing of the local farm animals involved more personal intimacy than was considered acceptable for an Anglican vicar. In comparison, atheism seemed a minor offense.

"I see," said Wexford. "Sent to religious Coventry in death, was he? Was that his only sin?"

"A bit o' smuggling, Cap'n, when he were younger. Brandy, mostly. That sort o' thing."

"And just what is it you believe your grandfather can do to help us?"

"He was a rare one for discipline, ma'am. Mum always said—he were her dad—Granddad was as like to blow the head off'n one of his mates, if they disobeyed his orders, as cover 'em with gold when they had a successful run. When I were small, he'd knock me and my brothers straight if we sassed Mum or Dad or didn't do our lessons." Sherman beamed.

"Very touching," said Wexford, "but how does that help us in this situation?"

Barrowman cleared his throat. "Cap'n, if we was to, uh, facilitate the reanimation of Sherman's granddad, it's possible he might be persuaded to help..." His eyes shifted to his boots.

"Are you mad? You're suggesting we dig up a body?"

"I know right where 'tis, Cap'n," said Sherman. "We allus' bring flowers on his birthday."

Wexford felt her grip on sanity's slender thread begin to slip. "Oh? And then what? Hoist the coffin onto the quarterdeck and spread the bits about?"

Sherman looked doubtful. "Could do that, I s'pose. Might be easier, though, to lower another mooring cable next to his bones and hope he's as full of vinegar as he used to be."

"And you think he might be able instill discipline and obedience into these...these damned voices?" Wexford rubbed the bridge of her nose with a doubtful forefinger.

All eyes turned to Sherman. She smiled nervously and nodded.

"He'd do anything to please me when he were alive, ma'am. Plus, I'm thinking he might enjoy gettin' some of his own back against them as put his grave outside the churchyard. He could hold a powerful grudge."

Wexford looked at the others. "What do you all think?"

"Seems to me," said Barrowman, "we've tried just about everything short of blowin' up the ship. This *might* work. O' course, we could wait for the voodoo bloke. He should be here any minute." He leaned toward Wexford. "He's bringin' a goat."

Wexford's hands curled into fists. Chickens were one thing. Goat guts smeared on the decks of her ship went beyond the bounds of endurance.

"Dig up your grandfather, Sherman! Master Chief, make it happen."

Barrowman and Sherman hustled down the passageway, boots ringing on the steel deck plates.

"Sherman!" Wexford called.

The sailor wheeled about.

"Keep him under control! Or I may conduct the next sacrifice."

"Yes, ma'am." Sherman scurried away.

"I must be mad," said Wexford, half to herself.

"I suspect we're all a bit mad at this point," said Goss. "It is risky, of course. He might run amok like the others."

"I shouldn't fret about it too much, Captain," said the Chief Engineer. After all, if it doesn't work—" He took another swipe at his greasy hands. "—it's just one more voice. Right?"

Wexford and Goss gazed over the rail. Far below, Sherman, Barrowman, and three other sailors bustled around a freshly dug hole near the churchyard wall. Within minutes, a long, rectangular box was uncovered, and Sherman jumped into the hole and began prying at the top. It gave way, and she threw herself backward against the earthen wall of the grave. The others took hasty steps away.

"I hate to think what that smells like," said Wexford.

"Indeed," said Goss, shuddering. "The cable handlers are awaiting your word, ma'am."

Four sailors, next to a winch filled with thick metal cable, peered over the rail with fascinated eyes.

Wexford waved a hand, and Goss barked out an order. The sailors hauled on the winch, and cable snaked ground-ward, gleaming in the setting sun's rays.

"God, I hope this works," muttered Wexford.

The crew below grabbed the cable and hauled it over to the hole. Sherman waved the others away. Staggering a little under the weight of the cable, Sherman laid the tip, very gently, inside the coffin of the late Edward MacKiddle.

Wexford halted outside the bridge hatch and leaned against the bulkhead. A storm of butterflies whirled around her stomach, each one a reminder that in just over an hour the Admiralty would lower the boom on her career. *Keep calm. Remember when the entire Hottentot fleet surrounded the Boadicea and shot fire-tipped arrows at the balloon? The crew thought the ship was lost, but you got them through it. You can get through this.*

Right. Time for a show of command confidence. Wexford squared her shoulders and stepped through the hatch.

Several sailors turned to stare at her, their eyes wide. Goss and the Officer of the Deck stared gloomily at the chadburn, and behind them, Barrowman rubbed his bald head with both hands.

Wexford cleared her throat. "Everything ready to get underway, Commander?"

Goss turned. His eyes were rimmed in weary red. "I'm afraid things just got worse, Captain."

Wexford forced her shoulders to stay erect, even as her butterflies descended into chaos. "I doubt that's possible. But tell me anyway."

"We've no control," said the Officer of the Deck. "All attempts to bring the boilers on line have failed, and when we try to talk with Engineering, those damned voices keep interrupting."

"What are they saying now?"

"All sorts of things, ma'am, some of it quite...quite crude. But the gist seems to be the ship will be going nowhere soon."

"Actually," said Goss, "it's just one voice now. Care to guess whose?"

Wexford gave up her pretense of calm.

"Get Sherman up here," she snapped at Barrowman. "NOW!"

Wexford glared at the diminutive figure standing before her.

"You assured me, Sherman, your grandfather would cooperate in our efforts to regain control of the ship."

"Yes, ma'am," whispered Sherman.

"That hasn't happened, has it?"

"No, ma'am."

"Why is that?"

Sherman stared at her steel-toed boots.

"ANSWER ME!"

Sherman jumped. Her hands shook as they gripped her cap. "Um...well, maybe...maybe he's revertin' a bit. To when he were young, and a bit...a bit wild."

What had Sherman said earlier about her grandfather? *He was a sort of sailor.*

"Sherman, just what *exactly* did your grandfather do as a sailor?"

Sherman swallowed audibly. "He were a...a...a pirate."

"Good God!" said Goss. His mustache bristled.

Wexford gripped both hands behind her back to keep them from reaching for Sherman's neck. She took a long, steadying breath.

"Tell us the whole story. And don't leave anything out this time! Understand?"

"Yes, ma'am." Sherman's voice trembled. "He ran away as a lad and joined the Navy, but he...he deserted. Took up with pirates. Edward Red Hands, he were called, 'cause he was right quick with a knife. Mum said the whole family were that upset with him, but after a few years he won his own ship, which made them all ever so proud." Blue eyes peeked at Wexford. "He sent home money regular, so we could go to school and better ourselves. Then, when he were old and couldn't crack heads together anymore, he come back here to retire, respectable-like."

Wexford sank into the captain's chair and put a hand over her eyes. Her career flashed before her...and crashed in flames beside an open grave near the wall of a small country churchyard.

"In the past two years," she said, "this crew has successfully repelled three of the Chinese emperor's best airships, downed four Ottoman Zeppelins, and laid waste to the Black Sea brigand balloons. But now—" She shook her head. "—We've been overrun. By a pirate. Who's dead."

"I'm sure he don't mean no harm, Cap'n," said Sherman.

"He's taken control of the ship, y'daft girl!" said Barrowman. "That's mutiny!"

Sherman cringed.

"Are we lost?" said Wexford. "Should I call the Admiralty now?"

Goss threw up his hands. Barrowman muttered darkly.

"Please, Cap'n." Sherman edged close. "Let me talk with him again. Maybe...maybe he misunderstood."

"Nonsense!" said Goss.

Wexford stared at Sherman. Talking *with* the dead implied a measure of cooperation, and thus far the *Boadicea*'s defunct invaders had engaged only in one-way conversations. Their way. What difference could Sherman make? She glanced at the clock that hung above the helm. Less than one hour left.

On the other hand, what choice did she have?

"Go ahead."

Sherman yanked the headset of the bridge's sound-powered phone away from one of the startled sailors and began talking urgently into the mouthpiece.

Wexford leaned back in the chair. Fatigue swept over her, a bone-deep weariness she hadn't felt since she was a junior officer standing too many watches in a row without sleep or sustenance.

Perhaps retirement wouldn't be so bad.

"He's willing to parlay, Cap'n," said Sherman.

"Parlay?" Wrath welled up like a tidal wave. "He dares to demand parlay?"

Sherman cringed against the bulkhead, clutching the sound-powered phone in one hand.

"He...he says he's got, um, demands."

"WHAT?"

"Just...just two, Cap'n."

Wexford's wrath surged higher, forming caps of icy rage.

"He's not taking control of my ship, dammit! Nor will I accede to any demands! I'll put all hands ashore and blow the thing up before I'll let a pirate have her. You tell him that!"

She whirled toward Goss.

"Sound Emergency Stations! Prepare to abandon ship."

A shocked silence fell. The Officer of the Deck turned pale. The watch standers gaped.

Sherman murmured urgently into the mouthpiece.

"Well done, ma'am," said Goss. "Perhaps this pirate chap and the other voices will float away if they think the worst was coming."

"Or," the Officer of the Deck swallowed, "we may join them."

"Nonsense, man! The captain's using sound psychological strategy."

Wexford grabbed the knot of Goss's tie and yanked his face down to hers.

"Do you really think I'm joking?"

Goss gazed into her eyes and swallowed. "Captain?"

"DO IT!" She released his tie.

Goss blinked at her. Then, with a visible effort, he pulled himself erect, straightened his jacket, and turned to the Officer of the Deck.

"Prepare to pipe Emergency Stations."

The Officer of the Deck looked bewildered.

"But...but how? The phone's being used to, um—"

"The alarm, man!" barked Goss. "Ring the damned alarm!"

A harsh clanging filled the air. Moments later, voices shouted, and boots thudded along passageways below the bridge. Wexford crooked a finger at the Officer of the Deck.

"Get to the quarterdeck," she shouted. "Once all hands are ashore, I want sailors on the road to stop keep villagers as far from the ship as possible. Oh, and once Goss and Barrowman are off, the First Lieutenant is to set the ship adrift from the mooring mast."

The Officer of the Deck fled.

"Goss, are the emergency charges in order?"

Goss involuntarily glanced through the skylights above, where the hydrogen-filled balloon floated peacefully, its colors bright in the afternoon sunshine.

"I conducted a zone inspection up there just last week, Captain. If...if they must be set off, they'll do the job properly."

"Good. I want you and Barrowman to go to the quarterdeck to ensure all hands get ashore. Then you're to follow them."

Goss stiffened. "I'd prefer to remain here with you, Captain." He pressed together lips that quivered ever so slightly.

"I'm stayin', too, Cap'n," said Barrowman. "You'll have t'toss me overboard before I'll leave you and the ship behind."

Wexford didn't argue. It was loyalty of the melodramatic, foolhardy kind that made her first impulse—throwing them both over the side—seem ungracious. Even insensitive. Besides, she didn't stand a chance of lifting Barrowman.

"Very well, gentlemen. Barrowman, get down to Engineering. We can't trust the damned phones, so if you hear the Emergency Stations alarm sound again, you're to give me just enough steam that Goss and I can maneuver the ship toward the river. An explosion there will do less damage."

The master chief hesitated. "Captain, what about the lass?"

"She'll be going ashore right away. I'll not make her pay for what that lunatic grandfather of hers has done."

Barrowman exhaled in relief and exited the bridge.

"Goss, shut down the alarm. Everyone should be off in a moment or two, and if I'm going to die, I don't want to die deaf."

The clanging bells fell silent, leaving behind a sharp ringing in Wexford's ears. The clock read sixteen-thirty-seven.

"Cap'n," said Sherman, "I think I've got everything straightened out with Grandda—"

"Stow it! Tell your grandfather this: Not one of Her Majesty's airships has ever been taken by mutiny."

"Yes, ma'am, but—"

"I want that clearly understood."

"Yes, ma'am. If you'll just—"

Wexford jabbed a finger toward the clock.

"You're leaving the ship, but before you go, tell your grandfather that if control isn't returned to me by exactly sixteen-forty-one, I will raise steam, steer the ship over the river, and detonate the charges in the ship's balloon."

"But if you try to move the ship—"

"I'll be damned if I'll parlay with the ghost of a—"

"It'll blow up on its own!"

74

"—mutinous, thieving son of a bi— *What* did you say?"

"Cap'n, Granddad says you must check the fittings for the steam supply valves in the boiler room. There's a problem, and that's why he won't let you move the ship. He says Mr. Peek convinced the others to muck things up all week, just to keep you from calling up steam."

Peek? Wexford mentally reviewed the Engineering staff roster and came up short a Peek. Which left only one possibility.

"Died near eight years ago," said Sherman. "He was engineer on a steam ship."

Of course.

"Goss," said Wexford, "have any valve issues been reported?"

"None. The Chief Engineer had some of the valves refitted recently, but he didn't report any problems."

"Ha!" Wexford turned back to Sherman. "It seems your grandfather is not only mutinous, he's ill-informed. Now, it's time for you to leave so I can—"

"Mr. Peek told Granddad four of them new fittings are brass."

"Nonsense! Only steel fittings are used for steam valves, and anyone can tell the difference between brass and steel."

"Not when they're painted the same color, like these!"

Hadn't the Chief Engineer mentioned a disembodied voice complaining about paint, as well as the valve repairs? Any valve through which passed super-heated steam temperature demanded the strength and endurance of steel. Why, brass would melt minutes after the boilers heated up, and the valve would explode. Steam would instantly cook everyone in the Engineering spaces, inside and out.

"Mr. Peek tried to warn the Chief Engineer," continued Sherman, "but he wouldn't listen. No one would. Granddad says even though Mr. Peek wasn't a proper sailor, him not having served in the Navy, he's got quick eyes for a foul-up."

This was absurd. How could a disembodied voice, whose owner was clearly incapable of finding his way to the Promised Land, diagnose a potential engineering catastrophe?

Goss stood beside the Emergency Stations alarm, watching Wexford, his face stiff with resolution.

She lifted a hand...and hesitated.

Two years earlier, a similar incident had occurred on one of the Royal Navy's oceangoing steam vessels. Brass fittings, painted the same color as the steel for the sake of some damned stupid idea of uniformity, had been used to secure a steam valve. The loss of life had been calamitous.

Wexford chewed her bottom lip. Blowing up the *Boadicea* and going down with the bits and pieces wasn't really her *preferred* means of retiring. Checking a few valve fittings would do no harm and, at most, would take only a few minutes.

"Tell your grandfather I want to speak with Master Chief Barrowman. Now. Without any interference from him or his friends."

Barrowman, at first leery of the voice on the phone that claimed to be his commanding officer, was eventually persuaded to descend into the steam room to check the valves. Minutes later he spoke breathlessly into Wexford's ear.

"Dunno how it happened, ma'am, but the ol' spook spoke the truth! Brass! Painted brass! If we'd got underway to head to the yards, or just to move the ship to the river, those fittings would've melted and *bang* we'd've gone, too."

Wexford's rage evaporated like a wraith at dawn. Her body felt weightless, as if at any moment she might float above the deck, buoyed by combined relief and astonishment. It appeared she might have a few years left in her career after all.

"Shut everything down, Master Chief."

"Aye, Cap'n."

Wexford thought she heard a soft sigh whisper through the headphones. She pulled these from her head and turned to Goss.

"Go to the quarterdeck. Use the semaphore flags and let the crew know they should return to the ship. Then get the engineers to replace those fittings right away. I'll be along in a moment."

Goss's running footsteps receded down the steel-plate of the passageway.

Wexford handed the phone back to Sherman, vaguely pleased her hands weren't trembling.

"Convey to your grandfather my...my gratitude."

"Yes, ma'am."

Wexford headed for the hatch.

"Um...Captain?"

Wexford slowed. "Can it wait?"

"There's one more thing, Cap'n. Granddad's second demand."

Oh, dear God, now what? Wexford's sense of relief deflated.

"Yes?"

"He and the others, they like it here, ma'am. They want to stay."

The hair on Wexford's scalp rose. "Stay? On my ship?"

"Yes, ma'am. Granddad says they're all much happier here than in the churchyard. Even Mrs. Pendleton-Shirt. They like being around the crew, you see, enjoying a little life."

"They're dead. They've had their quota of life."

"Well, one kind of life."

"That should be enough for anyone. Wanting more smacks of greed."

"Maybe. But they love life enough to've saved ours, Cap'n. And they saved the ship...or would've done, if we was still planning on blowin' it up, which now we don't have to 'cause of them. Besides, they don't take up no space. Don't eat 'n don't drink."

"That's beside the point. A ship filled with ghosts? Why, the last few days have been bloody hell! Which, by the by, is a place I wish they'd consider inhabiting, rather than my ship."

Sherman covered the mouthpiece of the phone with a grubby palm. "Begging pardon, ma'am," she said, with a frown, "but I don't think I should repeat them words."

A flush of guilt crept up Wexford's neck. "Yes, well..."

"Granddad says he won't let anyone interfere with shipboard communications anymore, and won't none of them cross him."

"Yes, but will *he* cross *me*?"

Sherman lowered her voice to a whisper. "It might be a good idea to say yes, ma'am. Master Chief Barrowman told the Officer of the Deck that all the singing 'n chickens 'n candles didn't do a bit o' good, and I'm pretty sure Granddad heard."

The deck seemed to tilt under Wexford's feet. A ship full of ghosts? What did that mean? Would the crew roster have to be expanded? And what about pay? A pirate was bound to demand some price for his cooperation, something beyond the hospitality of the ship, although what that would be she couldn't imagine. Chains to rattle? How would she explain any of this to the Admiralty?

Weariness swept over her. Right now, she didn't have the strength or energy to make a sensible decision.

"Tell him...we'll talk."

Sherman spoke quietly into the mouthpiece. She listened for a moment, then gave Wexford a quick nod.

It was time to head to the quarterdeck, make sure everyone got back onboard safely. She'd get some sort of message off to the Admiralty, and then she and the Chief Engineer were going to have a long and—on his part—painful conversation about quality assurance.

"Come, Sherman. We're done here for now."

Sherman hung the phone back in its holster. Her steel-toed boots clumped on the deck as she walked toward the hatch. She smiled at Wexford.

"Thank you, Cap'n. I don't think you'll regret letting Granddad and the others stay."

Regret? That airship had already sailed. Wexford stepped over on the threshold of the bridge hatch, then hesitated and looked back at the phone.

"I'll be damned," she muttered.

A gleeful cackle emanated from the mouthpiece.
"Like as not, lass," said a faint voice. "Like as not. But, eh, we'll have us some grand fun on the way!"

Her Majesty's Service

Lauren Marrero

A hand reached for Nandi in the pre-dawn, wrapping itself firmly around her waist. It was a strong, masculine hand, which she fondly remembered gripping her hips the night before, but it smelled like fish.

Nandi wrinkled her nose in distaste and began scooting away on the narrow bed. Of all the men she could have slept with, it was Nandi's ill-luck to choose a fisherman. At least the rooms he rented were close to the docks and her favorite tavern—facts that had been of the utmost importance during last night's drunken groping, but which left Nandi aching from the hard bed...and reeking of fish.

Next time she would set her standards a bit higher, Nandi promised herself for the hundredth time, but as a crewman on one of Her Majesty's royal airships, Nandi didn't stay long enough in any port to be choosy.

She hurriedly dressed and tiptoed out before he awoke. Once outdoors, Nandi stretched and gave her armpits an experimental sniff.

Aye. She smelled like fish and also the deeper, more masculine musk of the fisherman. They weren't due to sail for another hour. If she hurried, she just might have time for a quick shower before reporting in.

"You're cutting it close, ain't ya?" called a voice from above as she reached the ship. Nandi looked up to find

Ken, one of her fellow Spiders, dangling from The Virginia's many service lines. From the various tools attached to his belt, Nandi assumed he was supposed to be repairing something, but he looked like he was having far more fun practicing ballet moves in mid-air. "Need a lift?"

It was against regulation to practice lifts without a harness, but that didn't stop Nandi from eagerly lifting her arms—after a quick glance about to make sure no one was watching. Ken released his line, dropping like a stone, to land a few feet from the docks.

"Showoff," Nandi teased. Anyone else would have stopped much higher and then slowly lowered themselves to the ground, but not Kenshiro Mori. If he wasn't defying death, he didn't truly feel alive.

It was one of the many things they had in common.

Their friendship was one of the strange outcomes of Her Majesty's international expansion. Two war orphans from opposite sides of the globe had found each other and a home in the rigging of a British airship. Here, origin did not matter, nor eye shape, nor skin color. All that mattered was an ability to risk life and limb swinging from the ropes of an airship, and a desire to see the world.

Nandi grabbed his neck and locked her legs around his torso as Ken pulled another cord. It immediately retracted, lifting them high above the airship. Another cord released and they slid gracefully to the deck of The Virginia.

"Have you put on some weight?" Ken teased. "Our lift seemed a little slow that time."

"Cussed bugger!" Nandi playfully punched Ken's arm as he unhooked himself. Together they walked below decks where the corridors were bustling with activity. Nandi wasn't the only late arrival. She spied several hung over crewmen staggering into position before the officers arrived.

"Did you hear we have a new boatswain?" Ken asked as they stripped and headed into the communal showers. "Some rich bloke from Cambridge named Knightly. He's a well-to-do scholar with advanced degrees in something or other. He has all the ladies in a tizzy—and some of the blokes. You'll see him at roll."

Nandi snorted and ducked her head under the water to rinse. It didn't matter what the guy looked like. The odds of a Cambridge scholar and an officer messing about with an airship Spider were as likely as drowning in midair.

"Fools," she spat. "Toffs stick to their kind and we stick to ours."

"Come now," Ken replied. "What do I smell on you today, eau de fisherman?"

Nandi gave her arm a sniff, and then lathered herself again with soap. Did the guy wipe himself with fish? He must have been quite an Adonis for it not to have bothered her last night.

"You know what they say about Spiders: we can't keep our legs on the ground," Nandi called from under the water. "What is a boatswain doing with advanced degrees anyway?" she wanted to know. The boatswain was responsible for the rigging, cables, and anchors. They were officers of the ship, but it wasn't the most erudite profession, not like a commander or lieutenant.

"I don't know, why don't you ask him?" Ken was already pulling on his clothes. "Come on or we'll be late."

"Yes, Mother."

They hurriedly dressed and joined the rest of the crewmen streaming onto the decks for roll. Nandi wondered briefly if she should have said something to her fisherman before sneaking out this morning, but decided against it. He didn't seem like the sentimental type and neither was she. But if she ever came back to Cairo, Nandi would definitely look him up—provided he bathed first.

"Psst! There he is." A sharp elbow jabbed Nandi's arm, breaking into her thoughts. She followed Ken's gaze to a tall, broad-shouldered officer standing at the front of her line.

His head was turned, so she couldn't see his features, but Nandi was beginning to see why he would cause such a commotion. This was no emaciated scholar that spent his evenings with dusty tomes and a hot water bottle. Their new boatswain's muscles were clearly defined beneath his tight uniform. The firm cut of his backside begged for a friendly pat. His hair was still damp from a recent shower. The texture and pattern of his waves reminded Nandi of her lusty fisherman.

She shook her head at that comparison. The fisherman had made quite an impression on her if she was seeing him everywhere.

"Bugger me!" Nandi whispered, as the boatswain finally turned his head.

She had to be mistaken. Perhaps she was more hung over than she thought. Surely she could not be seeing correctly—because directly in front of her, in the crisp uniform of a boatswain, stood her fisherman...and he was staring directly at her.

is face didn't give anything away. Anyone else would assume he was merely inspecting his shipmen for the destructive influence of shore leave, but Nandi was not fooled. She could feel his bemused gaze burning into hers, though she forced herself to look straight ahead and not make eye contact.

What was her fisherman doing onboard her ship, and in an officer's uniform? Was he a spy? If so, for which side?

Perhaps he was like Nandi and had been in the mood for a little R & R before they sailed, but then why would he introduce himself as a fisherman? And when had she started thinking of him as her fisherman?

"Come on, then," Ken tugged Nandi's arm, anxious to get back up in the rigging. She stared at him blankly, having missed almost the entire general debrief. "How much did you drink last night?"

She blinked and pulled herself together. Whatever game the boatswain was playing, it was none of her business. What could she say against the man anyway, that he dressed like a local when he was on leave? That was hardly a hanging offense. She gave Ken her most lecherous smile.

"Sorry, my fisherman kept me up all night."

"Did he?"

Nandi froze. She recognized that voice. It had sent shivers down her spine, whispering naughty things the night before. She didn't think he would dare approach her once he discovered they were on the same ship—she certainly intended to avoid him. Nevertheless, her fisherman—and their new boatswain—stood directly beside her, studying her with a frown.

"Sir!" Nandi snapped to attention with a salute. Spiders were notoriously crude, but she knew to watch her language in front of an officer.

"I understand you were nearly late for roll," said Knightly. At least Nandi remembered his name from Ken's earlier gossip.

Nearly late? Since when did an officer berate a subordinate for something they almost did?

"I'm sorry, Sir," she replied. "It won't happen again."

Was he studying her for some hint of recognition? He wouldn't find it. She realized that he could be in as much trouble as she would be if the affair was discovered. Fraternizing was strictly forbidden between ranks.

"See that it doesn't," Knightly replied. "I am new to The Virginia, but not to command. I expect my Spiders to be attentive and disciplined at all times. If you are not early, you are late. Do you understand?"

"Aye, Sir!"

"Good."

With that he turned and left Nandi to stare after him in confusion.

"What was that about?" asked Ken. "Do you know him?"

"Of course not!" she scoffed. "He's a toff."

"Then why are you staring at his backside?"

"I am not staring at anything!" Nandi angrily averted her gaze. Why couldn't she have stayed aboard last night like a sensible woman? There was some devil in her blood that constantly encouraged her to seek out adventure every time they stopped at port. It was why she was so good at risking her life in the rigging of an airship. Her adventurous spirit had gotten Nandi into some interesting situations in the past, but nothing as bad as this. "Come on, let's get to work."

"You're staring again," Ken shouted above the hiss and clank of the steam engines. They were far below the deck, repairing one of The Virginia's many weather panels.

"I'm not staring," Nandi lied. She knew her eyes followed Knightly every time he appeared on deck, but she was powerless to stop herself. There was something odd about him, an indefinable air of mystery that had her watching him to see what he would do next.

"Do you remember the first time Kellie dropped towel in the showers?" Ken inquired. "I swore I wasn't staring. You didn't believe me then, and I don't believe you now. You're practically obsessed."

"I am not obsessed; I just think there is something strange about him."

A few days had passed since her first encounter with Knightly. She told herself to forget it, but she couldn't stop herself from wondering what else he lied about. Had he pretended to be a fisherman for entertainment or did he have another agenda?

"Where does he disappear after his shift? I saw him once wandering the ship, looking for God knows what."

"It wouldn't be outside the realm of possibility for an officer to inspect his ship," Ken replied. "This is his first tour with us. Maybe he is checking to make sure everything is working right."

"After his shift? He wasn't looking about; he was walking with a definite purpose. I think he's doing something below decks, something he doesn't want anyone else to know about."

Ken swung around, sliding along his cable until he hooked himself onto Nandi's belt and hung a mere inch from her nose. "Stop following him. You'll only get yourself in trouble. Why are you so interested in him? This isn't like you."

"I love a mystery." She unhooked Ken from her belt and gave him a not-too-gentle push, sending him flying across the bow. "Don't you think he's strange?"

"You're strange." Ken replied. "Have you seen something that made you suspicious? He singled you out that day for no reason that I could see. If something happened, you would tell me, right? I'll stand by you, even against an officer."

"I know that." Nandi wished she could tell him the origin of her suspicions, but it wasn't worth the risk.

Captain Wilson was a strict disciplinarian. If he discovered one of his officers had fraternized with one of his subordinates, they'd all be in trouble. "I'm just making up excuses to stare at his behind."

Ken shook his head sadly. "You give us Spiders a bad name."

A warning horn sounded from the deck of the ship, cutting off her laughter. It was the emergency alarm, calling the Spiders aboard. Nandi looked up to see several small dots on the horizon, approaching fast.

From the direction they traveled, and their formation, it had to be the Ottoman air force. They were officially allies, but that hadn't stopped minor skirmishes from breaking out as Britain sought to strengthen its position in the east. Whatever caused their arrival, from their fighting formation, Nandi knew they weren't coming for tea.

"Let's bring it in!" Nandi called. She checked to make sure her lines were untangled, and then tugged on the release. Instantly her line retracted, pulling her back to the ship with dizzying speed.

The deck was pandemonium. Officers were listening to the ship's phones and barking orders at the same time. Without having to be told, Nandi ran for the emergency lockers hidden directly below the decks and took out a battle suit. The thick armor wouldn't protect her from a missile, but it should stop a bullet—she hoped.

"You there!" Nandi looked up into the determined face of the boatswain. He was already in battle gear and looked ready to slay an army singlehanded. "Take me to the hangar deck."

"A...aye, Sir!" Nandi stuttered, astonished that he had chosen her. Since that first day, he had avoided her like the plague. She never expected to be singled out by him in the middle of battle. "Hold on, Sir."

She carefully hooked him into her harness, turning until they were spooned together like the lovers they pretended not to be.

Around them, Nandi saw others doing the same. It was definitely safer to travel through the protected inside of the airship, but nothing was faster than swinging along the side. During a battle, every second counted.

"On three," Nandi shouted above the cacophony. A spray of bullets peppered the deck next to them, sending many of her shipmates running for cover, but she ignored them. She couldn't run with the boatswain attached to her back and there were faster ways to get away. "Three!"

She yanked on a cord and felt Knightly's arms grip her waist. She often forgot that some people hated the feeling of being pulled through the air with nothing but a rope to support them, but to Nandi, this was life. It was the greatest expression of joy to hurdle through the air like an acrobat. If Knightly hadn't been holding on so tightly, she might have added a flip or two, but she didn't think he would appreciate the levity.

"Which hangar?"

"Alpha Niner," Knightly screamed into her ear. He sounded like he had just run a marathon—or orgasmed, Nandi remembered fondly.

"Aye, Sir!" She paused with her legs braced against the side of the ship and hooked herself onto another cable.

"One, two, three." She pushed back, releasing her cord, and letting the momentum swing them toward the correct hangar. "Ready to land? We're coming in fast."

Despite his death-grip on Nandi's waist, Knightly did an admirable job with the landing. She'd seen seasoned Spiders do something stupid at the last second and go tumbling with a twisted ankle or worse.

"Come with me," he ordered as Nandi unhooked them.

She shivered as he stepped away, missing the warmth at her back. It was pure luck and basic knowledge of ship design that brought them to the correct deck on the first try. She thought she knew every inch of the massive ship, but had never been to A9. It seemed to be always under construction, though none of the crew would admit to working there. She looked about with wide eyes, knowing she would never be able to relate what she saw there.

The Virginia wasn't a battleship, it was a cargo vessel. From the secrecy surrounding A9, Nandi suspected they carried some very controversial freight.

A man with wild black curls like a dark halo ran to Knightly, wringing his hands anxiously.

"This doesn't make any sense!" he cried. "We weren't expecting an attack. They shouldn't know I've left yet."

"It seems our intelligence was wrong," Knightly replied. "Or someone tipped off the Turks."

"But that's impossible!" replied the man. "No one knows about me. Oh God, what if they take me back?"

"Joseph, you know I won't let that happen. Allow me to introduce Nandi Magoro. She is one of the best Spiders in Her Majesty's fleet."

Nandi looked at Knightly in shock. Had he decided that before or after they slept together?

"Nandi, this is Doctor Joseph Hanan, an advisor from Beirut. But you already know that."

She blinked. There were no advisors from Beirut, not with the current political climate between the Ottoman and British empires. They were in an arms race for dominion of the east, along with Russia and Japan. Joseph was most likely a defector—a man important enough to bring the wrath of the Turks down upon their ship.

"Magoro?" Joseph enquired, taking in her dark skin and shaved head.

Nandi was so used to the multi-ethnic ship that she sometimes forgot how unnerving her appearance could be to outsiders.

"Are you African?"

"Ashanti." Nandi's chest puffed out as it always did when she spoke of her ancestry. From the widening of his eyes, Nandi knew Joseph had heard the gruesome tales from her homeland, stories of fierce battles and bands of female warriors. She grinned.

The boom of cannon shook the deck, sending them all scrambling for footing. The Virginia was responding with heavy cannon to their pursuers. That meant the enemy fleet was fast approaching.

"Where is it?" Knightly grabbed Joseph's arm and pulled him to his feet.

"This way." Joseph opened a small cupboard, unveiling what looked to Nandi like a mechanical backpack.

"What is that?" she inquired.

There were the usual straps that looked like her regular harness, but that was where the similarities ended. Instead of the normal, thick cord she was accustomed to, made of coated metal cables, this was a synthetic material that looked like a new type of rubber. It was much thinner than what she used, barely the size of her thumb. To a Spider, it looked like death.

"This is the future!" Joseph began excitedly pushing buttons, displaying his invention. "Until now Spiders have been tethered to their ships. You must be. The ropes only reach so far, and they are too heavy to move. So you swing from rope to rope along the side of the ship like monkeys in a jungle. This invention will change everything.

"Imagine a cord so light it can be carried with you. It is so small that meters of it can be easily stored on your back. It is impervious to the extreme temperature fluctuations that cause so many of our current cables to malfunction. The attached gun can propel the rope up to 100 meters, and like a grappling hook, it will latch onto any surface."

"This will completely change the way we fight," Nandi surmised. Airships generally fought from a distance. They were carriers for smaller airplanes that engaged in aerial dogfights while the ship-bound crew supported them with heavy artillery.

If Spiders could leave their ships, they could do all sorts of mischief to the enemy nearly undetected. Sabotage or assassination of senior officers could be done by a single fighter.

"It took years to convince Joseph to defect to Britain. I promised I would keep him safe and I have no intention of breaking my word."

Nandi looked up to see Knightly holding a small pistol in his hand. It was loaded and aimed at her heart.

"What are you doing?" she demanded, trying not to panic. No one knew where she was. Knightly could throw her overboard and no one would be the wiser.

"Stop playing innocent!" he snapped. "I know our initial meeting wasn't an accident, not after you showed up on The Virginia. Were you hoping I would lead you to Joseph before we sailed? Too bad he was already safely aboard by then. I wondered how far you would go to complete your mission. I must say, you are very good at your job."

"You're insane," was all Nandi could reply.

Did he really believe she was a spy for the Turks? That was crazy. If she was pulling in a second income she would definitely own some better boots.

"I'm not the spy—you are! You pretended to be a fisherman when we first met, and then transformed into a boatswain. You disappear for hours..."

"I have my duties to the crown," explained Knightly. "There is no point in pretending. I will never let you take him back to Beirut."

"I don't want to take him anywhere!" she protested. "I didn't know he existed ten minutes ago."

"Then why are the Turks here?" Knightly asked. "No one else saw me before we sailed. No one else has been watching me aboard The Virginia. It has to be you."

"I am not a spy!" Nandi cried in exasperation.

"There is another possibility," called a voice from the entrance.

Nandi spun around to find Ken standing there, holding a pistol.

"I told you to let it go, Nandi. You should have listened to me."

"Ken?" she asked in shock. "What are you doing here?"

"I followed you, of course," Ken replied. "And it's a good thing I did. I knew that as soon as the Ottomans arrived he would have to make sure Doctor Hanan was safe." Ken stepped forward, ignoring the gun in Knightly's hand. "Nandi, bring me the device."

"No!" Nandi refused to move an inch. "You knew Knightly was up to something, but you let me think I was a fool."

"I was trying to protect you," Ken protested. "Empires don't care about people like us. They crush us as easily as they would real spiders. But it doesn't have to be that way. Bring me the device. With it we can have whatever we want."

"What I want," Nandi replied. "Is to be a Spider."

"I'm sorry to hear that." Ken brought his pistol to bear on her chest. Years of friendship vanished in an instant, unable to compete with the promise of gold. "I really was trying to protect you from this."

He squeezed the trigger. For an instant she froze, hearing the bang of the discharge and expecting a mortal wound. Then she smiled and shook her head at Ken's mistake.

"That's why I always score higher than you in combat drills," she taunted. "What kind of Spider doesn't account for wind?"

Ken rushed forward, spraying them with bullets. What he lacked in accuracy, he made up for in brute force. They dropped to the floor, hiding behind whatever objects they could find. Unfortunately, in the sparse hangar, there wasn't much. Nandi ended up behind the same overturned table as Knightly.

"Do you believe me now?" she demanded.

"What was I supposed to think? You seduced me!"

" You seduced me!" Nandi countered. "Smelling like fish."

"That was part of my job," Knightly snapped. "I had to be a convincing fisherman to smuggle Joseph into port."

"And you wonder why I watched you! Give me your gun."

Knightly straightened his back and glared at Nandi in consternation. "I am a sharpshooter in Her Majesty's Secret Service. I know how to fire a pistol."

"Have you ever tried to shoot straight in a hurricane?" Nandi inquired. Spiders were the most mobile of an airship's crew and needed to be able to adapt to any situation, including combat. "Up here you're in a different world."

"I still don't know if I should trust you," Knightly grumbled, but he reluctantly handed over his weapon.

"This isn't exactly procedure. Be careful. It has a bit of a recoil..."

Nandi aimed and fired, hitting Ken on the barrel of his gun and sending the weapon flying. "Got it," she replied sarcastically. "Thanks for the warning."

"You aren't going to kill me," Ken taunted, rubbing his injured hand. "Not after everything we've been through. Spiders are like family."

"I wasn't family when you were the one holding the gun," Nandi pointed out.

"I knew I wouldn't hit you in here," he replied. "I just needed to scare you away from Doctor Hanan's device." Ken fingered the metal pack before slipping an arm through one of the loops.

The loud boom of cannons echoed again, shaking the deck. The Ottomans were getting closer.

"That's my ride. Are you sure you won't come?"

"Ken, stop!" she yelled. "I will shoot you."

"No, you won't. Once the Ashanti were warriors; once my father preached the code of bushido; but not anymore. We're civilized now, puppets of our mighty empires. If you stay here, that's all you will ever be."

"Do you really think we are nothing?" said Nandi, aghast. "No one else can do what we do. Why do you think they look for people like us to be Spiders? We aren't just the descendants of warriors, we are warriors. Without us, there would be no imperial fleets."

"That's not enough for me." Ken fired the gun attached to Doctor Hanan's device, ejecting the thin cord from its nozzle.

It crashed into Nandi, sending her flying across the deck. She skittered to a stop mere inches from the edge of the hangar and watched, breathless, as her own gun flew over the side. The cord retracted into the device, ready to be fired again.

Years of training kicked in, urging Nandi's fingers to inch toward the emergency rope located at the entrance to every hangar deck. She felt naked without something anchoring her to The Virginia, especially this close to the edge.

For some, it might feel better to stand on their feet, but on an airship, that safety was an illusion. A Spider would always reach for a rope before they reached for secure footing.

Seconds later, that training saved her life as The Virginia changed direction again to shake off her pursuers.

Nandi lost her grip, but was able to buckle herself onto a tether at the last second; ending what would have been a very nasty fall. Unfortunately, Doctor Hanan had no such training, and he went tumbling over the side, screaming like a banshee.

"Hold on!" Nandi yelled. Her tether was too heavy to move, but all Spiders carried small ropes attached to their belts. She swung it like a cowboy in the American West, catching Joseph's torso as he fell. "Doctor? Are you alright?"

"No, I am not alright!" he screamed. "Get me back on the ship!"

"Can you pull yourself up?"

"Are you crazy?"

Nandi muttered a curse and began hauling Joseph toward her. Rescuing Ottoman scientists was definitely not in her job description.

Once he was close enough, she hooked him into her tether, leaving him to dangle as she climbed back up to the hangar deck.

"Where are you going?" he shrieked. "You can't leave me like this."

"You'll be safe there," Nandi replied. "Just don't do anything stupid—like unhook yourself."

"That thought never crossed my mind."

Masculine grunts above drew Nandi's attention back to the hangar deck. Ken and Knightly were going at each other in a bare-knuckle brawl, fighting for control of Joseph's device. Any other time, Nandi would have stopped and enjoyed the show.

They were both exceptional combatants. Knightly was a military-trained boxer, while Ken learned to fight dirty in the streets. It promised to be a hell of a bout, but Nandi knew she had to break them up. They hadn't bothered to anchor themselves to the ship and were mere inches from going over the side.

"Hey, idiots!" she called, climbing back onto the deck. "Do you want to secure yourselves first?"

"Doctor Hanan," Knightly asked between blows— neither of them paused to tether themselves. "Is he...?"

"He's fine," Nandi replied, letting the men battle it out while she secured herself to another line. They could kill themselves if they wanted, but she had every intention of surviving.

A missile exploded into The Virginia's side, forcing the men apart as flames and shrapnel flew across the deck. Finally, Knightly dove for an emergency cord, but Ken had other plans. He ran into Knightly, tackling him around the middle, and sending them both overboard.

"I always knew that guy was crazy..." Nandi muttered to herself, watching the suicidal move.

She peered curiously over the side, not surprised to find both men still fighting, as they dangled from the end of a line. "Typical."

Knightly did well, but it was obvious he lacked Ken's skill on a rope. No one could defeat a Spider in aerial combat except another Spider. With a mental apology to her training master, Nandi slid down their rope, adding one more person to the brawl.

Three bodies on a single cord was insane. The well-used ropes were checked obsessively, but hangar A9 was an under-utilized part of the ship.

There was no way to know when these ropes were last serviced. The combatants weren't passively hanging either. They were wriggling about fighting for the backpack still hooked onto Ken's arm.

Nandi's training master would think they all had a death wish.

At least she had the advantage of being buckled onto another cord. It made her movements reckless, knowing she had the second line to protect her. She used Knightly as a distraction, slipping in close so she could unbuckle the device from Ken.

"Stop, or we'll all die!" Ken shouted, but he had no intention of stopping. She knew he was overwhelmed and hoped to scare Nandi and Knightly off their guards.

It worked for Knightly. The spy paused and looked down, closing his eyes briefly in prayer as he saw the vast carpet of forest below.

Ken kneed him in the groin.

"You fight dirty," Nandi berated him.

"I fight to win."

"Not this time." She finally pulled the device free, hooking it over her own arm. Letting go of Ken's rope, she dove for Knightly, catching his wrist.

"Let go," she ordered. She knew she was asking a lot.

Knightly wasn't tethered to the ship. The only thing keeping him alive was his grip on the rope, and thanks to that blow to his groin, that was growing weaker by the second.

"Trust me."

"Bollocks." Knightly let go, trusting Nandi's hold on his wrist to save him. It wasn't until he released his grip on the cord that she realized how surprised she was by his actions.

He really let go without a harness, she thought. Knightly was either incredibly brave or incredibly foolish.

They swung away on Nandi's cord, leaving Ken to curse and grumble after them.

"We don't have much time," she called.

Already Ken had pulled his release cord, taking him back up to the deck. In a few minutes he might climb down Nandi's line and they would restart their three person fight.

"Wrap your legs around me. That's it."

With her free hand, Nandi secured the device to her back and reached for her lasso. She tossed it at Doctor Hanan, catching his foot, and pulling them closer until the three of them huddled in a group.

"What are you doing?" Knightly demanded. "We have to get back to the airship."

"It's too late for that," Nandi replied, hating what was coming next. "Ken is already unhooking my line."

"Unhooking your..." Joseph looked up in horror.

100

Sure enough, Ken was busy at work on Nandi's cable. She was also held by Joseph's cord, but it would take only a moment to unhook that one too.

"Why is he doing that? He'll destroy the device."

"And the only evidence against him," Knightly surmised. "With us gone, he can pretend this never happened."

"This device of yours," said Nandi. "Has it ever been tested?"

She fingered the narrow cord protruding from the pack that Ken had sent crashing into her. It looked thin enough to rip in half with her bare hands. She tugged, but it held.

"I hung from the ceiling for thirty minutes," Joseph replied. "Although the ceiling of the aircraft hangar is only 40 meters high and I only weigh 13 stone..."

"We don't have a choice," interrupted Knightly, as Nandi's cord came loose. Now all three of them were dangling from Doctor Hanan's tether and running out of time. "Do you think you can make it work?"

"I've done all I can," Joseph replied. "The rest is up to providence."

"Then you should start praying." Nandi aimed the gun at the tallest, thickest tree she could find. She only had one shot at this. If she missed...well, it had been a good life. She took a deep breath and fired.

An instant later, the last tether holding them to the ship was released, sending them plummeting toward the forest below. She had been in freefall before—illegally playing around The Virginia without a harness—but she had never truly feared for her life. Not like this. Her eyes watched the hook as it shot toward the tree and blinked in disbelief when it actually hit its target.

"Bugger me!" she shouted, hitting the recoil button. Instantly, their trajectory changed, swinging them in an arc toward the tree.

They crashed through the canopy. Nandi expected at any moment to splatter on the forest floor, but the cord continued, incredibly, to pull them toward the tree. Instincts took over and she lifted her legs to kick them away from the trunk an instant before impact, but they still bumped into quite a few branches, swinging back and forth above the forest floor like a pendulum.

They were bruised and bloody, but miraculously still breathing by the time they stopped.

"Is everyone alive?" Knightly asked. From the tone of his voice, Nandi knew he must be in a lot of pain.

"Barely," Joseph groaned.

"Can you imagine the look on Ken's face when he realizes we survived?" she chuckled. Careful of her ribs, which she knew were at least bruised, if not broken, she unhooked herself and began climbing down the tree.

"Yes, well, we have other concerns at the moment," Joseph replied. "Do you have any idea where we are?"

"We were nearing Vienna when the battle began," said Knightly. "It's possible we are still somewhere in Austria-Hungary."

"Aren't the Austrians allies of the Ottomans?" Nandi helped Joseph from the tree, checking to make sure he was uninjured.

"Yes."

"Bollocks."

"Indeed." Knightly held Nandi's chin up to the light, frowning at the scrapes she had obtained from the fall. "You handled yourself well up there. Better than me. Have you ever thought of joining Her Majesty's Secret Service?"

Nandi regarded him for a long moment. She liked being a Spider. She loved the camaraderie of an airship crew and flying through the air with nothing but a cord to support her . Could she give that up for constant danger, travel, and adventure?

"Do I have to rub myself with fish?" she inquired doubtfully.

"I may have been a bit...zealous...in my role."

"It was believable," Nandi acceded. "Does Her Majesty have any rules against fraternizing among her spies?"

Knightly's cheeks turned an adorable shade of pink as he pondered the best way to answer that question. "It is generally frowned upon," he admitted, "but things sometimes happen in the field. That's where my best friend met his wife."

"His wife..." Nandi replied with a grin. "That's a big leap from partners."

"We have a long way to go." Knightly wrapped his arm around Nandi under the guise of supporting her while they limped through the forest. "Shall we get started?"

Doctor Hanan chuckled and swung his device onto his back. "With the two of you, I daresay this will be an interesting journey."

Nandi pressed her lips against Knightly's. He tasted of sweat, but thankfully, this time, not of fish. "I hope so."

A Wind Will Rise

Andrew Knighton

Dirk Dynamo pedaled frantically, legs going hell for leather to keep the pedalo-thopter's wings flapping. A fierce wind lashed at him, stray cloud brushing his face like Death's own icy fingers. He was glad he'd worn a thick jacket.

"Nearly there," Timothy Blaze-Simms called from the front of the machine, tailcoat flapping as he stood excitedly in his seat.

"We'd be nearer if you'd sit down and pedal," Dirk growled.

They burst out of the cloud bank into clear blue skies. Below them, the Atlantic was just as clear and empty, a carpet of rippling blue from horizon to horizon. The only other sight was their target.

The *Storm of the South* hung in the air ahead of them, looking for all the world like a whale of the skies. Most of the airship was made up of its vast gas bag, acres of treated canvas straining under the pressure from within. A lightning rod rose from the top, and Confederate battle flags hung from its bows, blue crosses dark against their crimson backgrounds. A stain on his country's recent history that Dirk would rather the world could forget. Stopping this floating menace, with its piracy and slaving, could only help.

"Are those seagulls?" Dirk asked as they closed on the airship. His legs ached like hell and he was getting short of breath, so he welcomed the distraction.

"Too big," Blaze-Simms replied, peering through his binocular goggles. "I do believe they are vultures."

"At sea?" Dirk leaned forward, pedaling faster for one last surge.

"One sees very few Confederates since they lost the war," Blaze-Simms said. "Why not vultures who have lost the land? Oh look, almost there."

The back of the gasbag was now beneath them. Dirk lifted himself off the pedals, checked the knife tucked into his boot and the Gravemaker snuggly holstered at his side. Both gave solid reassurance against the battering wind and the sea so far below to either side.

"Ready?" he called out as the pedalo-thopter started to wobble and lose height.

"Ready," Blaze-Simms replied, grasping his swordstick and securing his top hat with a strap.

"Then let's go."

They leapt. Dirk landed with a thump that knocked the air from his lungs. With one hand, he grasped a rope running around the gasbag, securing himself in place, while with the other he grabbed Blaze-Simms as the Englishman slid past.

They watched the pedalo-thopter bounce off the back of the airship and tumble forlornly into the sea.

"I suppose I shall have to make another," Blaze-Simms said. "But this is hardly the moment to worry about it."

"Damn straight." Dirk looked around for the nearest ladder to climb down by.

106

"I believe it's time for tea."

"Dammit, Tim, this is not the time." Dirk glanced around the compact space of the galley, wary that they might be caught out before they found the captives—slaves, Colonel Storm had labelled them, hostages and victims, their families insisted. Innocent folks either way.

"Thirst can be crippling to a chap's fighting capacity," Blaze-Simms replied, putting cups and saucers on the gleaming steel work surface. "And besides, who knows what intelligence we might find?"

"Intelligence? In the kitchen?" Above Dirk's head, pans and kitchen knives swung in the breeze around the air vents.

Blaze-Simms opened another cupboard, blinking in surprise.

"Actually, yes," he said.

Dirk peered over his friend's shoulder. Inside the cupboard huddled a girl, maybe twelve years old, pale and trembling, and wearing the remnants of a once expensive yellow dress.

"You alright there, miss?" Dirk held out a hand, but the girl shrank back, eyes wide with fear. He caught a glimpse of a tear across the back of her dress, and an all too familiar injury on the flesh beneath.

Dirk's blooded boiled. Hadn't they left this behind?

"Someone whip you?" he asked, as gently as he could.

"Bad man," the girl whispered, wrapping her arms around herself.

"Don't worry," Dirk said. "We're here to save you from the bad men."

She shook her head.

"Bad *man*." She held up a single finger.

"There's just one of them running this place?" Dirk frowned. That made no sense. A vessel this large...

"One man and the hundred captives he's taken off ocean liners," Blaze-Simms said, once more rummaging through the cupboards. He turned to the girl with a smile. "I say, you don't have any tea in there, do you?"

She shook her head.

"Coffee would do, at a push."

"Chicory," she whispered.

"Good lord." Blaze-Simms shook his head sadly. "What war's privations will do to a man's tastes."

"Tim, this really ain't the time." Dirk scratched his head. Something was bothering him, a piece missing from his sense of the situation. "If he's got no crew, then how's Storm capturing those ships?"

"By bein' an awful sight smarter than y'all," said a voice behind them.

Dirk spun around, hand going for his Gravemaker.

But it was too late. There was a bright flash of light and his whole body flared with pain. He fell to the floor, blackness closing in on him. The last things he saw were a beard like a shovel, and a pistol that seemed to glow.

Dirk woke to another jolt of pain. He screamed and snapped his eyes open. He found himself looking down at vultures circling above the wide blue of the sea. His body was being stretched out, hands reaching towards the ocean as he hung upside down, strapped by his feet underneath the airship.

To his left, hung Timothy Blaze-Simms, still unconscious—and still with his top hat strapped on. As Dirk looked at him, a screwdriver fell out of Blaze-Simms's pocket and tumbled end over end, glinting in the sunlight, until it was lost to sight against the vastness below.

Turning to the right, he saw another man standing proud amid the riveted beams of the airship's landing struts. The wind tugged at an all-too-familiar gray uniform, crisp and clean except for an old bullet hole near the right shoulder. The man wore a holster on one hip and a whip on the other. Above a thick, neatly-kept beard, blue eyes sparkled like hate-filled diamonds.

"Colonel Storm?" Dirk's tongue felt thick in his mouth, and every nerve tingled.

"Captain Dynamo." Storm spun his pistol one last time, the glass bulb on the back glowing, and holstered it. He gave a casual salute. "Or do you no longer go by rank, sir?"

"Not in a few years." Dirk heaved himself up enough to see the straps binding him to the beams. They were riveted in place, without buckles or laces he might undo. "I seem to remember we met during the war?"

"I crossed paths with most Pinkertons in my day," Storm replied, fingers brushing the ragged hole at his shoulder. "The War for Southern Independence made us some strange enemies, and stranger bed-fellows."

"We've all done things we ain't proud of." Dirk tried to keep the loathing from his voice; loathing for his own past as much as for this man with his slaver's suit. "Looks like you're fixing to do more now."

"Oh, but I am proud of my achievements, Captain. And I am proud of my country." Storm looked towards one of the Confederate flags hanging from the beams, and a tear sparkled in the corner of his eye. "You Yankees may have the upper hand for now, but a wind will rise from the South, sir. It will rise like God's fury let loose upon your vile Union. It will come a-roarin' and a-poundin' against the walls of Washington and New York and all your proud, gleaming cities. The South will rise, sir. The South will rise!"

Storm whipped out his pistol. Lightning burst from its barrel and jolted into Blaze-Simms, who woke with a scream.

Colonel Storm holstered the pistol, its globe glowing a little fainter, and took out his whip. He swung it in long arcs and the vultures circled in towards the hiss. Their eyes shared Storm's hateful gleam, and razor-sharp blades gleamed on their beaks and talons.

"I ain't bein' brought low again, boys." Storm cracked the whip. Pain lashed Dirk's cheek. Blood dribbled down his face and into his hair. The vultures screeched excitedly. "Not by the thievin' Yankee government. Not by the lyin' Pinkertons. Certainly not by some two-bit adventurin' club come boardin' my fine ship on a flyin' bicycle."

The whip cracked again and Blaze-Simms yelped. Blood trickled from his chin.

"Goodbye, gentlemen." Storm saluted the flag and disappeared up a ladder into the airship proper.

The vultures cried out and circled closer.

"I say, old chap," Blaze-Simms mumbled, patting at his many pockets. "What on earth is going on?"

Dirk heaved himself upward, stomach muscles tightening until his head came above his waist and his hands could reach his feet. Being upside down might be a problem for Storm's usual victims of trans-Atlantic emigrants and scared cabin boys, but not for a man who'd made the effort to build up his own body. He reached down the side of his boot, but—as he had feared—the Bowie knife was gone.

He felt a swift lash of pain as razor talons skimmed the back of his legs. Another vulture swept past his head, its beak ripping the back of his jacket.

"Ouch!" Blaze-Simms flailed wildly, as if his thin, flapping arms might deter the birds.

Dirk tried to twist his foot loose but it was no good—his ankle gave an agonizing pop, and the straps showed not the least sign of movement.

"You got any scalpels?" he called out, as another vulture tore a gash in his arm.

"Sorry, no." Blaze-Simms looked pale and frantic, his shirt and tailcoat ripped open in a dozen places, blood soaking the cloth.

"Scissors?"

"No."

"Match?"

"Sorry, nothing pointed or burning or argh!"

Blaze-Simms screamed as one of the birds raked its beak down his back.

"OK, then." Dirk looked back at the vultures. He needed something to cut himself free. He had nothing. Blaze-Simms had nothing. That left one option.

A vulture swooped in close, bladed claws reaching out towards Dirk. Instead of trying to avoid it, he swung towards the bird. It squawked in alarm as he grabbed hold, one hand around its wing, the other around its neck. Two-foot-long wings battered at Dirk while bladed claws hacked at his arm. He squeezed his fists tight and twisted. There was a crack as the bird's neck snapped and it went limp.

"Sorry," Dirk said as he yanked the blade from its beak. "It ain't personal."

He let go of the body and it tumbled away towards the sea, the other vultures chasing it down. Carrion birds always had an eye out for easy pickings.

"It was trying to kill you," Blaze-Simms said. "That seems awfully personal to me."

"Just an animal," Dirk said, heaving himself up to his foot-straps once more. "It's never the critter that's to blame. Always the owner."

He set to cutting himself free.

Dirk and Blaze-Simms crept out of a corridor and into the wheelhouse of the airship. Dirk limped, trying to keep the weight off his injured ankle while still staying quiet. He clutched the blade he had taken from the vulture, while Blaze-Simms wielded a mop handle they had found on the way up through the vessel.

Wind lashed at them as they emerged. The space was less a wheelhouse and more a wheel *deck*, wide open to the elements at the front. The great wheel was strapped into place, keeping them on a straight heading, and there was no-one to be seen. More Confederate flags flapped above the edge of the deck, where a plank protruded out into the open air.

"Stop right there, gentlemen," came the Colonel's distinctive voice.

Dirk turned to see Storm standing in the shadows of the far corner. The glass bulb on the back of his pistol glowed less brightly than before, but it lit his face a stark white as he pointed the weapon towards them.

"Drop that there blade." The Colonel walked slowly towards them, gun steady in his hand. "The stick too."

Dirk, letting the knife go, heard it and Blaze-Simms's mop handle clatter onto the deck.

"Now, over towards the edge," Storm said. "And don't you think of makin' any funny moves."

They slowly sidled across the deck, watching the Colonel's impatient scowl.

"Faster," he growled, blasting the floor by their feet with a bolt of electricity from his pistol.

"I say, that's a frightfully clever device," Blaze-Simms said, as they hurried over towards the plank. "Do you have a generator to power it?"

"Lightning," Storm replied. "Got me a mast catches the power."

"How ingenious!" Blaze-Simms's face lit up with excitement. "But it looks to me like you're running low on power."

"Then I guess I'll have to deal with you by other means." Storm raised an eyebrow, gesturing towards the plank.

"You gonna make us walk that?" Dirk asked.

"Reckon I am. You first, Captain."

"And if I don't go?"

Storm gave the trigger the slightest squeeze. The bolt of lightning that leapt out was small, but it was enough to make Blaze-Simms scream and fall to his knees, flames flickering from the top of his hat.

"Well, alright then." Dirk turned and stepped onto the plank. It was good, solid wood—pine maybe. It had a little spring to it, and he felt it start to bend beneath him as he walked. There were times he'd thought he might die beneath the Confederate banner, but not like this.

Not that he intended to die.

He bent his knees, his twisted ankle aching, and leapt. The plank gave him extra spring as he flung himself sideways, grabbing one of the flags and swinging on it towards the deck.

Storm screamed in fury at the desecration of his precious banner. Pain juddered through Dirk, frying his every nerve end, but he clung on tight. There was a ripping sound, and he free-wheeled through the air, slamming into the deck with most of the flag still in his hands, his heart hammering and his head pounding. Darkness crept into the edges of his vision as he staggered to his feet.

"Damn you, Yankee scum!" Storm raised the pistol, but there was barely any glow in the bulb now. It only buzzed as he pulled the trigger.

Storm reached for his belt, fumbling at a round pouch. Dirk staggered towards him, each step a strain on his screaming muscles, twisting the banner around.

The Colonel opened the pouch, and pulled out another glowing globe. Dirk lashed out with the tightly coiled flag. His improvised whip knocked the ball from the Colonel's hand.

Storm scurried after the globe, leaning down to grab it at the edge of the deck.

Before he could find his balance, Blaze-Simms flung his top hat, the flaming headgear hitting the Colonel in the back of the head. He gave a pained yelp, lost his balance, and went tumbling over the side.

Dirk leaned out and watched as Storm fell, end over end, towards the sea far below, his vultures circling down after him.

"Guess we let the prisoners out now," Dirk said, turning towards Blaze-Simms. "Take 'em all home."

His colleague staggered to his feet.

"Any chance of a cup of tea first?" he asked.

"Only chicory, remember?"

Blaze-Simms sighed.

"Of course. What more can one expect of a pirate?

Hooked

Rie Sheridan Rose

"I want to go on an airship!" Wynelda P. Darling stamped her foot, fists balled at her sides.

"But Wyndie, dear—" her father began.

"An airship!"

Mr. Darling sighed. "It is your trip, and you may plan it as you wish, but half the point of a Continental Progress is to see the Continent. The airships don't land just anywhere you happen to fancy. You will miss the finer points of travel..."

"Don't care, Father. I want to fly!" She spread her arms and twirled in a cloud of skirts. "Please, I'm finally old enough to travel on an airship, and that is what I wish to do. I need adventure. This may be my only chance before I must settle down and be adult."

Mr. Darling sighed again. It was true that Wyndie had been obsessed with birds and flight since she was a fledgling herself. An accident involving a young boy when she was still in swaddling clothes had led to regulations requiring all passengers on the mighty airships to be eighteen or older. Families had to forego air travel if their children were below the age of majority. Wyndie had been marking days off her calendar for two years, dreaming of the day she was old enough to fly.

Today was her eighteenth birthday.

When he had told her over breakfast that his gift to her was a trip around the world, this was the reaction.

"Very well. You shall travel by airship whenever feasible. Will that do? There are some areas not on the routes that I would hate for you to miss..."

"Oh, Father! You are the best, most wonderful man in the world!" She threw her arms around his neck and hugged him enthusiastically.

Whatever Wyndie did was always enthusiastic.

It took three weeks to book all the arrangements, but soon enough Wyndie stood before the air liner Neverland, the most luxurious transport available to the public. She gripped her valise in both hands, vibrating with excitement.

Mr. Darling, hands clasped behind his back, shook his head fondly. "I wish you the finest of trips, my dear. Be on your best behavior. You are representative of our whole family, so do not fail me."

Wyndie rolled her eyes. "I promise, Father."

He led her to the captain, and introduced the man. "Wyndie, dear, this is Captain Pan. Do as he says in all things. He knows his ship—and we can't have you falling off it."

Wyndie groaned. "I am not a child, Father. You will have the captain thinking I have to be lashed to the mast."

The captain chuckled, and then said, "There is no danger of you being taken for a child, miss. I am quite sure we're all in for a lovely voyage."

For the first few days, it seemed the captain was right. The sky was a field of cerulean blue, occasionally strewn with lacy clouds, and kissed by a perfect breeze.

But on the morning of the fifth day, Wyndie woke to masses of gray cloud outside her porthole, and the swaying of the airship as it was buffeted by gusts of wind. Being Wyndie, she immediately dressed in her warmest clothes, and dashed for the deck.

The captain stood at the wheel, fighting for control as the gusts sang through the rigging. Wyndie staggered toward him, bracing herself against the gale.

"Is this normal, captain?" she shouted above the squall.

"It's nothing to worry about, miss, but you'd be safer down in your stateroom."

Wyndie wound a bit of rope around her wrist. "I'm staying here. I've never seen a storm from the top before."

Pan scowled at her. "I could order you down below, but somehow I doubt you'd listen."

"And we have such a short acquaintance for you to know me so well." She batted her lashes at him.

The storm seemed to be growing in intensity, as rain began to lash the deck, making footing treacherous.

"Don't move!" Pan shouted above the wind. "I will not be responsible for you falling off the ship."

"I'm a big girl now." Wyndie glimpsed something in the distance and pointed at it. "What on earth is that?"

Pan followed the direction of her point, and swore under his breath. "I'd know that damn ship anywhere."

"Is that someone following us?"

Pan spun the wheel, fighting to turn the ship. "It's the bloody Jolly Roger—it's Hook! I don't know how he found us, but I will not lose my ship to a bloody pirate."

"A pirate!" Wyndie's eyes widened. "Are we in danger?"

"Not if I have anything to say about it." There was a grim set to the captain's features. "I strongly suggest that you go down below, miss."

"But you might need me!" Wyndie protested. "Where is the crew? I assumed they would be at their stations by now."

"We weren't expecting any trouble, and the meteorological forecast was for clear skies the remainder of the week; most of the crew disembarked at last night's stop to replenish supplies or take a leave. We've only a skeleton staff at the moment, and only one or two of them are sailors. The rest are passenger support personnel."

"Well that is convenient timing."

"I don't need your sarcasm, Miss Darling. If you really want to be helpful, take hold of that rope," he ordered, pointing across the ship, "and pull on it with all your might."

Wyndie braced herself and scuttled to the indicated position. She put all her weight into it, as she hauled on the rope. It moved six or eight inches before she could move it no further.

"That's all I can do, Captain," she shouted, before emitting a squeal of terror at the sight of the pistol in his hand.

"Duck!"

She dropped to the deck as the pistol ball whistled over her head.

"It isn't very sporting to shoot at a lady," chided an unfamiliar voice.

Wyndie glanced up to see a tall figure dressed in black velvet and red silk looming over her. Her mouth fell open. Was this a pirate? He looked so splendid compared to Pan's conventional green uniform.

A sun-browned hand reached down to help her up. She took the assistance to scramble to her feet.

"Unhand her, Hook!" The captain cried.

"What do you say, little lady? Should I let you go?"

Wyndie stammered, "I–I would really rather you didn't." She was standing very close to the rail, and the sky was a boiling sea of cloud beneath the ship.

The pirate threw back his head and laughed.

Wyndie took the opportunity to study him more closely. He was a rakish figure; dark wavy hair pulled back at the nape of his neck, brown eyes that sparkled with humor, a raised scar along his left cheek—the epitome of a pirate. It was almost as if he chose the profession because it matched his looks.

"You look like a lass who favors adventure," the pirate murmured in her ear. "Which would you rather, stay here and be safe, or board the Jolly Roger for questing and treasure?"

Wyndie glanced over the rail at the pirate's ship moored to the Neverland by a pair of boarding ropes. It was a much smaller ship in dark wood with a black and red striped envelope—she was proud of herself for knowing the correct name for the outer skin of the gas-filled balloon— and the skull and cross bones snapping in the gale. Her father would never approve.

She looked once more at the pirate, and he winked at her. A life of adventure, flying free without the constraints of polite society. That sounded much more to her liking. She would have to tell her father someday, but for now...

"I'll go with you, if you please."

"Then hold on tight," Hook told her, tightening his arm around her waist.

Wyndie put her own arms around his neck, only now noticing that his other hand had been replaced by a hook.

He caught her glance at the appendage and whispered, "Watch this." He raised the hook, aimed it at the Neverland's envelope, and jerked his elbow. The hook flew from his arm, splitting into three pieces to form a grapple. It punctured the silk of the envelope, as Hook jumped to the railing with Wyndie under his arm.

She gasped as they flew across the gap to the Jolly Roger, accompanied by the sound of ripping silk. As they landed on the pirate ship's deck, she looked back to see a gaping tear in the Neverland, and Pan leveling his pistol at them.

"Release that rope there, darling," Hook ordered, moving to the second mooring rope.

Wyndie did as she was ordered, and they sailed free of the falling Neverland, as Pan's shot once more went wild.

Hook fought his way across the deck to the wheel of his ship and pushed a series of buttons built into its stanchion. The gale stabilized into a steady wind that blew them away from the passenger ship as the clouds appeared to miraculously disperse.

"Were you controlling the weather?" Wyndie gasped.

"Just a little invention of mine. Comes in handy for a pirate."

"But what about all the passengers on the Neverland?"

"If Pan can't get that ship down safely, he shouldn't be piloting her. That rip will definitely ground her, but slowly enough to steer to safety."

Now that worry was out of her head, Wyndie had another question. "How did you know my name was Darling?" she asked Hook.

He laughed. "I didn't, but it seemed the right thing to call you. Now, my Darling, where shall we go?"

"Where ever the wind takes us."

"You are one for adventure, aren't you?"

"I suppose you could say I am well and truly Hooked."

Go Green

Ross Baxter

Running a floating brothel had never been easy, but—fortunately—Bruce Valmont always liked a challenge. Since the end of the war, he had done very little else and, as a result, thought he'd just about seen everything the business could throw at him, until now. He glanced down at his silver pocket watch; he had ten minutes before the crew would muster in the dirigible's bar and he decided he definitely deserved a drink before he broke the bad news. Donning his best satin frockcoat, he inspected himself in the mirror before leaving his cabin for the bar.

"What can I get you, Colonel?" smiled the barman, putting down the glass he was diligently polishing.

"If you could fill my flask Tom, I'd be much obliged," Valmont answered with a polite nod. Although he and the crew had left the Army Air Corps over half a decade previously, all of them still found it hard not to call him Colonel.

While Tom carefully decanted one of the good bottles into the shiny silver hip flask, Valmont looked around the well-appointed bar. Being early afternoon, the bar was empty, an ideal time for him to brief his loyal team. What he had to tell them would be a sure test of their loyalty, but given their history together he had few concerns in that respect.

"Can I ask what the meeting is about, Sir?" asked Tom as he handed the flask back.

Valmont smiled, but shook his head. "We'd best wait for the others."

As if on cue, the double doors opened and the engineering department walked in. Though only two in number, they were more than capable of running the twin coal-fired turbines, both generators, and maintaining the integrity of the converted Covenanter-class airship. Next came the cook, resplendent in freshly cleaned whites, closely followed by the two deckhands. Finally, the three sporting girls sauntered in, still tired from the night before.

Valmont nodded a greeting to each in turn and with a sweep of his hand indicated that they should sit at the tables. He was justifiably proud of how the small crew of just ten competently handled the dirigible's twin businesses of brothel and federal mail-carrier.

"So what's the occasion, Colonel?" asked Lou Mathabane gruffly. As Chief Engineer, she was effectively second-in-command on board, and usually the first to voice an opinion.

"Some challenging news," began Valmont, looking intently at the seated crew. "Earlier today, I met with Major Drake at Fort Carney. The final supply train before winter hasn't made it through, and—consequently—the two wagons of coal promised by the Army will now not be delivered until March of next year at the earliest."

"But we haven't enough coal to get us more than ten miles from the fort!" Mathabane cut in.

"I know," Valmont sighed. "Drake was under the false impression that we could run the steam turbines on wood. He claimed he had no idea that the lower calorific value and higher organic makeup of the timber would clog the particulate filters and stop the engines before we could even slip the moorings. All he can suggest is that we moor at Fort Carney for the winter. He seemed to think we would jump at the idea and we'd make a fortune through our bar and our ladies servicing the fort."

Hoots of derision rose from the gathered crew. They were only at the fort to deliver supplies and did not plan to stay.

The trouble with the military was that a private's pay of thirteen dollars a month did not go very far. A full winter moored in northern Montana would also play havoc with the dirigible. In addition, Valmont had secured a lucrative contract to deliver post over the winter on a circuit around Indiana, a deal which would treble their normal takings.

"So," Valmont continued, "unless we can come up with a plan, we're stuck here at Fort Carney for a very long winter."

"What have you got in mind, sir?" called Tom hopefully.

Valmont smiled, ever flattered by the seemingly endless faith the crew had in him. "Not much at the moment, but I suggest we all go ashore shortly and scout out other sources of coal. Maybe we can beg, borrow or steal sufficient from the farms and homesteads, or from the fort, to get us heading south. The Duty Watch will remain onboard, but the rest of us will meet back here in fifteen minutes, ready to go scouting."

Nods and sounds of agreement came from the crew as they rose and made off to get ready. Lou Mathabane stood and made her way towards him, nimbly picking her way through the chairs although she was as a big as an ox.

Sweat from the engine room still marked her face, glistening like tiny stars against the dark ebony of her skin.

They both went back a long way, from when Valmont had been forced to promote her during the war after his Chief Engineer caught a musket ball in the gut. The decision caused a storm of protest at the time; not only was she the first female Chief Engineer in the Air Corps, she was also the first Afro-American one.

Despite the objections, it proved to be one of the best decisions he had ever made. Not only did she know turbines and boilers inside out, but she had been the first to join him after the hostilities and had proved her loyalty countless times. She also kept the dirigible running on a shoe-string budget with just a single stoker.

"We'll need at least two tons of coal to get us to the nearest railhead," she warned.

"I know," conceded Valmont. "Let's just hope we get lucky."

After visiting two farms, Valmont was thinking they were just plain out of luck. Both farmers kept their coal securely locked in brick bunkers and neither was prepared to sell or trade despite generous offers. With the reliance on steam-driven machinery, the failure of the final supply train to reach Fort Carney was a disaster for all.

"I hope the other two teams are doing better than us," muttered Lou as they approached the last farm.

"I'm sure the sporting girls will come up with something," Tom chipped in, positive as ever.

Valmont nodded, thinking the same thing. Kate, Amelia and Drea always proved resourceful—and were always ready to turn their considerable powers of persuasion to anything.

Through the failing light, they made out a large two-story timber farmhouse ahead. It was much bigger than the previous two establishments and was flanked by a huge single-story brick building. As they approached, a door opened in the brick construction, and a filthy farm-hand appeared carrying a shovel.

"Evening," nodded Valmont. "Is the owner around?"

The farm-hand stopped and looked at them uncertainly for a moment.

"Are ye looking for work?" he said hesitantly, his eyes seemingly drawn to the imposing figure of Lou Mathabane.

"No," snapped Valmont, a little insulted, in that he had changed in to his best leather frockcoat and did not feel he looked like a farm laborer. "We want to discuss some business with him."

"It's a her," the farm-hand mumbled.

"In which case, where would we find the lady?" Valmont pushed.

"She ain't no lady."

Valmont stared hard at him, trying not to lose his temper. His strict upbringing had ingrained in him a need for politeness and respect for females, whether they deserved it or not.

"Where is she at the moment?" Lou cut in, anxious to prevent a scene.

"She's in the milking shed," muttered the hand, nodding at the building behind him.

Without another word, Valmont pushed past and strode to the open door in the large structure. Lou and Tom followed closely. Inside the building was huge, with row upon row of small pens stretching out in each direction, every enclosure holding a tethered cow. A network of pipes ran from the rear of each pen, each ending in brace of small cylindrical cups. The pipes led upwards and snaked across the planked ceiling towards a room at the far end which appeared to house large copper holding vats and smoke-belching pumping engines. Valmont wrinkled his nose at the earthy smell of cattle and manure.

"There must be a couple of hundred cows in here," Valmont marveled, trying to breathe through his mouth. "It looks like some sort of automated steam-powered milking factory."

"I think she's over there to the left," Lou offered. At six foot five inches, she stood half a foot taller than her companions and had a much better view.

Valmont led the way, gingerly picking a course across the filthy floor whilst holding up the hems of his moleskin trouser legs to ensure they remained spotless. As they approached the woman, their quarry stood and regarded them quizzically.

Prematurely gray, and with a skin darkened by the sun, the glint in her eye and heavy bunching of her arm muscles showed she was not one to be trifled with.

"Can I help you?" she asked flatly.

"I hope so," said Valmont, unconsciously turning on all the charm he could muster. "I'm the proprietor of the dirigible currently moored by Fort Carney. The failure of the last supply train to reach the fort has meant that the commanding officer reneged on his deal to restock us with coal. We're here to see if you'd be willing to sell us any."

"I'm afraid I can't," the farmer replied with a shake of her head. "The failure of that buffoon Major Drake to get the supplies here is a disaster for me too; the heating and milking machines for my herd here are all coal-powered, as are the engines which run the refrigeration plant where I store the cheese. I've only just enough coal to last a really mild winter. I don't have the labor to start cutting lumber, and so I'm going to struggle."

"What if my crew were to cut some lumber for you, would you trade then?"

The farmer made to answer, but was cut short by a huge fart emanating from the rear of a cow in the pen by which Valmont stood. Valmont flinched at both the volume and the light spray of dung which shot forth with the explosion of gas.

The farmer laughed. "I think that answers your question."

Valmont sighed, and flicked bits of manure from the leather sleeve of his frockcoat.

"Would you be willing to sell us a couple of your cows instead?" asked Lou.

"I suppose," replied the farmer. "That much less drain on the coal."

"Wait!" demanded Valmont angrily, turning towards his Chief Engineer. "What the hell do you want with two cows?"

"They might be good company if we're stuck here for the winter," Lou replied, the ghost of a smile playing over her dark lips.

"Have you lost your mind?" Valmont seethed.

"You need to trust me on this," Lou replied calmly. "Have I ever let you down, Colonel?"

"Yes," Valmont shot back, "at Pensacola in '69!"

"Okay," she conceded. "Have I ever let you down—apart from Pensacola seven years ago, when I couldn't fix that scrap boiler you won in a card game?"

"No," Valmont muttered.

"Then buy me the cows and give me twenty-four hours to get us out of this mess," said Lou.

Valmont looked at the dung-splattered sleeve of his favorite frockcoat and swore under his breath. Then he reached inside and reluctantly withdrew his wallet.

The colonel actually gave his Chief Engineer just twenty- three hours before he decided to check on her progress. Unable to wait any longer, he moved to swap his satin lounge-suit for the stained cotton overalls which hung behind the door. He quickly dressed and left the cabin to stalk aft towards the dark heart of the vessel. One deck later, he unlatched the heavy steel door and stepped into the claustrophobic heat of Engineering. It was quieter than usual, with only the reserve generator running, as opposed to the colossal twin cast-iron steam turbines which provided motive power. Over the steady throb of the generator he could make out the sound of heavy hammering and even louder cursing from within the adjoining boiler room. Stepping carefully over sizzling pipes and oil-soaked thwarts he traversed his way over to the open doorway and the source of the foul language.

"I see you're having fun!" Valmont shouted over the din of the hammering.

Lou swung the heavy hammer one last time before rising up from behind the steam duct. She squeezed herself out from beneath an access gantry and nodded a greeting. Sweat poured down her face to soak her overalls

"You only come to the bowels of the ship when you want something," she growled. "And you're early."

Valmont laughed and held up both palms in admission. "I'm ready to hear your apology for making me buy the two cows."

"Ain't gonna happen," Lou muttered, taking a stained rag from a pocket in her overalls and wiping the oil from her hands. "Would you care to step inside my office?"

Valmont smiled wryly as he followed, knowing her office was actually just a battered desk at the back of the engineering workshop. Lou pulled up a wobbly stool for him and switched on the fizzing sodium lamp hanging above.

"Coffee?" she offered.

Valmont glanced at the stained, chipped cups on the table and shook his head.

"You won't have to worry about spending the winter in northern Montana," she began. "Me and the cows have sorted the problem?"

"How?" asked Valmont.

"I've fashioned a set of injectors for the reserve generator and coupled it to the main drive shaft," she explained. "It's woefully underpowered, but should give us a steady seven knots. I reckon we can reach the coaling station at Missoula in around three days."

"But I thought we didn't have enough coal?" countered Valmont.

"We don't. But it's not coal-powered, it's cow-powered."

Valmont rolled his eyes impatiently. "It's not the time for jokes."

"It's no joke," she went on. "When I was a slave in Louisiana, the plantation had milking cows. I was always amazed by how much wind those beasts could pass. It turns out they produce four to five-hundred cubic feet of methane a day. Compressed, chilled, and then injected into the cylinders instead of steam, it produces enough oomph to turn the engine."

"Oomph?" asked Valmont.

"It's a technical term," she answered. "All you need to know is that two cows can produce enough methane to get us to the Missoula depot at quarter-speed. The cows are happily munching silage in the store room right now, and we can depart as soon as you're ready."

"You mean to say that the dirigible will be fart-powered?"

"I prefer to think of it as 'environmentally friendly recycled gas'," Lou replied seriously. "With a bit more development, and the right name, this could be the future of steam! I was thinking of calling it *Green Steam*."

"Fart-powered airships," Valmont muttered sadly, shaking his head at the thought.

"You can't sniff at a rip-roaring idea like this; we'll be able to completely trump the competition," Lou said. "Now let's get ready for blast-off!"

Lost Sky

Amy Braun

The sky used to hold hope for me. Now it held only terror.

I led Abby through the ruined streets, over blood-stained rock and broken glass. Darting behind the remains of a collapsed shop, I curled my arms around Abby's small shoulders.

"Stay behind me. I'm going to take a quick look," I told her.

Abby nodded, eyes glistening with fear and tears. Dirt was smeared along her babyish cheeks. Oil slicked most of her knotted blonde curls. The beige dress shirt she wore was too big, as were the dark brown work pants and boots, but she could run in them. Keeping her hand in mine, I lifted my head over the grimy stone.

The sky was stormy and gray, like the skin of a furious dead man. Hanging in the middle of it was the black monstrosity we called the *Behemoth*. After seeing it through a spyglass, I knew it had earned its name.

It looked like two ships stacked on top of each other. The upper half was enormous, a black man-o'-war covered in large rusted gears. Four rows of gun-ports carrying heavy cannons on the sides pointed an ominous warning down on us few survivors. Three tall masts with black sails shivered like ghosts in the wind. The bow and the stern curved upward like two horns, rows of spikes jutting out from their middles. Just above the rudder was an exhaust port which coughed out dark smoke that poisoned the clouds.

Chained under the *Behemoth* was a smaller vessel that was nearly its replica, except for the slots where the skiffs would berth.

The skiffs were backing out of their docks to go on hunting missions. They were charred metal rowboats with pointed masts and inky black sails. Heavy, gushing smoke spewed from their sterns when they steered. Their figureheads were pointed, conical spears, used to impale an unlucky victim and hoist them to a fate worse than death.

"Are they close?" Abby whispered.

I held my breath and watched the six skiffs chug out of the *Behemoth*, spreading in various directions.

"I don't know yet," I muttered back. "But we're about to find out."

No one knew where they had come from. They simply appeared three years ago between the night clouds and the moon, descending in their evil ships and carrying away the children. The adults who resisted were slaughtered, torn to shreds by demons with black razor teeth, onyx claws, and blood-red eyes. We called them Hellions.

They used to only come at night. The men and soldiers would attack them with their own airships in the daylight, thinking they could overcome them by surprise.

Every ship sent up was shot down, or captured with none of the crew to return. Now they came even during the day, erasing any vestige or illusion of safety.

The few pilots that survived the attacks spoke of a tear in the sky, a rip between two worlds—ours and theirs.

They said that beyond that tear was an obsidian fortress. A few rebellious, possibly insane, pilots ventured through the tear before the daylight attacks. When their crews returned in shambles, they hastily told us that the Hellions had a commander that was dying, and needed blood to be gathered to preserve his life.

No matter how valuable the information was, it served to damn us further. After that daring daylight mission, the Hellions became smarter. They found the crews, butchered them, and began to wear their clothing. It hid them from the sun, and gave them a greater advantage in destroying the few survivors that remained grounded.

I came out of my thoughts when one of the skiffs turned in midair, rapidly making its way toward us.

Cursing under my breath, I dropped down and pressed my back to the rough stucco wall. Abby was silent, watching me with nervous green eyes.

I wondered how she saw me—ten years older than she was—lean and tough, wearing a stained black blouse, scuffed boots, and gray work pants with a utility belt. I was an engineer to my core, and it had saved us more than once.

"Stay low, we have to run," I whispered.

Abby nodded, tightening her lips as tears filled her eyes. I kept her hand tightly in mine then started shuffling away from the broken building.

We raced across the street to a boarded-up shop with a locked door. I hid Abby by another pile of rubble, and then knelt in front of the lock. It was held in place by a simple but effective chain looped around the door handles. I pulled some bolt cutters from my belt and placed the clippers over the chain. I applied pressure until it cracked sharply, separating the lock from the door handles. I grabbed the broken chain and yanked it free. Just as I did, I heard an ear-shattering scream.

My body tensed, head whipping around and looking for the source. It hadn't been far. They were closing in on us.

I grabbed Abby's hand and helped her up. Pulling open the door, I shoved her inside, closing the door behind me. It wouldn't keep the Hellions out, but it was better than nothing. I backed up and looked around to see what kind of store we'd stumbled into.

The floor was littered with glass from broken windows and shattered jars. Areas of the floor were dusted with brown, pink, and white salts. I smelled dried sage and spicy paprika mixing with metallic blood. A spice emporium.

I ushered Abby toward the hip-high counters lining the walls. Their glass covers had been smashed, but the wood bases were solid and would still hide us.

We slipped behind them and edged along the wooden boards, being careful of the broken glass lightly scratching under our feet. I directed Abby toward the storeroom door across from the entrance. Hopefully, it would lead us into a back alley so we could keep running.

The doors exploded open, smashed apart by a ruthless force.

My heart leapt to my throat. Abby's eyes widened with fear, but she covered her mouth and remained still.

I took the pocketknife from my belt and unfolded it quietly. Fear started to fog my mind. I had seen this happen before. They made a grand entrance from the *Behemoth*, then drifted unseen until they found their prey, dragging them into the darkness, ignoring their screams and cries for mercy, wrenching of their masks and tearing open their throats—

Stop it, Claire, I ordered myself. *Just stay put.*

I closed my eyes and forced myself to breathe as quietly as possible.

My relief splintered when glass crunched beyond us.

Abby jumped and squeezed her eyes shut, as if she was in pain. I turned away from my sister's distress and listened as the intruder entered the shop.

Crunch, crunch.

Every step was closer than the last. The Hellion would stop for a moment, presumably to look around, then stalk through the shop again.

Crunch, crunch.

My heart pounded visibly in my chest. I told myself they couldn't smell me; that their senses were dulled from their masks and the scattered spices, but the lies didn't settle my pulse.

Crunch, crunch.

Time stopped. It was at the counter. I clutched the knife to my chest, knuckles white, and risked tilting my head back.

Only the top of the Hellion's helmet was visible—a black piece of hard plastic that refused to reflect any light seeping into the shop. A black tunic covered the hulking body, straining over its muscles. I could see the edge of the respirator around its mouth, but couldn't see the rest of its face.

One quick glance was enough. I looked back down and swallowed the whimper building in my throat.

Crunch, crunch. Crunch, crunch.

My stomach flipped and the whimper nearly burst free. Another Hellion had entered. Our chances of escape were now slim to none. They each had the strength and speed of three men. Two of them would literally tear me in half before I had the chance to scream.

The thought of what they would do to Abby was enough to loosen the terror constricting my heart.

I pointed over Abby's shoulder. She glanced over at the back door then at me. She nodded warily, biting her lips to keep them from shaking. Abby stayed in her crouch and started moving. I followed close behind, watching my feet and avoiding the glass scattered under me.

The Hellions started speaking a language I didn't understand. Their voices were raspy and rough, becoming scratchy squawks when they were excited.

Abby had stopped, their awful voices making her jump and stare at the counter. I wondered if she could see them, if the sight was freezing her resolve. I herded her along by putting my hand on her back and giving her a light shove.

The sharp, wheezing conversation stopped. I slowed down to listen to their boots. Glass was still crunching in the middle of the shop, but it was difficult to tell where each Hellion was positioned. My heart skittered beyond my ribcage and I was practically crushing the knife into my hand, but I kept us moving.

We can make it, the door's right there—

The counter behind me creaked as something heavy landed on top of it. I turned, holding out my knife, and stared up at the shape that appeared there.

The Hellion was dressed in a black jumpsuit with blood-red buttons along the left breast. Its heavy boots, leather gloves, and round helmet almost made it look like a police officer, aside from the gas mask with two black glasses for eyes, staring at me like an insect's. A respirator with a pointed needle on the end covered the Hellion's mouth.

I cringed at the sight of it. I'd seen that needle stab into the necks of helpless victims, heard their screams as their skin turned ashen, blood leaving their bodies at a dizzying speed.

There was another loud thump and Abby screamed. I turned around, seeing the other Hellion had vaulted over the counter and was now standing above of her.

I reacted without thinking. I twisted away from the monster behind me and shot to my feet, charging for the Hellion in front of my sister. It saw me coming and batted my hand away with a hard slap. The stinging pain made me drop the knife. Before I could move again, the creature struck me with the back of its hand.

My chest slammed against the counter, a flash of bruising pain burning along my ribcage. I saw the Hellion perched on the counter scrambling toward me. It moved too fast for me to evade it, its hands lifting me by the shoulders and launching me into the middle of the shop. I landed hard on my stomach, broken glass scraping along my palms.

Something dropped behind me and grabbed the back of my neck, jerking me to my feet. I roared and thrashed furiously, hoping to get in a lucky strike. It whirled me around and swung its fist into my jaw.

Everything tilted as my head snapped to the side, pain swelling across my lower face. Leather fingers knotted in my hair and wrenched my head back. I swung my far fist awkwardly at the Hellion. It clamped its hand around mine and twisted my arm so hard I thought it would be torn from its socket.

I grimaced and blinked, staring at the masked face above me. Terror fuelled the blood in my veins, tunneling into my heart and straining it relentlessly. I tried to glare at the Hellion with hatred, but all I could focus on was the needle on its mouth.

It looked even more terrible up close. A slim spike stained with dried blood. No wider than my smallest finger, but capable of doing irreparable damage. One quick stab, and the blood would be drained from my body. It would flow into the monster, blinding it with hunger, and it would consume me until I was just a husk of skin.

"Claire!" my little sister cried. I couldn't see her. I didn't know if she was crying for help, or pleading for mercy.

"Don't look, Abby!" I shouted back to her. "Don't look—"

The Hellion holding me looked at its companion as the other hissed. I turned my head as much as I could to see what was happening.

The second Hellion had come into the front of the shop, gripping my little sister by the back of her neck. Tears shone on her cheeks; her whole body shivered.

Both creatures screeched and shrieked at each other. I desperately looked for a way to fight, but the Hellion refused to release me.

Then, an agreement seemed to be reached. The monster holding Abby started to drag her away. She cried and struggled, but it carried her like she weighed nothing.

"Claire!" she wailed, fear widening her eyes.

"Abby!" I screamed. " Abby!"

Something heavy struck the back of my skull. I felt myself falling, crumpling onto the ground. I fell into darkness, my little sister's desperate voice still ringing in my ears...

"Hey, she's moving."

I opened my eyes slowly, squinting against the sharp throbbing in my head while everything focused.

Two men and a woman, about my age, stared down at me. The man on the left was stocky and well-muscled, his biceps nearly exploding from his navy blue work shirt. Black stubble covered his head and his eyes were nearly as dark as his skin. At first I was scared of him, but there was no anger or ill intent in his face. He was even smiling a little bit.

On the right was a pretty woman with tanned skin and a whirlwind of dirty blonde hair cut to her shoulders. She was lean and petite, wearing a brown leather vest that curved to her shape. Her baggy black pants were held up by a leather belt decorated with pistols, knives, and brass knuckles. None of those weapons seemed to match the sparkling vigor in her dark brown eyes.

Between them stood a man in a dusty leather jacket with tarnished gold buttons and gray piping. Thin gray shoulder cords dangled under the right shoulder board, and the outside of the high collar was designed with gold waves and swirls. It was a military coat, yet there were no medals on his chest. Under the jacket was a loose white shirt with the three top buttons undone, revealing smooth, tanned skin underneath. He wore black leather gloves, buckled pirate boots, and black pants with a forest green cloth belt wrapped around his waist, tying a flintlock pistol to his hip.

He had high cheekbones and a slightly crooked nose. His chestnut hair was thick and tousled, and he stared at me with roguish, tawny eyes.

They stepped back to give me space and let me slowly stand up. My head felt ten times too big as it pounded behind my eyes. I let out a small groan and put the heels of my hands against my eyelids. Once the pounding went away, I could take Abby and—

A sharp pain tightened my chest. *Abby.*

In a single flash, the gravity of what had happened minutes ago crashed over me. Was it minutes? What if it was hours? What if she was on that horrible airship?

I dropped my hands and looked at the strangers. "Did you see a little girl with curly blonde hair? She was wearing boy's clothing, and she was taken by the Hellions—two of them. Did you see them? Where did they go?!"

The rogue raised his hand. "Calm down."

I glared at him, not caring that he and his friends were armed. "Don't tell me to calm down! Tell me where my sister is!"

The rogue stared at me, no expression crossing his face. "You were the only one we found," he told me. "Your sister is gone."

I fell into a trance of despair. My heart felt like it had been carved out, the emptiness pulsing with pain instead of blood. I gasped air into my lungs, which only made my chest ache more. My head started to spin, but I held my ground.

The rogue took a step closer to me, and I got a better look at his clothes. I froze, looked at his friends, and recognition hit me.

"You're Marauders," I breathed.

The rogue shrugged, trying to seem innocent.

Before the Hellions, Marauders had controlled the skies.

Daring and deadly, they had staged bombing raids through the clouds, capturing any vessels they could and disappearing again before they could be caught. I'd never faced any of them before, but I knew two truths about them.

They loved explosives, and hated being grounded.

A reckless plan formed quickly in my head.

"I can get you back into the air," I said. "I can get you the *Behemoth*."

The three Marauders looked at me as if I was insane. Then they started snickering.

I dug my nails into my palms, the only way I could control my anger. I glared at them hatefully until they finished.

"Going into the clouds is suicide," the rogue said. "Even if you could get us there, we can't pilot that ship. It will be infested with Hellions."

"And if we went in daylight and blew holes in the ship, like the first soldiers did? The sun would filter in and destroy them."

"Or us," the woman added unhelpfully.

"Not if they were small, concentrated blasts in the right areas," I corrected. "I can tell you where to place the charges."

She folded her arms over her chest. "Spend your free time making bombs, do you?"

"No. Repairing their damage," I shot back. "I'm an engineer. I can break as easily as I can fix."

I took a deep breath and looked at the Marauders. Dangerous, selfish pirates, every single one of them. But I could see the longing in their eyes. They wanted to fly again, to feel freedom and power. To sail the Hellions' ship would give them all the respect and fear they could ever desire.

"If you help me rescue my sister, I will make the *Behemoth* yours. The sky will be yours."

It was a steep promise, but one I could keep. At the core, all airships were the same. It might take some time, but I would figure out its operations and make it work for the Marauders. In addition to being a talented engineer, I kept my promises.

After taking a minute to consider my offer, the rogue turned to his friends, the man first.

"Nash?"

He shrugged. "Not like we got anything better to do."

The rogue looked at the woman. "Gemma?"

She grinned wickedly. "Might as well use those sticky bombs we saved, Sawyer."

The rogue—Sawyer—matched her smile. His tawny eyes turned to mine, shining with excitement.

"What's your name?"

"Claire," I answered hesitantly.

His grin widened. "All right, Claire. We're in."

That was great news, until I remembered that my plan had simply been to obtain their help. I had no idea how to get to the *Behemoth,* let alone what to do if we made it inside.

But I couldn't back down. Not when thoughts of what could be happening to Abby ruled my mind.

"Do you have a way to get us up there?"

They chuckled quietly. I wasn't sure whether to be relieved or unnerved by that.

"You could say so," Sawyer smirked.

I don't know how they had stolen it. Taking anything from a Hellion seemed impossible. But there I was, sitting in one of their skiffs. I scowled at the sight of the black metal, the dark splotches of dried blood on the hull and the pointed tip. Just the thought of needing to be on it sickened me.

But it was a gamble that paid off. If any Hellions below saw us, they probably assumed we were flying back to the main ship with fresh victims for their dying master.

Slowly raising my head, I stared at the expansive *Behemoth* above us. It blocked out the sun, drowning us in its huge shadow. I should have been more terrified, yet truthfully, I was amazed.

The airship was a marvelous, if twisted, creation. I could see all the detail and careful construction. Every gear had a purpose, the entire machine needing the smaller pieces to work the larger ones. It was a sight to impress any engineer.

Though I still wanted to see it burn.

Sawyer was piloting the skiff with expert skill. He glided us higher, moving quickly but never enough to draw attention to us. Since the other skiffs were still on the hunt, we were going to be the only one docking under the main half of the airship. I wanted to think that luck was on our side, but I had no idea what we would find once we entered the hideous ship.

"Nash, Gemma, get us ready to dock," Sawyer commanded.

The two Marauders at the front of the skiff lurched up and moved purposefully as they uncoiled the harpoon guns from the compartment under their seats. Gemma dropped her rucksack, filled with sticky explosives, next to my boot. I frowned and inched my foot away from it. I was told they could only detonate after they were timed, but that didn't mean I wanted to be near them.

They retrieved the harpoons and began loading them into the guns. I glanced nervously at the *Behemoth* again. It was now the only thing I could see when I looked up. There were no sickly clouds or thickening smoke. There were only the crunching gears and screeching wheels of the Hellions' ship. Instinct kicked in, and I hunched down. I didn't want to be anywhere near this monster. I wanted to be back on the ground, running from danger instead of approaching it.

But Abby's in there. She needs you.

The thought seemed to stir a little more courage into me. I pulled my eyes away from the *Behemoth* and looked at Gemma and Nash. Sawyer turned the skiff so it was directly facing an open dock. A row of holes lined the inside of the gate. Clear shots for the harpoon guns. Once we were straightened, Sawyer left the helm and smoothly walked to his friends.

Nash and Gemma didn't need instructions. They lifted their harpoon guns and fired at the same time. A thick metal spear shot out of each barrel, a heavy rope darting toward one of the gate locks. It shot into the lock, the rope snapping and going taut. They dropped the guns and began to pull the ropes.

Sawyer was helping Nash adjust a knot in his rope, as Gemma stared at them impatiently. I got up from my seat and grabbed the rope behind her. The pirate woman turned her glare on me, but I just glared back.

We pulled the chain when Sawyer gave the command. Our combined strength hauled the skiff into its dock until it snapped loudly into place. Once it was secure, I looked at the black walls beside the skiff. Each side held a watertight door with a large hand wheel. Sawyer and Nash walked to the door on the right, both of them taking a side of the wheel. Together, they pushed and pulled on it. It screeched as it twisted, but soon enough the two young men had opened the door. They held it so Gemma and I could slip through, and then Sawyer swung himself inside, quickly followed by Nash.

It was pitch black within the docking bay, but I could see well enough. The corridor we entered was narrow and plain, with a single staircase leading upward. It curved around after about a hundred steep steps, which would lead to the top half of the airship if its outer design could be trusted.

I didn't wait for the others, bounding up the stairs as fast as I was able.

By the time I made it to the top platform, my legs were rubbery and my lungs were burning. To my relief, I wasn't the only one winded. The Marauders behind me were bent at the waist, gasping in air. As my heartbeat slowed, I looked up and saw another watertight door blocking us from the interior of the ship. When we'd caught our breath, Sawyer turned to Gemma and Nash.

"Remember what Claire told you?" he asked.

They nodded. I had explained how to space the explosives evenly during our flight up to the *Behemoth*.

"We'll go look for her sister and take the ship. Once you plant the bombs, get back here, wait thirty minutes, and then blow them. Whether we're back or not."

"Sawyer, are you sure about this?" Nash asked, seeing the seriousness on his captain's face.

"Sure enough. But you know the rules. Pirates aren't patient."

It must have been some kind of code, because neither Nash nor Gemma contradicted him.

Sawyer beckoned Nash. The big Marauder followed his captain, taking my place by the wheel on the door.

I stepped back to give them space, studying Sawyer. Could the *Behemoth* really be worth all this risk? Did he want a life of adventure back so badly? Did he just want to spit in the eye of the Hellions? Or was this pure selflessness? The chance to save an innocent life from the monsters that had taken so many? Sawyer was a mystery I doubted I would ever solve.

Sawyer and Nash opened the door, which was just as cranky as the last one. I slipped through, with Sawyer trailing behind me.

It was like stepping into a monster's belly. The hallway before us stretched until it was lost in shadows. The floor was smooth, bolted iron that gleamed red in the pockets of light skimming across it. That light came from rectangular gaps in the walls, flaring behind slim archways which curved like ribs under the hundred foot ceiling. The red glow made me think of the dozens of furnaces which must work to keep a ship this size running. The air tasted thick and smelled like ashes. I heard flames crackling, saw their light shove against the shadows and skitter along the walls.

Fresh sweat trickled down my neck, spine, and temples, not just caused by the boiling heat. I knew Abby was here somewhere—that she was terrified and desperate for help—but my body didn't want to move. It didn't trust the darkness or the red lights. It didn't want to turn a corner and find flames, or Hellions, or my sister's unseeing eyes as she lay on a pile of corpses.

Something touched my shoulder. I jumped.

It was Sawyer's hand. I caught a glimpse of Nash and Gemma moving down the hall behind him. Sawyer stared at me blankly, but calmly.

"Come on. There's another door over here," he said, pointing to a tall, rectangular shadow on our right. "Let's start there. Maybe it's a secret path that'll lead us to your sister."

I found my voice quickly. "What about the ship?"

"It can wait." Sawyer turned and started walking away.

I stared at his back, dumbfounded. "You only agreed to this because you wanted the *Behemoth*," I burst out. "Why would you want to find my sister first?"

Sawyer stopped walking. His shoulders stiffened for a moment, and then went slack.

"I had two little brothers," he said, so quietly I barely heard him. "I couldn't save either of them from…this."

He didn't turn and let me see his heartache, but I heard it. He'd felt the pain of losing family to the Hellions. He didn't want me to suffer the way he had.

"I'm sorry, Sawyer," I told him.

"Don't be," he replied roughly. "Once we find her, alive or dead, you're going to keep your end of the bargain."

If he hadn't just bared part of his soul, I would have argued with him. Instead, I bowed my head and followed him.

We moved quickly, entering the door and rushing through another dark corridor until we came to a cool room lit by bleak yellow lightbulbs. The shadows in the room were thick, but I could see what I needed to see.

Rows of metal plates about the size of a man lined the walls, each with leather straps at the top and bottom. To the left of each was a clear tube attached to a blocky, black electrical pump at the base. Held in place by those straps were a dozen half-naked humans with a large needle in their necks. The clear tubes steadily pumped fresh blood into the mechanisms at the base of the metal plates. The wires connected to these pumps snaked along the blood-spotted floor and connected to a large tank next to an even larger circuit breaker. The breaker was lined with numbers and lights, some glowing green while a couple blinked red. I looked at the survivors, watching the short, slow rise and fall of their chests. Most of these poor people were sickly gray, their breathing shallow and short. Some weren't moving at all.

Horror and sickness filled me, almost making me vomit. Men, women, boys, and girls of all ages had been stolen from their homes, captured and tortured, drained of blood to feed a monster that wasn't even on our side of the rip.

The plate nearest the breaker caught my attention. It held a little girl with unkempt blonde curls and oversized clothes. My heart leapt into my throat.

Abby.

I ran to my sister, stopping in front of her plate. I clutched her shoulders as gently as I could.

"Abby! Abby!"

She didn't answer, didn't open her eyes. I stared at the tube, watching it drain the blood from my sister's body. Her skin still had some color to it, so perhaps she was brought here as a way to tide the Hellions over until they could gather more victims. Disgusted by the thought, I grabbed the tube and steadied myself to tear it out.

"Claire, wait!"

I glared at Sawyer over my shoulder.

"Find a way to stop the machine," he said reasonably, stepping closer.

He was right, damn it. The sight of my sister's closed eyes and ashen skin had made me lose focus.

I took a deep breath and stepped back. Forcing myself not to look at her, I turned to the humming circuit breaker. Near the bottom was a square piece bolted onto an otherwise solid chunk of iron. I knelt down in front of it, drawing a screwdriver from my belt. The bolts were easy to unscrew, dropping with soft clatters onto the floor. I peeled away the panel and studied the wires inside.

There were hundreds of them, but past the smaller wires was one large black cord about the size of my fist. The power cable. Just what I needed.

Placing my screwdriver back onto my belt, I reached inside the opened panel and felt around the bottom of the cord. It was attached to the floor by four heavier bolts. I grabbed the battery-powered drill from my hip and ducked back into the machine. It was difficult to work both of my arms into the small, square hole, but I managed to find the first bolt and drill it out.

It took little over a minute to get the rest of the bolts unscrewed. I put the drill away and grabbed the tube, giving it a fierce yank. The cable make a loud, angry pop as it was released, air hissing into the new space.

Then the whine of machinery began to dull. I pulled my arms back and stood up, turning to Abby. Blood had stopped flowing into the tube. It had worked.

I unstrapped Abby from the plate, starting with her legs. As soon as I undid the straps around her chest, she toppled forward. I caught her, tears forming in my eyes.

"It's okay, Abby," I whispered, smoothing down her tangled curls. "It's okay, baby sister."

There was a slight breeze against my neck.

"Claire?"

Her voice was hoarse and frail, but it warmed my heart.

"I'm here, sister," I told her. "We're getting out of here."

I looked over my shoulder when Sawyer approached. He glanced at my sister, then at me. "We need to move. I'll carry her."

I hesitated, but nodded. I looked at the other dying humans in the room. "What about them?"

Sawyer glanced at them and sighed. "There's nothing we can do for them. We can't carry them all and even if we could, look at them, Claire. They're almost dead. We'd just be taking corpses back to the ground."

He lifted Abby into his arms, turned, and started jogging from the room. I chased him through the dark corridor into the hallway, barely seeing where I was going until he skidded to a stop and I nearly crashed into him. Abby screamed and buried her face in Sawyer's chest.

A dozen Hellions were blocking our exit.

They must have just returned from hunting, because their masks and gloves had been removed. Lank black hair hung on either side of splotchy white faces. Serrated black claws protruded from their fingertips. Glowing red eyes shone like flaming coals. The monsters opened their jaws and revealed two rows of jagged teeth.

In a flash of movement, Sawyer twisted and handed Abby to me so he could draw his pistol, but he was probably thinking the same thing I was.

We are going to die.

There was no way we could survive when the Hellions charged us. Abby should have run when I told her to—

The *Behemoth* shuddered violently. I bent my knees to keep my balance on the vibrating floor. The Hellions chittered and shrieked at each other, trying to figure out what was happening. Then the airship rocked again, and I knew.

Gemma and Nash had triggered the explosives.

I turned my head to look past Sawyer at the hull of the *Behemoth*. A speck of gray light filtered into the ship's belly, and then another, and another, and another. Each speck of light grew larger as it edged closer, blasting away the shadows and bringing daylight into the airship.

The Hellions realized their danger, and that they had no way to escape. They panicked and started to run for the shadows, scrambling to put their protective gear back on and forgetting all about us. Any Hellion that was able to get their mask and gloves on was immediately shot in the head by Sawyer.

I grabbed my sister's hand and sprinted with her and Sawyer to the door beyond the panicking Hellions. They were spreading out, cutting off any chance we had of sneaking around the edges. There was no choice but to run through them.

More sharp, sudden explosions rippled through the *Behemoth*, making us stumble as we rushed through the invaders. Sawyer shoved away creatures that shifted too close to us, lashing out with a punch when he could. I would swear there was a grin on his lips.

The pockets of light were gaining quickly, murky gray beams shining through the holes. The Hellions scratched, clawed, and bit each other, crazed in their desperate attempt to escape the light.

But we're nearly there. Just a few more steps—

A chunk of the hull burst inward off the ship, clanging loudly against the iron floor. Two unprotected Hellions were trapped in the light, both of them dropping to their knees and screaming in agony. I watched their skin blacken and peel, bloody muscles singeing and catching fire. In seconds, I saw the creatures turn into humanoid flames then crumble to a pile of black dust.

The next shock was stronger than the last. It threw us onto the ground, sending pieces of shrapnel tumbling over us. Sawyer landed beside me, quickly rolling onto his front and covering his head with both hands. I grabbed my sister and pulled her close, shielding her as much as I could from the deadly metal.

Thunderous wind and animal howls reverberated in my ears. The floor trembled under me. I smelled smoke and burning skin. I thought it would never end.

But then, it did. I could still smell smoke, but heard no more screams. I raised my head carefully then took Abby's hand and stood up with her.

A dozen smoking ash piles lay around me, tiny flecks being swept away by the wind. Pale light filtered in behind me, pushing away the shadows. Holes at least six feet high and six feet across peppered the hull of the *Behemoth*. The damage was extensive, but the ship's powerful engines would keep it afloat. For now, we were safe.

The Hellions were dead.

My little sister abruptly threw her arms around me, and I smiled.

"I knew you'd find me," Abby whispered.

My heart ready to burst from relief, I stroked her hair, and then looked at Sawyer. He was sitting across from me, watching us with contentment slightly marred by sadness. I nodded my gratitude. He returned the gesture.

The door behind us, which had survived the explosions, was thrown open. Nash shouldered his way through, Gemma right behind him. Both of them smiled with relief.

"Thought you weren't gonna make it out," Nash said.

Sawyer grinned crookedly. "You forgot how lucky I am."

Nash and Gemma chuckled at that. Sawyer looked at me again.

"I want to make a new deal," he said.

I narrowed my eyes. "What kind of deal?"

Sawyer held my eyes.

"There's nothing down there for you and your sister," he said. "Any food or materials are going to be snatched up by whoever has the fastest hands. There will be riots and murders. You won't be any safer than you were when the Hellions were around. If the rumors are true, this is the only ship those animals ever had. Their leader will probably die off in a few months. We could very well have seen the last of them. If you join my crew as an engineer and help me fix this ship, you won't have to worry about protection ever again. We look out for our own, and we could do with a clever engineer."

The playfulness in his smile reached his eyes.

"So, would you rather struggle to live off scraps, or would you rather sail through the clouds?"

All eyes turned to me. Nash and Gemma looked interested, even a little hopeful. Sawyer was expectant. I glanced down at Abby, whose face was filled with wonder, excitement...

Hope.

It had been so long since I'd seen that look in her eyes, so long since I felt its warmth fill my chest. There was only one choice. I looked at Sawyer and smiled.

"We'll choose the sky."

Miss Warlyss Meets the Black Buzzard

Diana Parparita

Miss Isabella Warlyss was inspecting the delicate engraving on the mahogany panels that covered the walls of her cabin with the air of a connoisseur. She had already identified the country of provenance—Ardesia—and the style and period they belonged to—early eighteenth century pre-Victoriana—and was now discussing their aesthetic merit and praising the workmanship to Colonel Austeria Hazelhold, her host, chaperone, and jailer aboard the *Glass Maiden.*

What Isabella was actually looking for, as she brushed her fingers over the intricate details of the woodwork, was the switch that would open a secret passage...her ticket to momentary freedom should Colonel Hazelhold take her eyes off her for just one moment. She hadn't seen any blueprints of the *Glass Maiden*—all information on Imperial vessels was strictly guarded—but she had yet to see blueprints of any airship that didn't have a secret exit for their first class passengers.

"My dear, there is nothing to be found in that corner you are so greatly praising," Colonel Hazelhold said rather abruptly. "And, at any rate, there can be nothing of interest for a young lady aboard an airship like the *Glass Maiden*. I should say, nothing of interest that could be found *outside* this cabin.

"If you wish for a better view of the sea of clouds below us, we can go out on the deck for a little while, and you will notice that you are equally bored outside the cabin as in it."

"There are plenty of interesting things on an airship," replied Isabella. "There's the engine room—"

"—Which you are forbidden from visiting," Colonel Hazelhold interjected.

"But I could learn so much there!" Isabella pleaded, clasping her hands before her in a most imploring stance.

"There is nothing you can learn from watching a bunch of men throw coal into a furnace," replied Colonel Hazelhold. "And all a young lady like you needs to learn is how to look pretty, be obedient, and wear her dresses without staining them. I assume your father, Governor Warlyss, has already informed you that you are to be married as soon as a suitable husband can be found. Your duty, my dear—to your father and to your country—is to secure a foreign husband whose political influence will strengthen our position in these barbaric territories. There is *nothing* you can learn in an engine room that would help you with *that*."

Isabella did not seem too thrilled at the prospect of marriage. She had always abhorred her father's business associates back home, before he'd bought his governorship and she'd been sent off to the *Pensionnat*, and she imagined his political allies would be equally boring.

Having spent the past ten years of her life cooped up in Madame Belchagrin's *Pensionnat for Young Ladies*, reading forbidden periodicals of science and romance by the light of a dim candle, she was now eager to explore the world and its wonders. Instead, she found herself confined to her cabin, under the ever-watchful eye of her chaperone, and bound on a one-way trip home to Chipateria, and a marriage of convenience to an odious man—for he was bound to be odious under the circumstances—chosen by her father to better *his* political interests.

Her bitter thoughts were brusquely interrupted by the most unromantic sound of a siren going off in the communication tubes and erupting from the brass funnel above her head. Colonel Hazelhold jumped up from her armchair, her hands reaching instinctively for the pistols strapped to the twin belts that decorated her uniform.

"Incoming ship!" the voice of Captain Arabald boomed from the communication tubes, echoing throughout cabins and corridors. "All hands on deck! All military personnel to the bridge!"

Colonel Hazelhold's lips twitched in disgust. She wasn't used to taking orders from a captain. But aboard an airship of the Imperial Fleet, all troops, whether regulars or passengers, were at the command of the ship's leader.

She gave Isabella a curt nod, marched out of the cabin, and locked the door behind her. A moment later, her rushing footsteps pounded down the corridor and up the stairs.

"Imperial ship, straight over our heads!"

Captain Jack Coggs of the *Black Buzzard* tipped his tricorn over his left ear and shouted over the deafening sound of the engines.

"Double the speed! Increase altitude! Prepare grappling hooks! Get ready to board this beauty!"

His words were met with cheers and aye-ayes, and a belch of dark smoke from the *Buzzard's* furnace. The smaller ship burst out of the cloud that had kept it hidden from view, and darted in pursuit of the imperial vessel, buzzing and whirring from every valve and hinge.

On its deck, below the balloon that kept it in the air, a handful of men in colorful clothes were readying their pistols, aiming them at the still distant ship. Below the deck, the *Buzzard's* only gunner, Steve McSteam, was loading the guns with his special grappling hooks, meant to grab hold of the enemy ship and wheel her in, to bring its treasures closer to hand. On the bridge, Captain Coggs had taken the wheel into his own hands and was pushing switches and pulling levers to adjust her speed and altitude.

The skies above Chipateria were known for their daring pirates, ready to attack any ship that might fly by. The imperial vessel did not, therefore, waste time in trying to ascertain the identity of the approaching ship. A siren, loud enough to be heard from the *Buzzard*, rallied the troops it had aboard, and a burst of cannonballs immediately followed.

"Watch out, boys, the Empire sends its regards!" Captain Coggs shouted, deftly maneuvering the *Buzzard* up and sideways, to keep it on the imperial ship's tail, where its cannons couldn't aim. The larger ship turned, trying to keep the *Buzzard* in view of its starboard cannons, but it was too slow, its movements hindered by its bulk and its heavy cargo. The *Buzzard* zipped behind it in a crazy game of tag.

"This is Captain Arabald of the *Glass Maiden!*" a voice boomed from the larger ship, magnified by the communication funnels. "You are approaching an imperial airship. Surrender now, and your lives will be spared."

Captain Coggs burst into a fit of laughter.

"They're taking us for idiots," First Mate Fumes noticed, readying his gun and aiming it at the imperial vessel. "Want me to take them down now? One well-aimed shot at that balloon filled with hydrogen is all it takes."

"Not before we take their treasure, Fumes. Get ready to shoot some soldiers, we're closing in. McSteam, we'll be in position in five! Four! Three!"

The *Buzzard* doubled its speed, advancing along the balloon that kept the *Glass Maiden* in the air, until the two ships were side by side.

"Two! One!"

The *Buzzard* suddenly dropped in altitude as McSteam pulled a lever on the firing mechanism, making its five portside cannons release their grappling hooks all at once. Five sturdy ropes tied the *Buzzard* to the *Glass Maiden* as the pirate ship hovered below the imperial ship's line of fire.

Captain Coggs released the wheel into the hands of his helmsman and drew his pistols, shouting at his men to follow him. Nimble as monkeys, the pirates climbed the ropes onto the imperial ship.

They were met by a squadron of soldiers with muskets ready. Guns fired, releasing smoke and bullets. Blood splattered on the precious wooden panels and wide windows of the *Glass Maiden*. Soldiers and pirates alike fell in agony, but for every bullet the soldiers had ready, the pirates had three. Shooting with both hands and drawing charged pistols from their belts one after another, the pirates quickly incapacitated their enemy.

In a matter of seconds, the soldiers were lying on the ground, holding their shoulders and arms where they'd been hit, trying to stop the blood flowing out of their fresh wounds. The pirates didn't bother to tie them up. They broke up into groups, one headed for the engine room to ransack its supplies of coal, another headed for the cargo area to load whatever wares the ship transported onto the *Buzzard*.

Captain Coggs and First Mate Fumes ran to Captain Arabald's cabin and helped themselves to whatever they could find; from Port wine and fine cigars, to maps and sextant, and a compass in a mahogany box. The looting was swift and in under half an hour the pirates were gone, sliding back down the ropes to their ship and severing ties with the *Glass Maiden*.

Captain Coggs took the wheel once more and the *Buzzard* zipped back into the clouds below the imperial ship, disappearing as if it had never existed. In their rush, however, the pirates didn't notice they'd taken on a stowaway.

The woodwork had not failed Isabella. There was indeed nothing in the corner she'd been inspecting, but there was something on a panel behind Colonel Hazelhold's armchair.

An elephant's tusk turned forty-nine degrees to the right, a tiger's tail rotated counterclockwise for a whole three hundred and sixty degrees, a hunter's rifle nudged downward by two degrees and one final push on the center of the engraved sun, and a panel slid open to reveal a sturdy oak door that opened outward into open air.

A gust of wind greeted Isabella as she stepped outside, onto a narrow ledge circling the ship's hull. Loose strands of copper-colored hair, freed from the tight bun imposed by the austere fashion of genteel society, brushed against her cheeks as she grabbed tightly onto the metal handrail suspended some three feet above the ledge.

A moment later, the ship's guns went off like deafening thunder.

She held on to the handrail, unwilling to relinquish her freedom for the safety inside. A second burst of gunfire made her skirt fly most improperly as a cannonball erupted from just below her feet. She looked about for the enemy, but only a loud buzz betrayed the existence of another ship.

The next round of gunfire she heard was of pistols, and sharp cries told her that their soldiers had been hit. For a moment, she thought she recognized Colonel Hazelhold's voice in the commotion.

She proceeded along the ledge, turning around the prow of the ship. She could see, now, a small vessel below her feet, just below the line of fire of the *Glass Maiden*'s guns, tethered to the imperial ship with long, sturdy ropes.

It was, no doubt, a pirate ship.

Above her head, imperial soldiers were screaming in pain.

She glanced behind her, at a world under her father's dominion, where the threat of an unpleasant marriage hung above her head. Before her, on the pirate ship, there was danger—to her person, as well as to her innocence, if the forbidden romances she'd read spoke the truth. But there was also freedom.

Carefully, glancing down at the sea of clouds below, she climbed up onto the handrail. She took a deep breath, closed her eyes to think through her options one more time, opened them again, and jumped, reaching for a rope directly in front of her.

The flying island of Rumnia was the perfect pirate den. Hidden in the skies above Chipateria, and constantly changing its position, it could only be found by pirates who knew where it was going to be next. Several ships were docked there to exchange supplies and let the men enjoy the pleasures of its seven taverns.

Captain Coggs's ship was always welcome, as was his crew, and it was said the seven tavern keepers fought every night for the captain's generosity, as did the tavern wenches. Captain Coggs was young—not yet thirty years of age—and devilishly handsome, in spite of the deep scar dug into his left cheek.

He had a nice voice too, and was known to sing a pretty ballad when he'd had enough of Boozemaster Swine's special brew. To top it off, he was rich—having amassed the most treasure of all the captains that visited Rumnia Island—and he was generous, always ready to give a gold coin where silver would suffice.

He had only one flaw in the eyes of the islanders. He liked to spend more time in the engine room than in the taverns.

But that was never the case on the first night after a successful raid, when all the crew was celebrating. So, as soon as they docked, at nightfall, the *Buzzard* was left deserted and unguarded, its gold making swift legs toward the nearest tavern.

From her hiding place, Isabella waited for the sounds of voices and footsteps to die down. And she waited half an hour more, just to make sure she'd be safe, counting the seconds by her heartbeats.

Her father's business associates had been boring and unpleasant indeed, but judging by what she'd heard in the few hours since she'd stolen onboard the *Buzzard*, it seemed the pirates she'd ended up with were far worse, worse indeed than even the scariest of the novels she'd read.

It seemed every other word they uttered was a curse word, and even the words in between sounded rude and vulgar, though she was willing to give them the benefit of the doubt because of all the technical terms she wasn't familiar with.

She was beginning to think that she'd made a mistake. But then, as long as they didn't see her, here—at least—she could keep her freedom. Though it was little freedom indeed, in the tiny closet where she was hiding.

At the end of half an hour of perfect silence, Isabella pushed open the door of her hiding place, looked out into the deserted corridor, took a deep breath and set about exploring the ship.

Perhaps the smartest thing to do would have been to sneak off the ship and find some less dangerous place to spend the night. Perhaps it would have been wise to find a ship bound for the continent below; for instance, one of the smaller trading vessels that the tavern keepers used to get supplies. And perhaps, this was what she would have done, had she not stumbled straight into the engine room.

Engines had always been her weakness, even more so than the forbidden romances she read at the *Pensionnat*. A lady had no business soiling herself with soot, as Madame Belchagrin used to say, and so the scientific journals she read were equally forbidden, but she'd done her best to keep herself well informed on the subject.

Still, she'd never seen a real engine before, only diagrams that didn't quite satisfy her appetite for knowledge. The *Buzzard*'s engine possessed, therefore, an inescapable attraction. She could not leave the ship without examining the tangle of pipes that constituted the ship's innards.

She had to see them, touch them, test them. Nothing in here fit the neat diagrams she'd seen. The entire place was a mess. Dust and grime covered the whole room, and rust was beginning to eat at some of the screws holding things together.

Things that should not have been connected were tied together, things that should have been connected were tangled and clogged. Her heart ached to see the engine and pipes in such a state.

Her mind raced over the diagrams in her head, over the tips and tricks she'd committed to memory, over hundreds of pages of periodicals read by candlelight with her heart racing in fear of the terrible Madame Belchagrin.

Before she knew it, her hands had reached for a wrench and she was working on improving the engine, on modifying it, on fixing it, her mind already concocting schemes that would double its power and speed.

Around midnight, there were footsteps on board, but Isabella didn't hear them. She'd made a fine mess of herself, her muslin dress covered in oil and soot, and her copper curls loosed from the constraints of the bun that had held them properly at the back of her head. She looked like no lady—that much was certain.

But the man who walked in and disturbed her certainly looked like no gentleman either. His clothes were in a state of disarray, with his coat and shirt unbuttoned and stained with rum, the smell of which wafted from him like cheap perfume. His long, dark hair was tied back in a messy ponytail, almost as mussed as her own hair. And his face—though handsome, and not without an air of nobility to its features—was covered by at least three days' worth of stubble, and marked by a deep scar on his left cheek.

Furthermore, the man swore like no gentleman, and he spent the first five minutes after walking in deeply engaged in this occupation, much to Isabella's consternation, before he interrupted his string of invectives with the words, "What, in the Devil's name, are you doing to my engine?"

Isabella thought it best not to give him time to resume his cursing, and hurried to explain exactly what she was doing, in a string of technical terms that betrayed long familiarity with her forbidden collection of scientific journals.

This effusion left the man speechless, his mouth wide open and his jaw dropping. He didn't seem to regain the ability to curse until after she'd finished.

"By all the cogs in Beelzebub's butt," he said in answer to her explanation, "I'll be damned if I understood a thing! Listen, Missy, I don't care who you are, or how you got on my ship, but I built that engine myself and I won't let anyone mess with it. So put down that wrench nicely, or I'll shoot you."

And he accompanied his words by reaching for his gun, though, judging by how unsteady his legs were, it was not certain whether he could aim.

The gesture was still menacing enough to make Isabella lower her wrench. She bent down and left it on the floor, and pushed it away with her foot to appease him.

"Good," the man said. "Now go to some sailor's bed, where you belong, and leave my ship alone."

"I beg your pardon," Isabella answered sharply, her cheeks burning with his insult, "but I think I belong *here*, with that wrench in my hands *fixing* your *mess* of an engine."

And she proceeded to explain, in just as baffling terms as before, everything that he'd done wrong in building the thing. A lesser man than the gentleman before her might have been enraged by such criticism, but he actually seemed to begin to understand her and her jargon.

He came closer to look at what she'd done. The smell of rum wafting from him made her dizzy as he leaned over her shoulder to inspect the pipes. She wished she'd kept the wrench to use as a weapon against him, in case he turned violent, but he seemed mollified by what he saw. Even his swearing had lost its intensity, and some of his curses sounded almost appreciative.

"Look, lady, you obviously know a few things," he finally said. "And I wouldn't be a gentleman if I were to throw you out in a place like Rumnia.

"Perhaps we should start over. I'm Captain Jack Coggs of the *Black Buzzard* and this is my ship."

He gave her an awkward bow and took her hand, leaning in to kiss her grimy fingers.

"And I'm Isabella Warlyss, runaway daughter of Governor Warlyss of Chipateria and I'm in need of a place to stay as much as this ship is in need of a good mechanic."

"Warlyss..." Captain Coggs said with a frown. "I don't think you'll find anyone willing to risk his neck to take you on board, not with your daddy hunting us down like a madman if we do."

"I was thinking a *brave* pirate captain like yourself wouldn't be afraid of my father or of anyone else."

"It's what you'd do to my ship that I'm afraid of," Captain Coggs answered, scratching his rugged jaw. "And it looks like you've been busy already."

"I can make this the fastest ship you've ever seen. Faster than any ship in the Imperial Fleet," Isabella hurried to assure him. "You've done a great job building it, and with the improvements I've made and a few more tweaks, we could be unbeatable. Just let me stay."

Captain Coggs gave her a long look, scratching his chin once more.

"And you'll want your own cabin too, I reckon," he complained. "I'm not saying 'yes' until I see what this ol' girl can do. And if you've messed it up, I'll have you walk the plank above your daddy's mansion, understand? There's a merchant vessel coming into Chipateria two days from now. We'll test your 'improvements' then. They'd better be good."

"Imperial ship, straight over our heads!"

The *Black Buzzard* darted noiselessly out of the cloud that had been hiding it. The imperial ship greeted it with a burst of gunfire, but Captain Coggs quickly maneuvered the *Buzzard* out of harm's way and on the ship's tail. He made the smaller vessel dance around the slower merchant ship, taunting it. A low purring rose from the pipes as the engine reached its top speed.

"Looks like we got ourselves a new mechanic," Captain Coggs said, nodding to Isabella. "McSteam, get ready to fire the grappling hooks! We'll be in position in five! Four! Three! Two! One!"

Plunder in the Valley

Libby A. Smith

"I'm just a poor, wayfarin' stranger, travelin' through this world of woe..." When Miss Bea stopped singing, so did the rest of the choir, followed by the congregation. Not only was she the unofficial church lady, she was the town matron. It wouldn't do to keep singing if she wasn't.

Instead, she tilted her head, listening to a distinct *chugga-chugga* sound getting louder and louder. "What is that racket?"

Constable Vernon Hicks dashed out the sanctuary door. "Anyone expecting something by Airship Express?" he called back.

"On a Sunday? Ain't fittin!" Miss Bea announced. All adults muttered their agreement as she walked from the choir loft down the aisle. The church had no choir robes, so she wore her Sunday-best apron which had been handed down from her grandmother. Covered with barely-faded flowers, it'd been made from store bought fabric.

"That airship is black," Vern said, scratching his head.

"Never heard of such a thing," Bea commented. "What kind of company flies about hin and yan with a skull on their flag?"

"Pirates! That's a pirate ship. Get back inside, Miss Bea. Pirates are invading our valley! Everyone back inside!

I've got to go get my rifle! Stay calm everyone, no need to panic."

"Appears to me that you're the only one panicking, Vern. Pirates are just folks with a naughty streak." Miss Bea shaded her eyes with her right hand as she stared upwards. "The way that thing is weaving about and getting lower, I'd say it ain't long for the air. I'm surprised it made it over the mountains. Seems to be heading for your place."

"Dang it all!" The constable took off running down the road, most of the congregation following him.

The valley was surrounded by high, rocky mountains, accessible only by foot, burro and airship. Anything out of the ordinary was considered a big event, and no able-bodied citizen risked missing a moment of it.

"Come on, Buster!" Miss Bea called.

An old brown hound dog who'd been curled up beside the church steps roused with a yelp before trotting to her side. Miss Bea lifted up her long skirt, dashing after the crowd.

The faster the crowd ran, the faster the ship came out of the sky, finally resting right on top of Vern's outhouse and the nearby chicken house. The ship was a small one, roughly half the size of the church, and much more compact than the Steam Express vessels which sometimes delivered mail-order goods. Still, it smashed the wooden building to smithereens.

As the dust settled, a door started lowering from the ship with the loud grinding noise of metal gears in need of oil. Vern reappeared with a gun, cautiously approaching the ship with the weapon aimed.

"Vern! Put that thing down. Now."

"Look what they did to my property, Miss Bea!"

"Whatcha got your temper up for? Neither you nor any chickens were in residence. No harm, no fowl."

"That's not funny."

"Wasn't meant to be. You haven't had so much as a laying hen since you started calling on the Widow Hopkins ten years ago. Fact is, you ought to do the right thing and get hitched to her while you are both spry enough to get up to marital antics."

A thin, pale woman, whose gray hair was still carefully pinned into a bun despite her run, stepped forward. "You tell him, Bea. I'm tired of waiting."

"This isn't the time to talk about my private business."

"Your private business?" the widow snapped. "We go heading off down the road, hand in hand towards the tavern every Saturday night, Vern. That's hardly private. I demand to know your intentions."

The men in the group suddenly became very attentive to the cleanliness of their fingernails or shoes.

"Excuse me, fine townspeople…"

"I don't have any intentions!" Vern shouted.

"Excuse me…"

The Widow Hopkins swung her cloth handbag at his shoulder.

"Excuse me—would someone please call this animal off my dog!"

Miss Bea turned around. A stocky, short person in a metallic rick-rack trimmed black waistcoat and trousers stood on the ship's lowered ramp, flanked by two taller men with drawn swords. She figured the stranger for a man, until she noticed the bosom bumps causing a strain on her shirt buttons.

175

Just in front of the woman was a potbellied stove turned on its side. Only it had legs—and a dog-like head with smoke steaming from its ears. Buster stood a few feet away, baying.

"That's a dog?"

The woman smiled. "In a manner of speaking. I call it 'Smokey.' I have a slight issue with the real thing, seeing as they smell like dogs. Especially when wet, I've found. All I have to do for Smokey is to add coal to his chest several times a day."

"Buster, you come over here. Don't judge those who are different. It's Sunday."

After one last bark, Buster obeyed. By the way his ears remained pulled back, Bea could tell he wasn't happy about it.

Vern stepped in front of Miss Bea. "We were speaking of intentions, stranger. Just what are yours?"

"The repair of my ship. I'm Captain Isabelle Stewart of the Piggy Plunder."

"That's the name of a pirate ship?" Vern asked.

"Don't judge, it's Sunday." The captain looked very pleased with her own wit. "Tell me, handsome sir, are you engaged with one of my gender?"

Vern grinned slightly. "Me? Naw..."

"Yes, he is!" shouted the Widow Hopkins. "He's mine."

The Captain nodded acknowledgement of the claim. "Too bad for me, I'm sure."

"Vern, you're grinning like a lust-struck tomcat." Miss Bea placed a hand on his shoulder, forcing him back a few steps. "Pirates or not, we ain't ones to turn away a traveler in need. If we supply what you're looking for, will you forget about any plundering?"

"I assure you, we have no intentions of plundering this settlement. We reached the limits of our plunder license for this quarter in Saline City just over the east mountain."

"You plundered Saline City? Why didn't you say so! That's worth the loss of my outhouse. Worthless lot of lazy-ass thieves is what they are," Vern explained.

"Never mind him. Their mayor's son beat him at a greased pig contest when they were young'uns." Bea held out her hand, pleased when the Captain shook it firmly.

Her pa always said that was a sign of strength and character.

"While Vern here is helping gather supplies, why don't you let us cook y'all a hot meal? We'll push aside the pews in the meetin' house, set up the table, and have a proper celebration of you promising not to plunder."

Captain Stewart smiled. "That would be quite acceptable—and much appreciated. However, I insist on helping with the preparations. Have you heard of song-catchers? Perhaps they have visited here, collecting your quaint folk songs and putting them on paper for others to enjoy. I do the same with various cuisines from around the region. Just a pastime, mind you."

Bea crossed her arms, glancing in Vern's direction. "That ain't nothing dirty is it? I think it's been made clear Constable Vern there is claimed. Like I told them song-catchers that come around here some years ago, we don't cotton to dirty ditties."

"Recipes...I collect recipes of cuisine, of...vittles."

"Ah, well, why didn't you say so using plain language? The Good Lord has crashed you in the right place! Go grab your apron and let's get cooking."

Looking down at her feet, the Captain sighed. "I'm afraid I don't have one."

Miss Bea motioned with her right arm, smiling an invitation. "Come with me. I've got one to spare."

"I've never seen Miss Bea without an apron," Vern said. "She's even got some full ones that'll cover your bos...pardon me, your blouse."

"I'm touched you noticed my...blouse. Please, select a few of your friends who might be of help, and my men will show you want needs to be repaired." Captain Isabelle came to Bea's side, keeping pace with her as they walked towards Bea's home. Buster and Smokey joined them, each lumbering in their own way beside their respective master. "Are all your aprons as beautiful as the one you're wearing?"

"Like this one? This isn't a working apron, it's a showing one. Handed down from my Grandmama. It ain't never been worn for cooking. It's strictly Sunday-go-to-meeting."

"Oh." The Captain pursed her lips together, making a clicking noise with her tongue. Her expression was one of deep thought. "I don't suppose you would kindly consider selling the one you are wearing?"

"Can't do that. Not even for all the tea in the Steam and Robots catalogue. Now, now, don't fret! I'll loan ya one of my others. They're quite sturdy and serviceable. Constable Vern was right, you won't get any spillage on your fancy duds. In fact, I'll gift ya with my newest one. I even spun the cotton to make the fabric myself. Made it to

178

gift to Widow Hopkins should Vern ever get right about her, only he's being slow about making her honest."

"Yes, thank you. I guess it will have to do."

For pirates, the *Piggy Plunder's* crew of five were right nice folks as far as Bea was concerned. She spent several days teaching Captain Isabelle all the tricks to biscuits, gravy, and even her surefire buttermilk pie recipe, not minding that the pirate wouldn't stop asking about her floral apron.

"Ah, well, I hate to see her go," Bea muttered to Buster as she washed the last of the pots and pans they'd used. As dusk darkened, she could see the faint glow of the ship's engines far beyond where her laundry hung on the line. Even with the time the Captain spent supervising repairs instead of in her kitchen, Bea had fallen behind in her chores. Not that it mattered. The night was warm enough her wash should dry by morning.

"Buster, I'll miss that Isabelle lady, for sure." The hound managed to raise up from his rug and lumber to Bea's side. She reached down, scratching his head. "I'm praying she'll pass this way again. My, all those adventures she's had. Might consider pirating myself if the Good Lord calls me to it."

Buster barked, his ears standing nearly straight up in alert. He spun towards the kitchen door, growling, just as Vern ran inside.

"Good grief! Wipe those dirty boots off before you come a'storming in on my clean floor."

"Miss Bea, I'm sorry, but it's those pirates..."

"I don't care! Go right back out that door and wipe your feet." She pointed her right index finger at him, and then the door. "This old hound dog has more manners than you!"

Vernon muttered some not-so-fit-for-mixed-company words under his breath before complying. In seconds, he re-entered.

"That's a little better, I suppose."

"Miss Bea, will you listen? I was saying my goodbyes to the *Piggy Plunder's* men when I overheard that lady Captain telling her first officer they'd be leaving as soon as she had the 'crowning glory' to add to her collection."

Bea put a hand on each hip. "She called my rhubarb pie recipe a real jewel. She didn't take notes while we were cooking it, though. I reckon she just wants to jot it down a'fore they take off."

"You don't understand—she wants your Sunday apron! She's plundering *aprons*. The hold was full of them, but I didn't think nothing of it, figuring it for merchandise or some such."

"Now how does it make sense her telling me right-out she didn't have an apron?"

"She lied!"

"Lied? I told you pirates weren't to be trusted! Where's your gun, they might get violent."

"I left it at home today since it kept getting in the way when we were wielding. Listen, you've got to get out of here. I'm sure they're right behind me. Let the Captain have the apron!"

Bea ran into the parlor as Buster started chasing his tail in the kitchen. She snatched her Grandpa's childhood pellet gun from its place of honor above the fireplace.

"That's not going to hold off pirates!"

Bea didn't slow down as she headed for the door. "Maybe not, but if I aim it right, they'll be mighty sore in the nether regions!"

She wasn't more than twenty feet from the door when she stopped suddenly. Vern collided with her from behind. "Dang nabbit it all down a rabbit hole, Vern. Watch it!"

"Where's the pirates? All I see is that steam-bellied metal mutt."

"It's heading towards my wash!" Smokey was moving faster than Bea imagined possible. Smoke not only poured out of its ears, but also its rear. The metal around its gut glowed from the heat.

"What's she feeding that thing? Gun powder?"

Just as Smokey reached the clothesline, Bea raised her gun and fired. As the mechanical dog hit one of the poles holding up the line, shot ricocheted off its metal. The pole fell, covering Smokey with her half-wet bloomers. It took a few more steps before falling over, the underwear catching fire. Immediately, Smokey righted itself, holding the corner of the floral apron in its mouth.

From the distance, Bea could hear the Captain shouting, "Run, Smokey, run! Come to Mother!"

Knowing she didn't have time to load the gun again, Bea countered, "Sic 'em, Buster! Get that apron!"

"What good is that going to do?" Vern asked. "That hound can't take down red-hot metal!"

Before Bea could reply, Buster caught up with Smokey, running right alongside. He raised his leg and started peeing.

"I ain't never seen a dog run on three legs while doing that," Vern said in amazement.

"I didn't know he could!"

Smoke rose from every joint and around every bolt on the mechanical creature's body. It stumbled. When it fell, its legs moved slower and slower until they stopped. The glowing slowly died out.

"You dastardly hill people! You murdered Smokey!" The Captain shouted.

Bea reached the body, grabbing the apron from Smokey's slightly-gapped mouth. "You lied to us! Said you weren't going to plunder."

"Of course I lied! I'm the captain of the *Piggy Plunder*. You may have won this round, but beware I will be back for that apron with...with two steam dogs." Captain Isabelle Stewart turned, disappearing in the darkness.

Bea started to go after her.

Vern grabbed her arm. "You've got the apron. Let them go. We'll be ready for them next time."

She pulled away, holding up the apron. "Look at that. Not only did that monstrosity get it dirty, there's a hole in it. She should count herself lucky I can mend it. Come on, Buster. I'm going to make sure every dog in town is kept well watered. There will be pee in this valley!"

The Clockwork Dragon

Steve Cook

The clockwork dragon came in for another strafing run and I ran to the pilot's cabin. The deck was dented from the constant pounding it was enduring, and I could see that the steps up to the cabin were all-but destroyed.

I cupped my hands around my mouth to be heard over the battle. "Captain! Incoming!"

Even as I spoke, I knew it was too late. I heard the roar of the dragon behind me and saw the grim set of the captain's jaw; the sudden reflection of flame and anger in the glass of the cabin. I turned, readying my cutlass for a futile effort.

The dragon flapped its massive metal-ribbed canvas wings once, slowing it in the air. The leather bellows in its chest blasted a gout of burning gases and oil onto the prow, and then another across the deck. Men screamed left and right; I saw one of the deckhands go overboard, trying to put the flames out on his sleeve even as his hair burned. The smell of burning flesh filled the air, almost overwhelmed by the acrid stink of the ship burning. At the prow, a metal cable twanged as it finally gave way, followed by another. I watched in horror as the cables flailed around and tore into one of the midshipmen, ripping him in half.

"The mast! 'ware the mast!" the captain shouted.

The fore propeller spluttered its last as the mast began to fall over to one side, and the entire ship lurched sideways as the controls bucked. The dragon dropped the last ten feet onto the prow and the entire ship tipped crazily downwards. It roared, gears grinding together, metal teeth shining in the light of our destruction. Chest proudly thrust forward, it measured easily the width of the airship, and half its weight. The beast's claws dug deeply into the wood of the deck. Its emerald eyes gleamed balefully, as its long neck snaked forward, brass plates clicking into line down its spine.

We plunged through the clouds, cold mist suddenly enveloping us, and then burst out into the storm below. Rain lashed down on us, soaking everything, but—at least—the fires began to diminish.

Bladed tail lashing, the dragon took a step forward, the entire ship shaking beneath it, and I bolted for the weapons locker. The door was hanging loose, all of the rifles missing, but the lightning-thrower was there at the bottom. I grabbed its long barrel, and checked it over. It was designed to throw little metal bolts pre-charged with the electricity stored in its amber battery, useless against something this massive, but it was all we had.

I was in time to see one of the lookouts disappear into its holding stomach, or at least her top half. The legs writhed and kicked for a moment, and then fell over.

"First Mate, I'd thank you kindly to get that thing off of my airship!" Captain Roth bawled, thunder booming as if in response.

"Aye sir!" I replied, and shouldered the gun. The dragon dropped what it was eating and thudded closer.

I pulled the trigger and the gun hummed into life. Each tiny dart rubbed past the amber and crackled out of the barrel, some stabbing into the brass plates of the dragon's hide, others clattering uselessly off its swept-back horns and the immense, greasy hinges where its wings met its barrel-like body. Every impact crackled and sizzled, arcs of lightning rolling over its rain-slicked casing, but the dragon kept coming.

"Captain," I shouted, but it was too late. The dragon swept one foreleg forward, pistons hissing, and I was flying through the air, gun lost. I slammed into the railing and lay, struggling to breathe, as the dragon advanced on me. It raised its wings in triumph and I licked my lips, steeling myself for the end.

A bolt of lightning arced out of the storm and struck it on the tip of one wing, instantly crackling over the darts I had shot into the thing. Uniquely conductive, they popped and sizzled, electricity dancing between them. The canvas wings immediately erupted into flame and white-hot light played all over its body. Like some sort of hellish angel with wings of flame, the dragon staggered backwards. Every part of it seemed to be flexing at once, joints moving jerkily, and I could see fire inside it, burning the delicate clockwork that moved it, consuming the leather and rubber parts.

"Tip—" I started, then coughed and drew in a ragged breath. "Tip the boat, Captain!"

The airship swung crazily one way, and then the other. With a roar every bit as loud as the storm's fury, the brass dragon staggered backwards, tore a hole in the railing, and was lost over the side. The sound of its roar seemed to echo on for many seconds, and then there was just the rain, the thunder and the groans of dying men.

We flew on.

Seven of the crew were dead. Two more would die unless we made port by the next day, which was unlikely. The remaining lookout would always walk with a limp, and my back was a mass of cuts from where the railing had splintered behind me. But we were alive...mostly.

I left the ship's cook, Gerolt, dealing with the wounded and walked up towards the poop deck. Both sets of stairs were a splintered mess, almost completely destroyed. Some of the supply crates on the deck had come loose, making an ugly pile that was just high enough to clamber on. My back screamed in agony as I climbed over the—miraculously—intact railing.

"Captain Roth," I said, breathing heavily. He gestured me over with a jerk of his head. He was tense, hunched over the wheel like it was the only thing supporting him, and I saw how white his knuckles were.

"How bad is it?"

He listened gravely while I gave the report, never taking his eyes from the storm.

"Damn it, Ben," he said when I was done. "Worst I've seen. Is the Stone still safe?"

I nodded. "Still in the cargo hold, battened down. Why were we targeted, Captain? You paid the Guild fees."

He was silent for a moment, thinking. "I reckon someone's sold us out. Someone who knows we was after the Stone of Kilnarnock, someone who knows that if we're in these clouds, we're prob'ly on our way back with it." He tutted, and added, "Or if we've not got it, just plain don't want to see us again."

"But a clockwork dragon, Captain? Those things are for pirates and smugglers, not honest—"

"Bah, the Guild's watchdogs are easy to repurpose," he growled. "Doesn't take much tinkerin' once you've caught one of the brass beasties. Done it meself a few times."

"Can't be anyone on the crew," I said, moving to stand next to the captain. "They'd have gone down with the ship. And anyone on the ship when we get back stands to receive a share of the profits anyway."

"Could be," the captain said. "Wouldn't be the first time." He cleared his throat and maneuvered us around a low cloud bank. Lightning crackled deep in the gray-black depths. "That was a quick bit of thinkin' of yours with the lightnin'-thrower."

"More luck than judgment, Captain."

He nodded. "Happens that way more often than not. Been in a few scrapes, haven't we, laddo? Like that time over Spain. You remember?"

"I remember. The Armada thought they had us pinned between their flanks, ships coming up from underneath to board us." I smiled at the memory. "If you hadn't told us to throw the cannons down onto them over the side, we'd never have made it."

"Aye. Destroyed their props, holed their hulls and lightened our load all in one go." The captain smiled grimly. "I knew we weren't shootin' our way out of that one, though. You questioned me, then. Tol' me it wouldn't work, crazy idea."

"That's my job, Captain."

"Among other things. You were right, though. Crazy idea." He paused and cocked his head, looking at me out of the corner of his eye. "Lifeboats all attached still?"

"Aye, Captain," I said. The lifeboats, small single-prop airships really, were moored on the side of the boat. They weren't safe, but they were safer than jumping overboard.

"Start them. All of them. I want the speed boost with that mast gone. Time we got back."

I stared at the captain for a moment, and he turned to face me fully. I could see the pain and loss in his eyes; a crew sundered, his ship damaged and his life in danger. All of our lives. I nodded, shrinking in the face of that bottled rage, and vaulted back over the railing.

The lifeboats chugged into life, their front-facing propellers sluggishly responding, and each time I felt a little tug from the deck beneath me as we gained speed. The rain was lessening now, and the deck was clearing as the healthy took the wounded below. I moved fore and inspected the damage.

The wooden decking was burned and blackened; there was a hole eaten clear through the deck into the galley, even melting some of the cast iron range. Gerolt would raise hell for that. The mast had left a broken stub, like a rotten tooth, and taken most of the railing on the port side with it, but we were lucky it had gone straight over. I'd heard more than one story of a collapsed mast fouling the other props, or even crushing the control cabin.

I heard a shout from behind me, and turned to see a figure running out of the cargo-hold, something clutched in his hands. Captain Roth charged out of his cabin, and I vaulted over the railing to land with a splash next to the stairs below. It was Gerolt, and in his hands something glimmered, clear against the gray of his apron. The Stone of Kilnarnock.

The captain got to him first, pistol out, grabbing hold of Gerolt's arm as he put one foot inside the nearest lifeboat. I nimbly skirted the remaining mast and skidded to a halt.

"Mutiny!" I shouted. "You were right, Captain. Someone sold us out." I grabbed Gerolt's shoulder and spun him round, snatching the stone out of his hands. It was a diamond bigger than my fist, throwing rainbows around even in the dim light of the gaslights on deck.

"Aye, lad," the captain said, and I frowned at the note of sadness in his voice. I looked at him, and the pistol was pointed at me. "Someone sold ye out. Now just give us the stone and be done."

"Captain, what is this?" I clutched the stone closer to myself, noticing as I did so that the hilt of a knife was sticking out of Gerolt's apron pocket. The rough facets of the diamond bit into my palm.

"You had the right of it. The guild dragons only go for pirates and smugglers," the captain said. "I din't pay their fees. I'm done with them, going back to the life I left ten years ago." His eyes narrowed. "I was hopin' the dragon would do for more of you, to be honest. Well, now I'm puttin' that right."

I heard the pistol fire, saw the muzzle flash, and felt an intense burning pain in my gut, more real than anything else. I sank to my knees, clutching at the hot wound just above my belt, blood seeping out between my fingers. The Stone clattered to the deck.

"Sorry, lad," the captain said, his voice echoing as my vision blurred. "Yer just too damned good at yer job..."

I was chased down into darkness by the sound of their lifeboat buzzing away into the clouds.

"And yet you survived."

"I did, Your Honor," I said, leaning heavily on my cane. "One of the lads heard the shot and came up to find me bleeding out. They managed to get me below, patch up the wound. Bullet was still in me, y'see."

Chief Justice Rutherford leaned back in his chair. His powdered wig had slipped slightly in the heat, sweat beading his brow, and he shifted uncomfortably in his black gown.

"Your former, ah, captain, Captain William Roth...he was a pirate. Caught ten years ago, turned King's evidence and had his sentence reduced from, ah, death." He picked up a piece of paper and consulted it. "The Guild saw fit to give him back his license and install him as a junior crewman, where he performed admirably, and after years of good service they gave him a ship, a crew, and a mission." The chief justice peered over his spectacles. "Perhaps, ah, foolishly, it would seem."

"Old habits die hard, Your Honor."

"Indeed."

There was a pause, the sounds of London from the street below wandering in through the open window.

"You want to find them, I'm sure," Chief Justice Rutherford said quietly.

"Aye."

The fat man leaned down and pulled open a drawer in his desk. He pulled something out and threw it at me. A scroll. I caught it, snapped open the seal and skimmed the contents.

"A ship of my own, Your Honor?"

"It's as your former captain told you." The chief justice leaned forward and smiled, crooked teeth barely holding in rancid breath. "You're damned good at your job. Find him. Find him and end him."

My crew were young, but capable, and it was with a certain wry satisfaction that I christened our ship The Clockwork Dragon. We made for the skies over Ireland first, making port in Dublin.

A deckhand there didn't know anything about Captain Roth, but for the price of a pint he did hear tell of a lifeboat matching the description found abandoned in a field thirty miles north, near Drogheda. We followed his directions, glorious green countryside rolling by below us, until we arrived at a field with a few cows in it. There was also a clear scar, a long line of churned-up mud in the grass; the lifeboat hadn't landed cleanly. The farmer who owned the field pointed us in the direction of Dundalk, stating that the men who'd landed had sold him the lifeboat for scrap in exchange for food, and we moved again.

In Craigavon, we found a crime-scene, just a few hours old; two men had stolen a gunship that was in for repairs and flown off to the north-east. We took up the chase, our propellers greedily eating up the miles.

Over the skies of Belfast, we had our first stroke of luck.

"Ship off the starboard bow!"

I fumbled for my telescope and scanned the horizon. Sure enough, there was a small craft, its smooth profile marred by the long barrel of its main cannon.

"There you are," I murmured. The crew looked at me expectantly. "Best speed! Grease those props! Man the cannons!"

There was no way to mask our approach. If I could see them, I could be sure that Captain Roth had seen me. The gunship's single propeller seemed to be having trouble keeping its rhythm, and I brought us alongside with grim satisfaction.

"Ready cannons!" I shouted.

"Aye, Captain," came the reply, and I looked over to the deck of the gunship. I could see Gerolt staring over the railing at me, while the captain stood ramrod straight at the helm.

"Fire!"

All four cannons roared, and the gunship seemed to lurch backwards in the air for a moment as Captain Roth cut the power. Three of the shots missed their mark, but the fourth tore through part of the engine housing. Instantly, thick black smoke began to billow from the gunship's exhaust.

Then the lookout's voice rang clear over the sound of the engines. "Captain! Port security!"

Almost before he'd finished speaking, the gunship was peeling off as a heavily-armed cutter interposed itself between us. I could only watch in frustration as Captain Roth's little craft began to spiral down for a landing.

The cutter's loudspeaker crackled into life. "Combat is prohibited in Belfast's airspace," an officious-sounding voice boomed. "You will land or prepare to be boarded." Several cannons pushed their way out of the side of the cutter's hull, and I narrowed my eyes as I saw the bulk of a clockwork dragon crouched at the center of the ship.

"What do we do, captain?" the first mate asked.

I pounded the rail in frustration. "We land, and try to pick up their scent from there. Fates preserve us from idiotic bureaucracy."

The harbor-master was unsympathetic, but yielded when he saw the bounty documents, and we were back on the trail with only a day's loss in time. The damaged gunship lay abandoned in a berth at the harbor, but—for more gold than most of us would see in a year—we found out that two men answering Captain Roth and Gerolt's descriptions had chartered a private airship bound for Edinburgh. The Guild was displeased, but they paid the bribe, and we continued.

It was in a dingy backstreet tavern—the *Whipper's Napper*—that we finally caught up to them. I had instructed the crew to stay with the Dragon, tethered in Leith Basin, not two miles away. The bar itself was suitably scummy, the floor clinging to my boots as I shouldered my way past the worst of Edinburgh's dock workers. The beer was weak, like brown water, but it took the edge off.

The captain and Gerolt sat at a corner table, discussing something. A single lamp, hung on the wall above them, was enough to see that they were both heavily into their cups, with hooded eyes and rosy cheeks. The captain was dressed as neatly as ever I saw him, blue long-coat, shirt, and waistcoat immaculate as usual in sharp comparison to the cook's sweaty bulk. I primed my pistol, took my mug of ale, and went over to their table.

As soon as they saw me, their talk stopped. I sat down on the only available chair and placed my mug on the table. As loud as it was in the tavern with the dull roar of conversation and laughter, for the moment, we inhabited a little pocket of quiet.

"Good evening, Captain Roth, Gerolt," I said.

Gerolt stared at me, and then at the captain. "What the—kill him. Kill him now!"

Captain Roth locked eyes with me and drained his pint. He set his mug down and wiped his mouth. I could see both hands, neither armed.

"No," he said. "I want to hear him say why he's here."

I rested my cane against the table. "See this, Captain?"

He nodded.

"I can't walk without it now. The bullet went in, did a lot of damage. Rattled around some. I'll regret this ale tomorrow. Can't stomach it anymore. Sugar, the same, when I can get it." I sat back. "Pain in my legs. Pain in my knees. Physicians reckon there's damage to my spine somewhere along the way." I shrugged. "That's life."

"Go on."

"I've tracked you all over the Emerald Isle and back, Captain. I've got a ship to call my own, a beaut she is. I've got guild money on board, and men who'll follow orders without question. All to find you. And the Stone, of course."

"Sold it," the captain said, waving his hand. "Last night. Got a good price for it. Gold's hidden away, somewhere no-one'd ever look." He leaned forward again. "You haven't said why you're here yet. You here to kill us?"

"Maybe."

"You want revenge?"

I shook my head. "Revenge is empty. I could kill you, Captain, but that wouldn't be revenge. I'd still wake up at three in the morning needing to piss, regular as clockwork."

"You were the best I ever had, laddo."

Was that regret I could hear in his voice?

"I know, Captain. They were good times."

I could see Gerolt staring back and forth between us. I could sense his nerve eroding with every word we spoke, sweat beading his flabby face.

"This is stupid," he hissed, accent thicker than ever. "Kill the little worm and have done with it."

"Alright," Captain Roth said. He reached into a pocket and pulled out a pistol—the same one he'd shot me with. He stared at me, and I stared back.

I felt the room behind me swim in and out of existence as the click of the gun cocking sounded, sweet and metallic, and then the gun fired.

Gerolt fell dead onto the table, face downward. There was a sudden silence in the tavern. Still staring into my eyes, the captain pocketed the pistol and pulled out a few gold pieces. The sound of the heavy metal clinking onto the wood seemed to let the noise of the crowd back in, like floodgates opening.

"Coming here was another crazy idea," the captain said.

"Either way, it was closure. How did you know I wasn't just going to kill you?"

He smiled then, all the warmth I had ever seen him show filtered into that one expression. "You still called me Captain."

He leaned forward. "Join me." The gleam of gold was in his eyes now, and his grin was pure avarice. "Together, you and me, we could scrape the skies clean of the Guild that robbed us of service and health, and for what? For nothing."

I found myself nodding along with him.

"You and I, between us, we know their routes. We know where they'll be." He squeezed his fist and shook it. "Let them try to send their dragons after us. We would be unstoppable!"

I allowed myself only a moment's pause before I matched his smile.

Adventures of a Would-Be Gentleman of the Skies

Jim Reader

Andrew Augustus McKinney, Andy to his few friends, just knew this was going to be the score, the Big Score. It would be the one that let him pay off some very insistent debt-collectors, repair and improve his airship, the *Lilly Mae*, maybe even buy his way into one of the big pirate gangs, like the Sky Stealers, or Cloud-Borne Scourge.

He stood beside his ship, the great sky-blue dirigible's body above him, as he and his slave Trajan checked every last detail. It wasn't as if he was even going to fly that day; it was a daily ritual ever since he'd finished building it: Check everything, every day. Check everything twice on a day he was going to take her up...although sometimes he was so excited by the prospect of piracy he forgot the second check.

"She looks to be in tip-top shape," Trajan said. "As always."

"She is," Andy replied, "and yet—"

"—Something is bound to break on her, no matter what," Trajan finished.

The two grinned at each other. Trajan had been a slave of his grandfather's...with Andy he was more of a co-worker and partner, albeit one who couldn't leave to seek work elsewhere. Andy even paid him for his efforts...when he had any money at all.

Andy left Trajan touching up a bit of paint on the gondola, and returned to the tiny shack the two of them lived in for the moment. He spread out his calculations on the table, these all involved with weight. After his attempt to hijack a load of exotic hardwoods making their way from New Orleans to Baton Rouge, he'd realized how important weight could be. He'd almost lost the ship, and his own life, and had barely gotten his ship back into the air with five of the long, rough-hewn logs, even after dumping all of the ballast bags he kept aboard—they helped to keep her on her keel in high winds.

The gold heist was a simple plan—he didn't bother to reflect all his failures had been simple plans as well...

Wells Fargo was transporting a load of gold, all secretive-like. Not many guards, not an obviously armored wagon. The route was Galveston to Fort Worth by a round-about route...lots of empty miles with not many places to hide. He couldn't get too close to either city—air pirates could get their ships shot out of the sky easier than not—but that left a whole lot of country he could ambush them in.

The *Lilly Mae* could handle the projected weight of the wagon and cargo, and if it were too heavy, he could always leave some of the gold behind, much as it would break his heart.

His plan was a sure thing, no doubt, no chance of anything less than success.

He had the information straight from the mouth of his darling *Lilly Mae* Hunkins—say what you like about Soiled Doves, they found out secrets better than anybody, and if you were good to them, sometimes they shared what they'd learned.

Hell, if things worked out, first thing he'd do was up and marry *Lilly Mae*, make an honest woman out of her.

You wouldn't think Andy was a buccaneer of the skies to look at him. A friend had once described him as "the boy who sweeps up at the general store"—completely forgettable in appearance, plain in his manner of speech as well as his dress, polite, respectful, and patently not dangerous.

But courtesy of his lineage, he was smart. Courtesy of his parents, he had book learning. From the dime novels he'd devoured, he had an overly romantic view of piracy, and from his grandfather on his mother's side, Yorick Aloysius Feargus, inventor of the Variable Suspension System for Wagons of all Kinds, he had an inheritance and Trajan—an inheritance he'd already spent on his airship and a slave he'd set free in all but filing the necessary paperwork.

From nowhere and no one had he inherited a lick of common sense.

The *Lilly Mae* had a sound design, and was well-constructed, albeit a bit on the smallish side where her gondola was concerned. Andy had designed her with an eye toward efficiency—he could easily handle most shipboard operations from his cabin at the front of the gondola, lounging in the comfort of his wicker chair. The only reason he needed to move was to go back and keep the firebox full of coal. Aside from his tiny cabin and the coal hopper, the rest of the space in the gondola was for captured booty and spare parts. The latter was due to a small gift of wisdom from Yorick: "There ain't never been nothin' designed or built by the hand o' man what won't break down sooner rather'n later."

His granddaddy had been right. Eighteen breakdowns in the short eight-month life of the *Lilly Mae*, and only two of them had been while she was on the ground. Andy had never considered whether he was afraid of heights or not, but had been reassured to find they didn't bother him much at all—the first time he had to hang outside the rear of the gondola, repairing the airship's engine thousands of feet above the earth.

The airship was armed to the teeth, in Andy's estimation, courtesy of four steam-powered dart guns firing knock-out darts of his own design. He'd killed a lot of cattle getting the approximate dosage figured out, eight men equaling one cow—and he hoped no one ever found out who'd been responsible for those dead cattle—and further occasional tests on humans during previous exploits had proved he'd gotten it right at last.

In the dime novel tales of *Captain Anson and his Gentlemen of the Air*, killing was frowned upon. Evil and devious villains of all kinds killed, and did even worse to women. Air pirates were a noble breed of aerial Robin-Hoods, stealing for the good of the common man.

Andy was sure newspaper reports of real-life air pirates killing and burning and worse were just an attempt to soil their good names by the bankers and bureaucrats who controlled the papers.

Nope, not an iota of common sense.

Andy rode his mare, Estelle, into Waterloo, Texas from where he and Trajan kept the *Lilly Mae*, outside of Talmidge. Another twelve hours, and he'd need to be soaring north-easterly, but he'd be damned straight to a Hell full of Papists instead of a more Presbyterian Heaven if he'd leave without another few, sweet hours with *Lilly Mae* herself.

He'd never had the courage to tell her he'd named his airship after her—had never really had the courage to tell her how he felt about her at all—but somehow, he figured she knew. None of her other gentlemen callers could spend time with her for free, although that was limited to when he took her out for a meal, or a show at the Waterloo Opera House. Even Andy wasn't silly enough to believe he could hide the calf-eyed, love-struck look he had on his face whenever he thought of her, much less was in her company. She had to know how he felt about her.

As Estelle plodded along, he winced at the jostling and bumping his bottom and legs were taking. Truer love hath no gentleman of the skies than to ride a horse along a rutted trail to see his love.

Afflicted by horse flies and mosquitos the size of dragon flies, Andy reflected on his first meeting with the lovely object of his affections...

The crowded barroom of Thredgull"s Saloon, the thick haze of nauseating cigar smoke, the sense of celebration in the air. It was only two days after the North agreed to peace terms with the Confederacy, due in no small part to the Southern Cause's apt use of airships in their war efforts. Everyone was still walking around almost in a trance; joyous in the Confederacy's victory, but after five-and-a-half years of bloody warfare, unsure of what a peaceful life would look like.

He'd gone to Thredgull's to have his first drink of whiskey, in honor of victory. He'd drunk beer, and had little love of it, but that day he made his way into town from his job at the Waterloo Dirigible Works determined to try harder drink.

It was all forgotten when he spied *Lilly Mae* coming down the stairs. Her slight frame, almost like a boy's, except where it delightfully wasn't, her precious crooked nose, the cascade of almost brown hair, the missing tooth that gave her mouth character. As she drew closer, he first smelled the perfume of her sweat—the only odor he'd found that made cigar smoke tolerable.

It hadn't started as a lust that would have raised the eyebrows of his Presbyterian family—it had begun as adoration of her angelic form and features. When she spotted him at the bar, sidled up, and asked him a question he couldn't even remember without blushing, the lust had come.

His times with her had been the purest form of magic, from that moment on...

Andy's mind returned to the present, as he instinctively whacked a giant mosquito with his hat. He could see the lights of Waterloo in the distance, and spurred Estelle to a slightly more spritely gait, in anticipation of *Lilly Mae*'s company.

Later that evening, after dinner at Nightbird's, while they lay sweating in the after-glow of their passion, he said,

"*Lilly Mae*, darling, I'm about to turn that information you gave me into a fortune."

Her breathing quickened.

"You are? Do you have..." she trailed a finger down his mostly hairless chest, "any plans after that?"

"Uh...uh...if you'd agree to come... uh...away with me," he blurted out the rest of his words, "themostgrateful-andhappymanintheworldifyou'dmarryme!"

She leaned over and kissed him, with even more passion than earlier in the evening.

"Andy, sweetie, you come back with enough gold for us to be rich, I'll be yours forever."

His heart soared as he bolted from the bed and began to dress.

"Then, *Lilly Mae* my love, I'd better get going so I can capture it."

The ride back to Talmidge passed almost without notice. In his mind, he was holding his beloved close, his head upon her breast, listening to every beat of her precious heart.

Upon arriving home, he left Estelle in Trajan's care, running through a last minute check of the *Lilly Mae* in a daze. Trajan made sure to follow after him, sure his owner was incapable of seeing any problem, much less a subtle one, the state he was in.

Once through, Andy leapt in, ignited the coal in the firebox, and began building up steam for the journey.

He leaned out the door, and shouted to Trajan above the boiler's noise.

"When I get back, we'll be rich!"

"We?" Trajan shouted back.

"You, me, and *Lilly Mae*!"

As the airship made its way into the sky, slowly turning to a north-east heading, Trajan watched it go, shaking his head.

For the most part, flying the *Lilly Mae* at night was rather unexciting. There was an occasional light below, most often from some small town, but for the most part, there was nothing but engine noise, the groans of the boiler—in itself, not so much a problem, but something to be watched—and the wind.

The boiler, the entire steam system in fact, was at the top of Andy's to-do list. If over-fired, the system produced more steam than it could handle. A tragedy had narrowly been averted during her first flight when Andy heard a bolt shoot from one of the pipes, quickly followed by another. He'd rushed back and vented all the pressure, as fast as he could, before something exploded.

He'd managed to land alright, and then had begun testing. Anything above around fifty percent of her capability was dangerous, but that still left him with power to spare, so he'd been content to let it wait for when he was flush. Taking out the boiler, pipes, and everything else in the system would be a major undertaking, and very expensive to replace.

He thought of the one time he'd brought *Lilly Mae* out to see his ship. He didn't have her name painted on it, as anonymity was often of value in the life of an aerial pirate, so he was able to relax as he took her up, taught her the controls, explained in general terms about firing the boiler, keeping the pressure up—even though he'd handled those chores while she handled the controls. He even showed her how to operate the dart cannons, and they'd gleefully shot at a flock of goats.

Like all his time with her, it had been heavenly. He looked forward to returning from the robbery, giving Trajan his share, giving him his manumission papers, freeing the old man, and soaring off with *Lilly Mae*.

She could fly, and perhaps he could catch some sleep. By that point, it would be well over thirty-six hours since his last rest. Perhaps he'd have her tell him where she wanted to go first, point her in the right direction, and sleep on the floor close to the pilot's chair.

It was a warm, cozy thought...

He awoke to see tree-tops on either side of the *Lilly Mae*! There were loud thrums as the dirigible's frame pushed its way through the trees, and he prayed his weariness hadn't resulted in punctures to any of the gas bags.

The ship kept shuddering, and shuddering more often. He brought the nose up, noisily throttled back the engine, and held his breath as the airship climbed, at a painfully slow rate, higher into the sky.

Andy was still trembling as the ship reached a comfortably undetectable altitude. He damned himself for not thinking to bring some coffee with him.

According to his compass, he was still on course, more or less. He wouldn't be able to make any fine course corrections until after the sun was up, and as he looked out to the east, he realized sunrise wasn't all that far away. There was already a very faint glow on the horizon, almost imperceptible, but there nonetheless.

He set the controls, and stood up to stretch, forcing wakefulness into his body. As he rolled his neck back and forth, he thought, "Not much longer." Then he went up into the frame to check the bags.

The sun was barely half-risen before he knew where he was. A small correction to his course, and he was sure he'd be in position by the time the gold wagon came down the road. Wells Fargo's route was north to Nacogdoches, then west to Fort Worth, and as a consequence, he was floating above the piney woods of East Texas. With the exception of the road itself, and occasional clear patches for a homestead or small town, it was a sea of green.

It wasn't his first trip to the area—he'd crossed it twice on the 'log job,' as Trajan called it, and his third attempt at airborne piracy had been in this area as well...

Much to his dismay, shortly after the War of Northern Aggression ended, his Confederacy had proven themselves no better than the damned Yankees where Indian relations were concerned. Despite treaties, promises, and allied operations in the war, the Confederacy had implemented a policy of enslaving the Indians just as they had the Negro. It had outraged Andy, and he'd taken off to rescue as many members of the Alabama and Coushatta tribes as he could.

It was a fine and moral undertaking, perfectly apt for a Gentleman of the Skies, and the plan, as usual, was simple. Fly in high during the day, stay on station during the night, sweep down and rescue as many as possible in the early morning dawn.

He hadn't stopped to think that if they were being enslaved, there would be guards, and soldiers, and guns.

Lots of guns. More guns than he ever wanted to see again. Ever.

He'd taken two bullets, one in his bottom and one in his left arm, and the *Lilly Mae* was shot so full of holes he'd made it back only by the Grace of God and, as Trajan had said, "more luck than any dumb boy deserves"...

He was shaken from his reverie by the sight of a heavily-laden wagon, looking like a giant black box on wheels, rolling around a bend in the road and coming into view.

The first part was easy. He powered ahead of them, brought the ship around, and laid out the 'Whip' and 'Shotgun,' courtesy of his darts. He was ready to drop down and handle the team of horses should they require it, but in spite of the great droning ship in the sky, they slowed down, and went to the side of the road looking for forage.

Carefully he brought the ship around, and down over the wagon's top; dropped the cables to attach to the wagon; and leapt out—dart rifle in one hand, a line to the ship in the other.

There was no stirring in the wagon he could discern, so he crept to the front, gently laid the rifle down, lowered himself to the box, and unhitched the horses from the coach. No way in the world he could lift six horses and their traces in addition to the wagon, just to have them thrash their way free and fall to their deaths.

Climbing back on top of the wagon, he was preparing to rig the first cable, when a voice said, "Boy, you need to stand up real easy and slow, or I'm gonna end you right here and goddamn now."

Andy did as he was told. As he stood up, he saw three men on the road behind the wagon, all of them well-armed, and all of them sporting the familiar badge of the Texas Rangers on their shirts.

"I suppose surrendering would be a good idea," he said, thankful his voice sounded stronger than he felt.

"Yeah, it would be, so would droppin' that kerchief you got over your face," the man in the middle said, his large handle-bar mustache bristling as he spoke. "So, you took the bait in Waterloo."

"The bait?" Andy replied, not making a move to drop his mask.

"Yeah, we left news of a different gold shipment in several towns, got men out all over Texas, waitin' to see who would bite. You bit in Waterloo. Won't take us long to find out what whore it was that told ya."

The man to the left, a greasy-looking younger man with a paunchy belly said, "Yeah, we got ways to make whores—hell, purty much anybody—talk."

Andy had been considering surrender. Rangers were tough adversaries, and he'd been caught dead to rights...but then they talked about *Lilly Mae* Hunkins. Catching him, he might allow. Hurting her...

He wrapped the line around his wrist with a quick flip, grabbed on with his other hand as well, and pulled hard on a second line, much thinner, and hard to see in the gloomy shade between the tall trees to either side of the road.

"This is gonna hurt something fierce," he thought, as the ballast bags on the outside of the *Lilly Mae*'s gondola—all eight-hundred pounds of them—released at once.

How he managed to avoid dislocating a shoulder or two, he considered to be a Deeper Mystery, best left to the ponderings of preachers and professors.

How he managed to avoid being shot was a lesser mystery, and no doubt his swinging madly back and forth beneath the dirigible, screaming and wailing like a banshee, had something to do with it, as did the sheer speed of his ship's ascent. He was not ashamed he'd somewhat dampened his trousers during his escape.

Once he crawled, hand over hand, up the line, and reached the cabin, he gave the *Lilly Mae* all the speed she could muster at the moment then went back and fed coal in until the gauge read sixty-percent, before giving her even more speed.

The Rangers had the telegraph, and a state-wide organization.

He had an airship, and a long way to go.

The trip seemed endless, but for a moment he tore his thoughts away from *Lilly Mae*, waiting, alone and vulnerable in Waterloo, and gave thanks for his second disastrous attempt at piracy...

Mexican silver, and he'd brought home enough of it to keep the debt-collectors from breaking his limbs, but he'd have brought home more if the *Federales* hadn't heard the groaning of his boiler, while he loaded the silver on board.

He'd crawled aboard, hiding from the bullets whizzing all about, and had gotten the ship into the air...slowly...much too slowly. He'd been throwing ballast bags out by hand, bullets shredding his ship, and it had come to him he needed a way to let all the ballast go at once. So he'd rigged it outside, able to be released by a tug on a single line, and swore he'd never leave the airship while on a job without both lines in his hand...

He rubbed his sore hands and arms, and rolled his shoulders, and was thankful as he could be for his prior failure.

"Trajan!" Andy yelled as he put the ship down.

The old black man came out of their shack, and started to tie off the landing lines.

"Didn't go the way you'd planned?" Trajan asked mildly.

"Not at all. I'm saddling Estelle and heading for Waterloo. They're gonna come for *Lilly Mae*!"

Trajan stopped, and looked at his master.

"Who's coming for her?"

"Texas Rangers! I gotta get there and get her out afore they grab her and hurt her!"

"So you'll be leaving as soon as you get back?"

"Yeah. Do up some more ballast, strap it on..." Andy walked into the shack, pulled papers out of his valise, and returned. "Here—you go to any county seat, you get these papers filed, you're a free man."

"You're going to need money to escape," Trajan said. "Have any?"

"No...I expect we'll just deal with that later."

"You could sell your tools and such...to me."

"How much you got?" Andy said, desperate enough to consider it.

"How much I have isn't rightly your business, is it?" the old man replied, gently waving his manumission papers in the air. "Fifty dollars for the whole lot—and Estelle, once you're through with her—and the wagon."

"Seventy-five."

"Done!" Trajan went in to rustle about in his own bag, and returned with paper money, backed by Confederate gold.

"All right," Andy said, once Estelle was saddled. "I'll be back."

"Let's hope so," Trajan replied, as Andy tried to convince Estelle a trot was an achievable goal.

Andy found *Lilly Mae* packed and waiting in the shadows behind Thredgull's. He took her bag, put it in front of him, reached down, and swung her up behind him.

"Be quiet, my darling," he said. "There may be men looking for you."

Lilly Mae held her peace until they were away from town, riding down a little trail to a ford on the Colorado River.

"Did you get the gold, honey?" she said, hugging him tightly.

"No...It was a trap, courtesy of the Rangers. That's why they'll be looking for you. They want to know who passed on the story about the gold."

"Well, did you get anything?"

"Away with my life," he said, gently urging Estelle into the water. The horse eyed him meanly. "Any more than that...hell, even that, was asking the Good Lord for more miracles than any man has a right to ask."

She snuggled back up to him, as they rode toward Talmidge, and asked no more questions.

"Trajan! Trajan, we're back!"

Andy saw the old man come out of the *Lilly Mae*'s cabin with cleaning rags in hand.

"Just getting her nice for you," Trajan said, grimacing slightly as he helped *Lilly Mae* down from Estelle's back.

She ignored him and headed for the airship, bag in hand.

"Here's Estelle," Andy said. "Think I actually got her up to a canter on the way back."

"Tonight's miracles never cease," Trajan said, smiling. "You take care of yourself, boy. You won't have me around to patch you up after your errors in judgment anymore."

"I will," Andy said, before he slumped over, dart in his neck.

Trajan stood still and waited for his. "Boy never did have even a drop of common sense," he murmured, before he too slumped to the ground.

"Somebody was tired," Trajan said as Andy finally stirred.

"I was going to sleep while *Lilly Mae* piloted...oh...shit... Tell me she's still here and the dart was an accident?" Andy sat up, and rubbed his face with a dirty hand.

"Oh, it was, it was! Followed by another accidental dart for me, and accidentally stealing all our money, and then accidentally stealing your airship! All most regrettable accidents."

Andy sighed, and looked up at the sky.

"I must've slept about six hours by the look of things."

"You did. What do you want to do now?"

Andy got up off the ground, and dusted his clothes off.

"Aren't you going to say 'I told you so'?"

"I was going to be kind and wait a while," Trajan chuckled. "But don't worry about it, I would have before we parted ways."

"Have you by any chance heard a distant explosion, like...a steam boiler blast?"

"No," Trajan replied, "but I have been praying for one."

"Well, I guess I'll go see if they're looking for help at the Waterloo Dirigible Works."

"Boy, you are the stupidest man I know! The Rangers are going to find out from the other girls about *Lilly Mae*, and they're going to find out about the young idiot making a fool of himself over her."

"I guess you're right," Andy said. "So I don't know. Guess I'll head for Galveston, take to the sea."

"Not so fast, Andrew Augustus McKinney," Trajan said. "Your granddaddy would rise up out of his grave and make me start talking, and working, like a field hand again if I let you go wandering about." Trajan looked his soon-to-be-former master over. "Might be I could use a partner."

"For doing what?"

"That remains to be seen...I hear there's good money to be made in aerial piracy, so long as you listen to someone with common sense." The old man slapped Andy across his sore shoulders. "Very good money."

"I'm a wanted man, Trajan, or I soon will be. That's going to make buying the supplies to build a new airship mighty hard."

The old black man looked at his former master, his friend, his partner.

"No suh, Massa Andy, no trouble a'tall. It be the same as when you had yo' head buried in dem plans and designs. I's go inta town, get what we needs, brings it back out to you."

"So you don't have a problem pretending like that? Even now that you're a freed man? Even now that you're, well, the senior partner of the business?"

Trajan grinned. "Boy, we bring in good money, I'll play that role with no regret."

Andy mused, "I've heard tell there's a lot of rich cargo—and just plain old gold—being shipped in and out of Galveston..."

"Always wanted to see the ocean," Trajan said as he started loading their wagon.

A Clouded Affair

Steven R. Southard

William Starling scowled as he gazed into the periscope, seeing nothing but two eagles battling in flight over a fish held in one bird's talons. It looked like the scarred eagle with the tattered wings might keep its catch despite vicious attacks by its faster, nimbler foe. *Loife is full o' bloomin' surprises,* William mused.

He hated the thought of another day without finding prey. His crew would become restless without ships to attack.

He made another sweep with the scope. "*There,* Gorblimey!" he cried. In their port quarter, a distant, dark dot grew larger.

"Nell, there's our next target," he said. "We'll stay 'ere in the cloud until we're in attack position."

His first mate, Nell Remige, acknowledged him with an "Aye."

"'Elm, turn left an' steer us ter the south-east," he ordered. Their seventy-foot long, steam-powered ornithopter banked left and flapped its canvas wings to head toward the target.

"She's a beauty," William said. "'Ere, 'ave a look." He backed away from the periscope eyepiece to let Nell see. He'd never quite understood why the young, blonde woman wanted to join his band of aging air pirates in the first place, but Nell had become a first-rate buccaneer, as if born to it. In fact, she'd been the logical choice to appoint as first mate.

William had come to regard her as a sort of half-daughter/half-son. Her hard facial lines and windblown skin gave her a masculine impression most times, but when she turned from the periscope, her smile seemed that of a little girl getting her first doll.

"A beauty, all right," she nodded. "A passenger dirigible, no defenses visible. Bound west to Chicago, I should think, without a care in the world."

He returned her smile, long used to the way her proper English contrasted with the way he and the rest of his six-man crew spoke. He turned to his men and raised his voice. "Listen, up yer filthy scum." He used the sort of congenial insult shared by tight-knit teams who've worked together for decades. "We might soon all become filthy *rich* scum."

That brought smiles to the men, and on some of them a smile looked scary. All wore beards, hailed from the back-streets of London's East End, and bore the signs of many years spent in air piracy. With their missing ears or noses, patched eyes, and hooks for hands, they'd each lost some piece of anatomy while battling in the skies over England. His own right leg ended in a wooden peg. Among them, only Nell retained intact—limbs and organs both—probably due to her shorter time engaged in the business.

"'Ere's the plan. We'll attack this dirigible by the bloody book," he told them. "We've 'eard the Yanks aren't onto air piracy yet, and don't defend against it like the blokes do back 'ome. But keep on your guard, in case that's rubbish. Arm yerselves with cutlasses and pistols. If yer 'ave ter use a pistol, aim low so yer don't ignite them bags o' 'ydrogen.

"Break into the pilot gondola first, tie up the crew, then 'ead for the passenger gondola. Stuff jewelry and money in your bags, then we cop out of there, right quick and tidy. Understan' me?"

He gazed into the eyes of each assembled crew-member, getting an "aye" in return. Each one smiled too, no doubt thinking of the jewelry and bank notes soon to be lining their ornithopter's hold, and later to be split among them as their prize.

The London slums had given William no chance to move up in society, but as a pirate he could do his bit to correct the world's unfairness. He fancied himself a sort of airborne Robin Hood, with his like-minded crew of Merry Men.

By contrast, Nell, who'd joined the crew later, had grown up in privilege. A banker's daughter, she'd become bored with upper crust society with its limits and expectations. She'd left home and taken up piracy for the adventure of it.

William managed the approach while the crew made their preparations. When William had started out in the trade, he could fly straight at his target. No longer.

Commercial airships across Europe had gotten wise to pirates over time, and now all of them employed defenses. All English dirigibles sported machine guns, readily manned for protection. They could also deploy anti-piracy netting. Some even flew in the company of armed escort aircraft.

These measures had so reduced their haul that William had decided to leave Europe for America, where targets would be less prepared, or so the rumors maintained. "New hunting grounds for the new decade of the 1920s," William had said. Leaving home had been difficult and winging across the Atlantic treacherous, but his crew had all come along.

"Come right one point," he said to the helm, while peering through the scope. "Nell, what's the wind?"

"Ten knots from the south'ard," she said.

"Aye." As always, the trick was to stay hidden in clouds until the last moment. Only the periscope, painted white, showed above the gaseous blanket.

He looked around at the long-familiar interior of their ship—his ship—the *Raptor*. The clanking, hissing sounds and oily smell of the steam engine comforted him. He knew every plate and piston, every lever and linkage from her six pounder Hotchkiss bow cannon to her canvas tail rudder. Though old-fashioned, perhaps even obsolete, the *Raptor* had proved rugged and reliable through many attacks over the years. He could have bought or stolen one of the modern, fixed-wing types with gasoline engines, but he'd never done so.

"Now," he said. "Full throttle, up twen'y degrees." He lowered the periscope as the ship leapt out of the cottony, cumulous cloud and flapped at high speed toward its quarry. His well-trained crew stood by the gunwale and readied their coils of rope.

Few things in William's experience matched the beauty of a steam ornithopter in flight. The engine's piston rods rotated a large flywheel. Gears and linkages connected this brass wheel to the vast, hinged, bat-like wings. Here, the supreme intellect of man had produced a beautiful machine that imitated—even rivaled—Nature's most graceful creature, the bird. Guided by its skilled helmsman, the craft swooped, soared, banked, and climbed in a style so rhythmically exquisite it must render eagles jealous. William exulted in the joy and exhilaration of standing in the open cockpit with the wind coursing through his hair.

When the *Raptor* drew abeam of the dirigible's pilot gondola, six grappling hooks sailed across the gap. Four latched on to the gondola and William's men began pulling the *Raptor* closer. The craft's wings folded back against the fuselage like a grounded bird. With practiced skill, the crew ensured alignment of the *Raptor*'s half-door with the dirigible's gondola door. Armed with his cutlass in his belt and his pistol drawn, William charged through the doors first.

Two men stood in the large gondola, one with both hands raised in surrender, and the other gripping the large rudder wheel.

"We're 'ere for yer cargo and yer passengers' valuables, then we'll be on our way," William said as his crew entered behind him. "And, mind, no trouble from ye."

He wondered if the cargo might be booze. Now that America had declared alcohol illegal, the price had soared, making it a commodity well worth stealing. He nodded to one of his men, who took over the wheel with no resistance from the helmsman.

"I'm Captain Potts, of the airship *Sky Challenger*," said the one who had his hands up. A pudgy man, his jowls jiggled as he talked. His face held a puzzled expression. "Who are you people?"

"We're pirates," William answered him. "Now take us—"

"Captain," Nell said, and William held up a hand to silence her.

"I don't want any shooting," Captain Potts said, eyeing the pistols. "We're unarmed. Say, are you from England?"

"Never ye mind that," William took a step forward with his good leg.

"Captain," Nell tugged his sleeve. "You really ought to—"

"*Not now*," William said, then turned to Potts. "Take us to your passengers."

Small but firm hands grasped both sides of William's head and snapped it to face the starboard windows. "Someone's coming, Captain," Nell said, and pointed.

His jaw fell. With improbable speed, another aircraft neared. A single-engine biplane roared toward them, its enclosed fuselage rivaling the dirigible's gondola in size. The all-black plane appeared menacing, and William thought his *Raptor* comically clownish by comparison.

"Never seen a pirate before." Captain Potts' brow furrowed. "And now twice in one day?"

With a graceful precision William couldn't have matched, the pilot of the black biplane pulled alongside the gondola and slowed. Tethered grapnels shot from its side, but William saw no crewmen heaving them. Hidden winches drew the plane closer as its propeller stopped. The gondola shuddered as the plane's upper and lower wings thudded against the side opposite where William had moored the *Raptor*.

"Birds of a whole different feather." Nell nudged him. "Don't you think so, Captain?"

William only nodded in admiration for the modern plane, and the skill of its pilot.

A door opened in its enclosed fuselage and six figures walked across the lower wing toward the gondola. Each one wore a dark suit with white shirt, a black Stetson hat, and carried a Thompson submachine gun.

"Draw pistols, but keep 'em aimed low," William told his crew.

The gondola's starboard door opened and the six newcomers—all men—filed in. They took stations opposite William's crew, facing them. The black-suited men all wore mustaches, evidently an identifying mark for their band. With grim expressions, they all eyed William and his crew, but kept their machine guns angled down.

"Who're you?" the one on the end asked. His mouth barely moved as he spoke, and he clipped off each syllable as if with a knife. With the brim of the Stetson shading the man's eyes, William found it hard to judge the other's age, but guessed him to be several years younger than himself.

"We're the pirates 'oo are attackin' this dirigible," William said, staring the man down. "That's 'oo."

His adversary shook his head and reached to his inner breast pocket with his free hand. When every pistol in William's band shifted in response, the man grinned and slowed his hand. He withdrew a cigarette and stuck it in his mouth. To William's great relief, the bloke didn't actually light the fag while aboard a hydrogen dirigible, but merely let it hang from between his lips while he talked.

"Youse in *my* territ'ry now, Pops," the man said. "So take your toy guns and antique ship back to your own century, see?"

A couple of his men sniggered at the comment.

Something in the man's stance reminded William of his own first attack as a pirate captain, decades ago. The proud swagger, the confidence crossing into arrogance, both made it seem like he stared across the years at a younger version of himself.

"I've been a pirate since ye were pissin' in yer diapers, me boy," William said. "We were 'ere first. This is me *own* prize, mind ye, so move right along. Maybe next time *you'll* be the early bird."

The man laughed and his gang joined in. They all stopped when he spoke. "You slay me, Gramps. Doesn't matta who got here first. Only mattas who owns the territ'ry, and that's me, see? Crank Deco's the name and I'm the boss here. Got it? So youse betta scram. Flap your way back to jolly ol' England..." He looked at Nell. "But leave the hotsy-totsy Sheba. Me and the boys are gonna—"

A half second later, the sharp point of Nell's cutlass reached within an inch of Crank Deco's crotch, restrained only by William's grip on her arm. Every Tommy gun muzzle pointed toward Nell, and almost every pistol pointed toward the pirate boss. William's shout of "No, Nell!" still resounded in the confines of the gondola.

"Don't make 'er mad," William said to Deco, slowly lowering Nell's cutlass. "She might add your testicles ter her collection. I think she's makin' a purse outa 'em."

Nell managed something between a smile and a sneer, conveying thanks for William stopping her rash action—and pure hatred for Deco. Most of Deco's gang winced.

William's threat wasn't true, so far as he knew. Still, anything to put them off their game. "Why don't we all lower our weapons, then, eh? The bladders up there are filled with 'ydrogen, and firin' a gun could blow us *all* ter kingdom come."

After a pause, Crank Deco lowered his Tommy gun and his boys did likewise. William's men lowered their pistols at the same time.

"Look, youse can take your bearcat wit ya when ya blow," Deco glanced at Nell, perhaps unsure whether 'bearcat' would make her mad. "Just vamoose."

William stared into Deco's eyes, sizing him up. Well experienced in these encounters, William saw past the tough-guy stance, the firmness of the jaw, the twist of the sneering lips, and the iron in the eyes. Deco's presence would frighten most people, but not a seasoned pirate leader. William didn't miss the glint of a single bead of sweat sliding down beneath the Stetson and in front of the right ear. Nor did he fail to spot a slight vibration at the end of the dangling cigarette.

Not so sure of 'imself, William thought. *'E knows I'm not afraid of 'im, and that 'e can't outkeen me.* But deep down, William envied Deco's youth. He missed the days when his mind judged things in an instant and snapped to a decision. He longed for his former body, free of aches, taut with muscular power, and possessed with two good legs.

"We're not leavin'," he kept his voice even and low, "without our prize."

"You could divide our cargo and split it even steven," Captain Potts said, holding his palms up in an offering gesture.

"Shaddap!" Deco shouted.

"Pipe down!" William yelled at the same time.

Deco tried to say something else, but William interrupted. He knew what the pirate boss would propose, the next logical gambit in the game. Deco must have been about to suggest the two leaders fight it out, and the rest of both gangs abide by the outcome. Ten years earlier, William would have proposed that idea himself, but doubted he could take Deco one-on-one.

"'Ere's 'ow we're gonna settle this," he said. "Yer've got a flyin' machine and I've got a flyin' machine. Whichever takes the other one down, gets the prize."

Deco didn't hesitate. "That's swell. My plane can take your flappin' bucket any day, an' twice on Satudee. Ain't that right, boys?"

A dutiful chorus of "And how" and "Yeah, Boss" showed their well-considered opinions on the matter.

William looked at Captain Potts. "To make sure ye don't go sneakin' off while we're out there, I'm keepin' one man 'ere in the gondola ter watch ye." He looked down his row of crewmen and chose his most junior man, the one least experienced with the *Raptor*. "Lefty."

The crewman—nicknamed not for left-handedness, but for possessing only a left arm—nodded.

"An' I'm leaving one of my boys to watch him," Deco said. He spoke a name, "Rocko," and got a grunt in return.

"'Ere's the plan," William told his crew when they'd returned to the *Raptor*. "Soon as we drop away, spread the wings, turn toward Deco's ship, and fire the 'Otchkiss. I want that bow cannon blazin' soon as ye see a clean shot. One good 'it and this will be all over. Ready?"

Everyone nodded.

"Cut the grapnel lines." William donned his brass-rimmed goggles.

William's plan worked, except the part where the biplane would be dead ahead, waiting to be shot. A fixed-wing aircraft, William recalled too late, needed a good bit of forward motion to get lift, and Deco's plane gained that speed by falling several hundred feet lower than the *Raptor*.

By the time William located the enemy, it was clawing its way up toward him, machine gun firing. Most of the shots went wild, but holes appeared in the canvas of the *Raptor*'s port wing.

"Turn toward 'im, Beak! Turn toward 'im!" William yelled at his helmsman. Beak had earned his nickname after losing his nose in a swordfight and having an artificial, metal nose attached in its place.

"I'm tryin', Cap'n, but 'e's too fast," Beak said.

No matter how fast the helmsman changed course, just as the gunner readied the mighty Hotchkiss cannon to fire, the biplane banked away. Worse, Deco took every opportunity to spray the *Raptor* with machine gun fire. Damage from these rounds added up, with gauges shattered, hydraulic hoses punctured, and tail appendages holed.

Both more maneuverable and faster than the *Raptor*, the biplane could work over William's ornithopter with ease, and he couldn't even bring his cannon to bear. One hit from that massive six pounder should tear the diesel engine airplane apart, William knew. He only needed one good shot.

"'Ead for the cloud. Let's 'ide there." William needed time to think. The cotton candy masses had merged into a vast cumulonimbus formation with an upper surface as flat as an anvil's. Before the *Raptor* could descend into it, Deco made another run and everyone ducked under the edge of the open cockpit. William doubted the fuselage's thin metal would protect them. The spray of bullets stitched two lines fore to aft along their aircraft.

One round ripped through Nell's leather jacket, grazing her shoulder. More holes appeared in the wings and tail. Pings resounded from the Hotchkiss cannon and the steam boiler where shots ricocheted off.

"Are ye 'urt?" William asked Nell.

"Never mind about me," she shook her head. "We must get that bloody Deco."

Something in the way she brushed off his concern without even glancing down at her shoulder impressed William, but he didn't see how he could take Deco down. The Chicago-based pirate had all the advantages. Now that the *Raptor* had dropped into the cloud, he hoped he could think his way out of this. He had to think of *something*. William regretted his decision not to fight Deco alone.

He raised the periscope and searched for the biplane, expecting to see it circling in a vain hunt for him.

Instead, his eyes met a bow-on view of two parallel lines, the wings, separated by a translucent circle, the propeller. Behind the prop, he saw the twelve radial pistons of the immense diesel engine. Rapid red flashes from just beneath the upper wing could only mean one thing.

"Blast! 'E's found us somehow. Duck beneath the cowlin'!" William lowered the scope and knelt in the same motion.

The swarm of bullets struck the *Raptor* making twin lines of destruction as they slammed home. The targeting sight of the Hotchkiss cannon shattered. Oilcan Boyle, the engine-man, caught a round that nipped the edge of his right ear. The boiler sprang a leak, hissing steam through a bullet-hole. The linkage controlling the left wing-tip snapped off.

How did the beggar spot us, William wondered, *'ere in the chuffin' cloud?* He looked around through the moist, white fog, the mist he'd trusted as his shield. His eyes fell on the *Raptor*'s two beating wings, flapping to keep them aloft. *That's it. Our wings disturb the bloomin' cloud surface,* he realized. Deco just homed in on the pulsating parts of a cloud that was otherwise unmoving and flat.

He gritted his teeth and shut his eyes in despair. The biplane could fire at will, and soon the pounding would accumulate to more than the *Raptor* could bear. All the while, Deco would endure no harm at all, because he could avoid William's bow cannon, never passing in front of the *Raptor*, out-maneuvering him by remaining in other quadrants.

He stared at the iron Hotchkiss cannon, fixed in place at the bow. A prize won in combat years ago, the cannon would sit unused if he never got the chance to fire it. The gunner, one-eared Quoin, looked frustrated that the muzzle never pointed toward the agile biplane.

We've got ter move the cannon, William thought. *It's the only way.* "Right, then," he shouted. "We're gonna unbolt and 'aul the 'Otchkiss amidships."

The crew looked at him, mouths agape.

"Captain," Nell said. "There's nary a place amidships to bolt it down."

"We're not boltin' 'er down. We only need one fine shot. Quickly now, before Deco makes another bleedin' pass."

Nell blinked, slowly nodded, then rounded up men and wrenches to attack the cannon's mounting bolts.

On the biplane's next run, its machine gun delivered a massive hammering to the *Raptor*. The rounds struck aft and amidships, so missed the crew huddled in the bow. One landing talon got clipped off and fell away. The water storage tank got punctured in several locations, and fresh water streamed out from each hole. The engine's speed-regulating governor broke off and spun away. A left wing strut bent, but stayed in place.

"Now heave away and lift that cannon, men," Nell said when the last bolt came free. "Move it amidships. Your lives depend on it." She bent down in a way William found alluring, but put her back into lifting the heavy gun right along with the rest.

Though the Hotchkiss weighed over a quarter ton, the crew lugged it, their muscles throbbing with the strain, until they'd reached just forward of the steam engine. They aimed the seventy-four-inch barrel out the starboard side, over the lip of the open cockpit. The middle-aged men stood slowly, hands rubbing aching backs, faces dripping sweat.

"Yer'll only cop one go," William spoke into Quoin's only ear. "So aim true, and don't stand behind 'er when ye fire."

Another hail of machine gun bullets slammed into the *Raptor*. With a rip, the fabric of one section of the starboard wing tore free. The upper mirror in the periscope shattered. The pings of ricochets resounded as shells glanced off the boiler. The engine's steady 'chuff-chuff-chuff' became an irregular 'chuff-a, chuff, a-chuff' as something inside the engine came loose.

"Me bloody arm!" Beak yelled as his left bicep turned bloody indeed.

One bullet punched a hole through William's peg leg, and the force of it sent him sprawling.

"'Ow's the bloomin' engine, Oilcan?" William shouted as he struggled to stand. "Are all the important bits in workin' order?"

"It's 'oldin' togeffer well enough," Boyle replied in a strained voice, clutching a greasy rag to staunch his ear wound.

William closed his eyes in a private, thoughtful prayer. *Lord, just let me crew survoive this. Let 'em live and I'll give up me piratin' ways forever.*

"Now!" William shouted to the helmsman. "Full throttle, up twen'y degrees."

Like a gooney bird flapping and running along a beach to take off, the *Raptor* clanked, rattled, and lurched its way above the cloud.

True to the confounding, bedeviling rules of an uncaring universe, Deco's biplane appeared on their port side, swooping in for another attack. William cursed that his cannon pointed the wrong way.

"Turn right!" He screamed.

The *Raptor* struggled to swing around, and presented her tail to the enemy as he came within machine gun range. A hundred projectiles shredded the tail. The swerve to the right continued.

In moments the biplane got close enough that it had to begin its own avoidance turn.

William saw Quoin sighting along the barrel of the Hotchkiss as they came beam-on to Deco's aircraft. A smile crossed Quoin's face and he turned the firing crank.

Quoin jumped out of the way just in time as the recoil sent the un-mounted cannon speeding backward across the deck. It smashed through the port side of the cockpit, tearing a gaping, clean-edged hole through the metal fuselage like a hydraulic punch. Down the precious cannon fell, beginning its four mile plunge to the State of Indiana.

William looked at the biplane, which must have crossed well into its turn when the six pound ball struck. With its propeller and half of the diesel engine block sheared off, it could no longer fly, and could barely glide. He fancied he saw Deco himself in the forward cockpit windshield, cigarette drooping, giving him a hand gesture as the biplane descended out of sight.

Watching it go, William heaved huge sighs of relief. No one let out a single 'hurrah' over the victory, which William found appropriate. Deco had been a worthy opponent, and the battle had very nearly gone the other way.

"They'll make it all right," William told Nell. "'E can glide down."

Remembering his solemn promise, he gathered his fellow pirates around him. "Listen up, ye filthy scum. Ye've been the finest bloody crew a Captain 'ad any right ter serve with. It's been me 'igh 'onor ter lead ye these many years. But although we defeated Crank Deco and 'is men today, I think..." He paused and looked into the distance. "I think the future belongs ter the likes of ' im. The day of steam is over, lads, and that means me day is done too. It's time for me ter retire."

They stared at him as if he'd just sprouted wings.

"I wouldn't want ter leave you lot in a lurch. So I'm makin' Nell the bleedin' Captain and givin' 'er the ship."

Nell looked around and laughed. "A ship that's all torn up, barely flies, and lost her only weapon?"

"Not this ship." William smiled. "No, the *Raptor*'s done for. I'm meanin' that one." He pointed up, and they all gazed where the *Sky Challenger* floated, vast and serene. "If we can cop to 'er aright, she's yours. Ye can sell 'er and buy the best pirate craft ever. Better than Deco's biplane. Wot ye think, Nell?"

She put her hands on her hips and glared at him with narrowed eyes, though with a bit of a smile. "A ship, then? You thought I worked so hard so I could have my own *ship*?"

"I...well...wha' else, then?" William felt confused.

Nell shook her head and rolled her sky blue eyes. "You're utterly hopeless. I never wanted a ship." She looked directly into William's eyes. "I rather fancied a Captain."

"Ooh," chorused the rest of William's crew, all wearing smiles, pointing, and jabbing each other's ribs.

"Wot?" William couldn't believe it. "Ye and me, then, eh, luv? But I'm an ol' man. Me body is twenty years older than yours."

She winked at Oilcan Boyle then looked at William and lowered her voice to imitate Boyle's Cockney. "Are all the important bits in workin' order?"

William laughed and tried to recall Oilcan's earlier reply. "It's 'oldin' togeffer well enough."

Nell raised her hand in a 'stop' gesture. "Mind you, just because you want to retire from piracy doesn't mean I'm retiring from adventure. If you want to smuggle alcohol, or go barnstorming at air shows, or pilot a plane around the world for the first time, I'll be at your side. But I will not settle down in a house without wings, is that clear?"

Whatever Nell meant to William before, she was all woman now, and strong-willed, too. All eyes were on him, and everyone awaited his response.

"Adventure, is it then? Well, 'oo am I ter argue with the new Cap'n of the *Sky Challenger*?"

Without warning, Nell rushed to William and kissed him.

"Gorblimey!" William said when the kiss finally ended, amid hurrahs from the crew.

Suddenly feeling free as a bird, William turned to his helmsman. "Beak, see if ye can cop this antique, flyin' bucket back up ter the chuffin' dirigible. We've got ter pick up Lefty, decide wot ter do with that blighter, Rocko, and then get ye, Oilcan, and Nell to a doctor."

William Starling smiled and rested his hands on the gunwale, letting the wind blow through his graying hair. Somewhere below them, an eagle screeched. Me and Nell *Remige,* he thought. *Loife is full o' bloomin' surprises.*

The Climbers

D. Chang

prttEEk twitched her left tertiary whisker, bringing her Leafwing alongside the great Hearthbough. Pneumatics hissed and warm steam wreathed the bridge as the calculating machines adjusted the cutter's final docking with the massive battlenaught.

prttEEk's nose quivered. In many ways, she was a throwback—a climber more comfortable chitting commands to a hard-clawed crew than whiskering them in front of the cold input lens of an analytical complex—but she was adaptable. Climbers who did not adapt soon stopped climbing.

Tails bobbed respectfully as prttEEk left the bridge and scurried up an access rope. At deck level, she leaped over to a boarding tube and admired the view as she scrambled across the long dramatic expanse between Leafwing and the legendary flagship.

Ah, the Hearthbough. His many war-blimps, chitterguns, and gliderbombs had decimated the human fortifications, but prttEEk admired him most not for his efficacy, but for his beauty, because—at his core—Hearthbough was as much a live oak tree as a vessel. Birthed in the gravity-free embrace of a nutritive satellite, he exceeded every climber's expectations in scale and grandeur, the finest statement of an arboreal culture.

The warship's metal skin glowed with puissance. That shiny mesh protected his limbs and the vast aethersacs populating his innards, which in turn gave him much of his destructive and propulsive power. prttEEk could only guess at the panic that churned in the human psyche when they raised their eyes to the sky and saw that their colonizers had flown an enormous sacred tree through space to destroy their civilization.

prttEEk scrambled through the starboard tunnels like it was her own vessel. Proudly she waved her tail at the bridge entrance. "Second Claw prttEEk reporting for Phase Three."

"I'd be more okay with it if the goddamn aliens had been taller." Frankie spat in the corner of our subterranean den and took another drag on her last cigarette. Other than a little indirect glow from the central warren that came through the ventilation shaft, it was the only light we had.

"Yeah," I said. I was bone-chilled and my stomach grumbled. "The whole thing is insulting. When they said we were being invaded by alien mammals, I thought they'd be more impressive, you know. Wolfmen, maybe."

"No shit, girl." She paused, cocking her head at the faint sound of yet another of their airships fluttering in to land. Up close, it's a hellish aural torment, like a thousand pounds of dry ice being dumped into a boiling swimming pool. "They have robots and spaceboats, but there's no pussyfooting around it. There's nothing more insulting than being enslaved by jumbo squirrels."

"I bet I could think of something," I said, scooping some dirt out from under my butt in another vain attempt to get comfortable. When your bed is a cold pothole, it's nigh on impossible.

"Please don't," Frankie said, flicking an ash into the waste trough. With that, we fell back into silence.

I scraped at the overhead lid of the den with my digging stone for an hour. The next hour was more scraping, this time at the corner, in hopes of finding a weak spot or maybe an abandoned subway tunnel. Then I slumped back into bed, neck aching, frustrated and disconsolate.

Before the conquest of Earth, three weeks ago, Frankie had spent her days snowboarding upstate, tattooing herself, and prosecuting tax dodgers. She'd gained some minor notoriety by killing five squirrels during the second revolt using nothing but a pencil. Her arms and ankles were crisscrossed with deep squirrel bites.

My credentials were a little less imposing. I'd been a high school dropout and a specialist in a pet store. As a gerbil girl, I knew a rodent's ideal nutrition sources and how to bring out the gloss in its fur and the gleam in its eyes.

I made a small side income as a rodent psychic, reading hamster and guinea pig fortunes and communicating their medical complaints. I was the perfect person to make our captors as attractive, happy, and healthy as they could possibly be.

I scratched at my bed. I'd forgotten what it felt like to not have dirt under my nails. Rest was important, but it was hard to sleep knowing we were buried alive like ants in a bottle. What time was it on the surface? Where were my parents, my brother?

"Listen," Frankie said. "Maybe this is it." We could hear the sound of dozens of little claws running on dirt. The squirrels never ambled or wandered; it was always little neurotic bursts of energy.

We stood as best we could, glaring up at the earthen mouth in the ceiling.

The door came to life and rumbled to one side, quickly followed by a heavy object that fell wetly on my shoulder. A food pack. I could smell the distinctive grassy odor right through the soft outer membrane. "Thank god," I said. The door closed again with a thump.

"Yeah," Frankie said. "But it's off-schedule. Something's up." She crawled over, punched a hole near the top of the pack with her fingers, and began hungrily sucking fluid through the opening.

"They must be doing something on the surface."

"Yeah."

"Just before I was caught, I heard the Canadians and the Russians were still fighting," I said. "The rats hit Europe the hardest, but they weren't ready for Canada."

"Canadians, really?" Frankie chuckled. "You saw what they did to our boys."

"True." I took a deep pull on the food pack.

Our den trembled as a robot stomped past, hissing, its tail thumping against the corridor walls.

"Do you think the energy project would've worked?" I asked.

"What, the space guns? I don't know. I just got sick of all the ads begging us to save electricity. Did you go dark?"

"Sometimes, sure."

"'An hour a day keeps the squirrels away.' Bullshit. It was a hot summer."

"I remember. It was a blazer." Just thinking about it made the air even more stifling.

Frankie shifted the rapidly emptying food pack. "I'm glad it was still daylight when they arrived. We got to see everything. In Europe, it was already nighttime."

I remembered. "Their fleet was majestic. Solar sails glowing with the heat of reentry. The bright green and silver piping on the gunwales and the engine nacelles. Their tails braided and painted, twitching in concert."

"What the hell is a gunwale?"

"The edge of the boat. You know, where you'd put an oar, if you were rowing a spaceboat."

"Just say 'the edge of the boat.' It'll make everybody happier."

"Good point," I said. "Did you see the space guns shooting?"

"Yeah. Pathetic."

"We gave the squirrels history's best lightshow."

Frankie laughed at that. "True. Best pyrotechnics ever. It was a hell of an entrance."

A squirrel woke us a few hours later by opening the den lid and scalding us in our beds with one of the helmet-mounted hot steam guns they love so much. I stared up at it, unsettled by the wary intelligence in its beady eyes, half expecting it to start singing a tune from The Jungle Book. It was a large one, maybe the size of an adult golden retriever.

"I can tell it's hungry," I told Frankie.

"Shut up."

Hissing warm mist, one of the big clanking monkey-robots clambered down into our cell, fixed a clear, semi-inflated membrane bag around the entrance, and unceremoniously pushed us up into it using both hands and tail. We couldn't damage the bag, although it wasn't for lack of trying.

More steam jet and robotic prodding. We stumbled down the packed-earth corridor. It joined with another corridor, and then a much larger passage. Our ball fogged with condensation and sweat. We found ourselves crawling down a vast dirt tunnel the size of a superhighway with thousands of other men, women, and children. Most were bagged in pairs, but I spotted some singles and a few triples. Dark branching wooden pylons ascended the tunnel walls and spidered the roof like tremendous angular veins. Perhaps they had been crafted by the robots, because they were clearly beyond the abilities of the tree-rats themselves.

People were crying, some were screaming, and some tried to fight through the bags to no avail. Some simply sat in the way, curled up and unresponsive to the steam jets that were trained upon them until other humans shoved them forward. Perhaps they were dead. I know I saw one sad man, blistered and soiled, who must have been dead in his bag, his head turned at an unnatural angle to his body.

From the perspective of the squirrel overlords in their flying whirligigs, we must have looked exactly like the universe's biggest, slowest, saddest hamster ball race.

We came to a vast crater. All we could see was the bowl of heat-seared earth and an empty sky. It was a perfect sky, lightly draped with clouds, the first sky we had seen since the invasion.

We were herded into large open transports, wooden skiffs on wheels, each powered by a large grumbling bow-mounted engine. Shoved on top of each other, lumped on top of another struggling pair, Frankie and I waited and sweated in our membrane bag for several hours. Conversation seemed pointless. Then the transport vomited a great gout of white smoke, trembled into motion, and crawled over the curved lip of the crater out into New York City.

We gaped at the landscape. The skyline was gone.

Instead, it was ridged earth as far as the eye could see. Occasionally we spotted a relic of the metropolis breaking the monotony: a concrete embankment, the hindquarters of a bus, the peak of a roof, or a traffic signal poking up at an unexpected angle.

"They rototilled my city," Frankie said in a weak voice.

"These look like furrows."

"Huh."

"What do you think they want us to grow for them?"

There was a disturbing light in Frankie's eyes. She looked like she wanted to scream, but she started to giggle instead. "Do you think they buried the Statue of Liberty?"

"I...I don't know. Why?"

"You know. In case they want to crack it open later and look inside it for food."

I blinked. "Seriously, Frankie. Pull yourself together."

"I think they want nuts. They want pecan pie."

"Come on, be serious. We're talking about the enslavement of the human race."

"Nutter Butters?" She burst into laughter at her own joke.

"Please stop, Frankie."

"Go to hell," Frankie said. She shoved me to the other side of the ball and slumped against the wall, either laughing or crying, I'm not sure which. Everyone else in the transport clearly wished we would flop out of the vehicle to be crushed under the giant spherical wheels, and in a way I did too.

High in the mesosphere above New York, rEttOk shifted in his flight harness to nod at prttEEk. "I cannot wait until the first tender shoots rise from the garden. It is truly glorious."

prttEEk twitched her tail in agreement. "Yes, Your Honor." She trembled with the desire to share with her distant littermates the view from the bridge of the Hearthbough.

The setting yellow sun blessing the rich earth with warmth. The soft fertile soil stretching in uniform waves for miles in every direction. In the distance, the first green shoots of Phase Two would already be extending to the sky. Soon it would be verdant with young firs, cedars, larches, and pines, all seeded and watered and aching for spring.

"Your plan was inspired, Second Claw," rEttOk said. "The digger charges accomplished their dual purpose of shattering the skinned's cities and freeing the sanctified earth beneath them."

"Thank you, sir," prttEEk said, fur flattened in humility. "But I did not foresee how rich the soil truly was under their cities."

"Far more charged than anything on Hometree—or on this planet for that matter." rEttOk adjusted his monocle with a paw, admiring the rich purpling hues of the darkening clouds. "It astounds me that the humans burned all their cone trees and built stone trees instead," he said.

"Stone trees bear no seed," prttEEk said, unable to resist the old adage.

"Today's briefing is about the inland territories, prttEEk. I have glad news for you."

prttEEk bowed. "Your Honor, I climb to serve."

rEttOk nodded. "There is another phase, dear Second, a phase you will lead. Phase Four will bring prime trees to those inland acres and song to the hearts of generations of young climbers."

prttEEk pressed her belly to the deck. "Your Honor, I am not worthy."

"You are most worthy. Your work with the skinned is beyond our wildest expectations."

"Thank you, sir." prttEEk trembled. "But I fear our generals may be right about the skinned."

"They can be dangerous, they are terrible diggers, and their flesh is indeed savory. But they are skilled gardeners. Look at their form. With their awkward posture, oversized heads, and bovine temperament, they were born to manipulate dirt. We were born to rule."

prttEEk's sharp eyes caught sight of a pair of bright objects flaring earthward. "Sir...!" she said.

rEttOk laughed. "Look, meteorites punctuate my grand speech!" He petted prttEEk on the head. "I appreciate your security concerns, Second Claw, but no object of that size poses any threat to the fleet."

A scuffling came from the bridge entrance and a cadet entered with a bedraggled charge: an advance scout, probably hundreds of generations removed from his proud ancestors. He was a disgusting sight, a fraction of the mass of the average climber, skull flat, tail ragged, eyes close and dull. He stank of rot.

rEttOk waved the cadet away and turned to the scout. "What is your name?"

"Fluffybutt," the scout said, trembling. "Me Fluffybutt."

"You and your kin were remiss in not alerting us to the riches of this world more promptly," rEttOk said, voice neutral. "Why did it take so long to contact Hometree?"

"We sorry, dude...we real sorry. We knew Big Seed important. We no eat Big Seed. We work hard. We figure out how to shout with Big Seed." He rasped his claws against the deck, front paws going forward, rear paws going backward.

prttEEk found herself tempted to look away. The other climbers on the bridge evidenced a mixture of reactions: amazement, shock, and disgust.

"Yes, the seed was a transmitter," rEttOk said, demonstrating a depth of patience unique to a Great Climber. "An aether-transmitter."

"Eater," Fluffybutt said. "Eater." He threw his head left, then right, staring at the crew like they were skinned.

rEttOk twitched a whisker.

Fluffybutt recoiled. "No eat. No eat me."

rEttOk patted the scout with a forepaw. "There will be no more killing." The cadet ushered him out to the tunnels.

"A fearsome reminder of the sacrifices of our forebears," prttEEk sighed.

"Hometree knows of their failings, and of their successes." rEttOk blinked sagely. "Perhaps they did not want to share paradise."

"These things are killing me," Frankie said, throwing her digging gloves down. I looked around to see if the foreman squirrel might sic a robot on us for disrespecting their crude tools, but of course there was nothing moving in the gathering gloom except a bedraggled string of human diggers.

"I think we might be spending the night out here, squirrel style," I said.

In the distance we could hear the cadence of heavy footsteps. "Robots coming," Frankie said.

"I'm sure they're bringing the new mandatory tail prostheses that we have to ram up our asses."

Frankie slapped me on the butt. "Nice one, kid!"

The footsteps neared, preceded by a strange susurrus of whispers and comments.

"Frankie!" hissed one of our furrow-mates. "They want Frankie!"

Two bulky figures stepped out into the moonlight. The leader's helmet hissed open, revealing the grinning face of a septuagenarian Amazon wreathed in fine silver hair.

"Superintendent Esther Van Dusen at your service," she offered in a hoarse whisper. She extended a metal-gloved hand to us. "Canadian Mounties, Special Services. I hear you are American Frankie and her sidekick."

I spluttered, while Frankie smoothly took the proffered hand. "Damned straight. How can we help, superintendent?"

Van Dusen shifted slightly, clanking, and I realized her bulk was due in part to her pockmarked power armor and the steaming jetpack clamped to its struts, tailpipes still glowing. "It's an honor, American Frankie. We have me and Constable Carver here, proud descendants of lumberjacks as it happens, and we flew over with a little volatile present for the nutters. I hear you're the two who can help us deliver it, eh?"

"Won't blowing up the flagship only piss them off?" I said.

Frankie hissed. "Wouldn't you rather piss them off than dig their goddamned holes?"

This was greeted by an amiable chuckle from the other Mountie. Carver, a bald youth with a handlebar moustache the size of my fist, chimed in, "You both have fine points, lassies. And here's a third: if we break the back of their offense, we believe it will bring other human forces into the fight."

Frankie nodded. "Excellent. Let's get shipping." We began walking, toward what destination I had no idea.

I suddenly stopped dead. It appeared I was actually going to save the world with my rodent skills. "Uh," I said.

"Yes, dearie?" asked Van Dusen, motioning for Frankie to restrain herself.

"We have to stop off at a dairy upstate for some cheese." I was surprised to realize it was my voice.

"Really?" Frankie opened and closed her right fist in frustration.

"Really," I said. "I think we're going to find it very useful."

prttEEk strode down the corridors of the Leafwing, her tail proud but her mind heavy. The inlands would need more time, more fertilizer, and more seed. And what if rEttOk's lofty harvest expectations couldn't be met? Would there be more famines on Hometree? And why was she so damned hungry?

A scurry of undisciplined claws broke her train of thought. Did some foolish cadet stow his younglings on her cutter? If so her wrath would be quick and harsh.

She scrambled to follow the sound of giggling and little feet. Down, down she ran through the belly of the ship, panting, unused to such a frantic pace and slowed by her uniform.

Her pursuit brought her to the broader corridors of the engineering section, dimly lit and festooned with control lines, steam pipes, and aether-channels. She hadn't run this hard since she was chasing her brothers through the challenge lines on Hometree.

Her stomach was churning. She scrabbled at a stanchion to spin around a corner and finally caught a brief glimpse of her fleet-footed prey—not younglings after all, but two advanced scouts, their ragged, crooked tails unmistakable! What were they doing on the Leafwing? Could they possibly be conspiring with the skinned?

"Fluffybutt, stop!" she screamed, although her tongue was confounded by drool. The pair ignored her, or simply were too dense to realize they were pursued by an officer.

The two scouts darted left toward a dead end. Fools. prttEEk took a moment to straighten her uniform and catch her breath.

prttEEk's next sight was one that drained all the blood from her paws. Around the corner was one of Leafwing's massive airlocks. Through the closing outer door, she could see two—no, four!—figures in spacefaring gear, jetting away from the ship. Bipedal figures. They flew in pairs, the smaller ones strapped to the backs of the bigger ones, gesticulating crudely.

Of more importance was what they had left in the airlock, a large spherical object of warm variegated harvest colors, big enough to envelop a full-sized climber. Somehow, she knew it was edible, a calorie source more bountiful than anything she'd ever encountered.

Warm saliva filled her mouth and dripped unheeded to the oaken deck. The ball magnetized her gaze so completely that she barely saw the four (now four!) scouts frantically punching at the controls. In fact, now they'd stopped punching at the controls and were simply watching as the inner airlock door swung open.

Maybe the generations of nutritional hardship had heightened the sensitivities of the scouts. Perhaps they had foresmelled this transcendent visitation because of their keen awareness. Such things happened.

prttEEk blinked, her senses overwhelmed by a divine aroma that preceded the object as it slowly rolled toward them. It was like relaxing into a warm pond of sensation, a scent as rich and welcoming as her own mother's milk, but spicy and mature and enhanced by a chorus of delectable roasted nut smells.

Roasted nuts! What a concept! It was completely heretical, of course, but by all that was holy, maybe the heretics were right. Tears began to run down the fur of her nose. She had been wrong, oh so wrong, and the only mammal she had hurt was herself.

She could see those nuts rotating into view as the ball approached. Pecan. Almond. Brazil. Hazelnut. Pine. Cashew, oh cashew. Sweet, sweet cashew.

Joining the scouts, she fell upon the ball and knew its flavor only briefly before it spoke.

Deep within the concrete tomb known as Gorbachev Baikal Security Centre Annex, General Maximillian Maravich II watched his monitors impassively as his staff shouted, laughed, and brashly sang their best approximation of "Oh, Canada." The screens were frantic with exploding aether-tanks and flaming oak limbs as the smaller warship drove its prow deeper into the squirrel flagship and the two tore themselves apart from the inside.

Two precious crates of vodka were bashed open, uncorked, and sampled in order of rank, with the general declining his portion with a flick of his head.

Maravich raised the index finger of his remaining hand and silence immediately blanketed the war room and the adjoining thousand-seat command complex. He stood as straight as he could and regarded the room for a long moment.

"Comrades!" he bellowed. "Alert the rocket carriers and unmuzzle the Storm Huskies. Tonight we launch the dogs of war!"

A Steampunk Garden

Wynelda Ann Deaver

Mrs. Medlock stood in front of Lord Archer's desk, shaking with fury. "She's an unnatural child, she is. That...that...that girl broke every one of the dolls you bought for her!"

Archer shook his head. He'd been gone for only a few weeks, hadn't he? How had the addition of one girl add so much hysteria to the household in such a short time?

He had plans to go over, experiments to conduct. Letters to the Queen to be written. Ten thousand things large and small to occupy his attention, and now this.

"I thought you said she was too old for the dolls anyway?" Hadn't he received an aether-gram regarding that? She wasn't a ten-year-old girl. Instead, his new charge was a seventeen- year-old young woman. That had been discussed, hadn't it?

The rod in Mrs. Medlock's back became even straighter at that. "That girl willfully destroyed her room, making more work for the staff..."

"I thought you'd mentioned locking her in the room, and not allowing anyone else entry, as well? How did she manage so much damage on her own?"

Mrs. Medlock was either losing bits of her memory, or was hiding something. He narrowed his eyes at the woman. She ruled his home absolutely in his absence—he had to be able to trust her. Could he?

"I allowed her to keep one of the mechcani-mans."

Perhaps it was time for that to change.

"Send the girl to me. At once." Archer bit out the words, wanting to curse at the woman. Gentlemen didn't do that, but the temptation to give in to unreasonable anger was about to overwhelm him. *Deep breaths, old boy. Deep breaths.*

Mary ignored the glee on Mrs. Medlock's face when the old battle axe came to fetch her at Lord Archer's command. A glance around her room determined that everything had been, in fact, tucked away nicely. It was so easy to fool the woman, it almost wasn't worth it.

"Come, Flit," she commanded. The mechani-man rolled forward to follow behind her to the study.

Mary halted in front of the desk, Flit whirring softly behind her. Lord Archer sat behind the desk, staring at her. She reciprocated. He wasn't as old as she'd thought he would be. Nor as...infirm in the head as her parents had been.

Of course, he hadn't spoken yet. But if he were, in fact, as smart as he looked—

Goodness, she was going to have to work at keeping things rolling along to her satisfaction here.

"What happened to the clicking in that mechani-man?"

He surprised her with his first question. Odd, that he would recognize Flit as having been fixed. Or having made the clicking sound to begin with.

"I repaired it." She kept her voice neutral, her face like stone. No use giving him anything to use against her.

Or telling him how minor a repair it had been. Or that there were the other adjustments she had made.

"Mrs. Medlock informs me that you destroyed several things of value." He kept his gaze locked with hers, looking for any flicker of emotion, she was sure.

She would not give him—or Mrs. Medlock—the satisfaction of a reaction. "Yes, I did."

"Why?" His voice was soft, gentle. As if he cared.

Mary watched him, chewing her lip. *Tell the truth?* How far could she trust this stranger who was in control of her life? *Mayhap just a bit of the truth?*

She turned to make sure the large oak door was shut firmly and Mrs. Medlock was on the other side of it. "There was some sort of listening device in one of them."

He leaned forward on his desk. "How did you know of it?"

Mary fidgeted. *In for a penny...* "The sound of it irritated me beyond reason. It was poorly-made. I-it... *whistled.*"

"Is there one in here?"

Mary cocked her head to the left, held her breath. Nothing near the desk. Slowly, she walked around the room until she was sure there were no unaccounted for listeners. She shook her head no.

"What did you do with the device?"

"Flit, come." Mary waited until the little mechani-man rolled to a stop between her and the desk. Made to look like a small snowman, she pressed lightly on his third button. With a swish, a panel opened revealing the small aether-tube device.

Lord Archer's face hardened. "Is there anything else you would like to inform me of?"

Mary looked him dead in the eye. "If Mrs. Medlock ever slaps me again she shall require a mechanical appendage."

"Is there anything else you require?"

Mary stood still, feeling the air around her. Her heart beat loudly in her ears. Oh yes, there was something she required. Something she wanted more than anything else in the world.

Deep breaths.

"Might I have the walled off garden? The one with the cottage?" A place of her own—with no interference. A place where she could experiment and build with no one trying to peer over her shoulder, or bothering her about food and bedtimes. She was a woman grown, not some idiot child just because she'd had the misfortune to be born female.

"To live in?"

A short, sharp burst of hope. "Yes, a place of my own."

He shook his head and her spirits deflated. "Walk with me in the gardens."

She dropped a minimal courtesy. "Yes, Lord Archer."

Mary had to practically run to keep up with Lord Archer's brisk pace. Soon, they came to the walled-in garden with the small cottage. He went unerringly to a spot in the ivy, pulling it away to reveal the door. With a quick look around, he produced a key and let them into the garden. "I wonder where the gardener has gotten to?" he mused.

She stared around in wonder. It was perfect. She had never been inside before, just able to see the roof and chimney from the main garden paths. A gravel path meandered through beds filled with flowers. A trickle of water flowed through part of it, a tiny creek perfect for warm days. Trees shaded the house, which resembled a witch's hut. Lord Archer went straight for the cottage door, motioning her to follow him inside.

"I have a proposition for you," he began.

Mary drew back, startled.

"No, no, nothing of an improper sort. Except, well…" He dragged a hand through his hair. Mary maintained her silence, waiting. "I have a spy in the house. As well as plans for Her Majesty's Naval Fleet…"

"Plans for what?" Mary looked around the cottage, noting where her work table and tools would go.

"For an airship." His voice was bland.

"Why? There are already thousands of designs, I'm sure one of them would work." She moved around him, to the small sitting room.

"There are none that will bear the weight of both armor and heavy artillery."

A large low table occupied the middle of the room. The sort of table that invited one to sit on a pillow and make their designs. "The problem isn't with the ship. You need lighter weapons. And possibly a different sort of armor. Are you trying for metal? No…that would never be practical for air troops. What about—?" She began tracing in the dust on the table.

He watched over her shoulder. She could feel his presence, right there, behind her. His breath tickled her ear as he whispered "That's amazing. I'll have to copy this…"

"Mmmm...bring Flit. He can take an aether-impression of it."

"Flit?"

"The mechani-man I repaired. You left him on guard duty in your office." She ignored the receding footfalls and the soft click of the door as he left. Finally, she was free to dream mechanical with no thought of her parents or Mrs. Medlock interfering.

Lord Archer returned way too soon, Flit rolling behind and both carrying supplies. She listened as coal clattered into the stove, and a tea pot was placed upon the stove.

Mary stood, stretching her back. "Flit, come. We'll need more light, Lord Archer."

He quickly complied, lighting all the lamps and candles in the cottage.

The round mechani-man rolled to a stop next to her. "Impression protocol, Flit."

A small scope popped out of his head, allowing her to focus on the area of the table where the diagrams she'd been playing with were.

"Thank you, my girl, you have saved us valuable time. Now to find the turncoat in the house."

"It's Mrs. Medlock." Mary kept her voice flat, devoid of emotion.

"She's been with me for years!" His outburst was funny, really.

"Why else was there a listening device in my room? Why is she so angry that I am not a child that is easily controlled?" Mary began ticking reasons off on her fingers.

"Even if it is true, we need proof." His face was stern again.

She bit her lip to keep from laughing. "Will you give me this cottage for my own when I obtain it?"

"Yes. But you will have to be chaperoned. It would cause unwanted speculation for you to live alone at your age."

"Beatrice. I like Beatrice." Bright chatter, but left Mary's things alone. Yes, Beatrice was a perfect fit.

"You will also have to make appearances in the manor occasionally, and at any dinners I may give."

"Shake on it." She held out her hand, squeezing his just a bit as they shook. Mary was gratified by the slight wince.

Tools built strong hands.

"Here's what we will do..."

Mary resigned herself to life—temporarily—without Flit. It was amazing how much she had come to rely upon the small mechani-man, but he was needed in the office.

Lord Archer had the staff move her things into a more adult chamber, with Mrs. Medlock glaring all the while. All she needed now was for everyone to go to sleep so she could sneak up to the nursery and steal back her tools.

Her nightgown was laid aside, replaced by work clothes. Trousers, a large, soft man's shirt, and a vest with multiple pockets. A small leather satchel sat on the floor at the foot of her bed.

A clock chimed the hour, night had turned to morning. *Time to go.*

Mary crept down the hall to the stairs, a hand on the wall for guidance. Her foot was on the stair to go up to the nursery, when she stopped. A whisper of sound, a woman's giggle— accompanied by a man's voice, a door opening and closing. Mary sat down on the stairs, in the shadows, praying she was well hidden.

She remained, still and quiet, until finally she was rewarded with Mrs. Medlock's retreating back. There was no sign of the gentleman.

No time like the present. Taking a deep breath, she stood with her satchel and fled up the stairs to the nursery. Mary worked for a few hours before making her way back to her new rooms just before sunrise.

Once there, she collapsed on her bed, chuckling. Tomorrow was looking to be very promising indeed.

At breakfast, she served herself from the sideboard, filling her plate with sausage, eggs and toast. And marmalade. Such a lovely accompaniment to toast. Lord Archer came in and served himself before sitting across the table from her.

Mary waited, a bit cruelly, for Mrs. Medlock to come into the room before asking, "Did we have company last night, Lord Archer?"

"No, none that I recall." He raised his brow at her and continued plowing through his heaping plate.

"I went to my old rooms last night to retrieve something I had forgotten, and I could have sworn I heard voices in the hall by your office." Mary primly sliced her sausage as a large crash sounded behind her. She bit her lip to keep herself from showing any sort of reaction. "If you don't need me, Lord Archer, I believe that I shall take a stroll in the gardens."

"See me before leaving the house, please." He waved to Mrs. Medlock, catching her attention. "Have Beatrice go down to the village and bring Dickon up."

Mary quirked her brow. Dickon was Beatrice's brother, just returned from his service in the Air Navy. Whatever could Lord Archer want with him?

No matter. They would have their answers and she would be free, and soon!

Once in her rooms, Mary paced, fighting a yawn. Obviously, Lord Archer had taken her clues.

What he did with them was up to him. For Mary though...she had to plan what to take out to the cottage today. Later, she would bring everything over in the open. But for now she had to hide herself, who she truly was.

Not so much difference between now and when her parents were alive. Except, perhaps, there was. Someone liked her abilities, *admired* them. He didn't make fun of her. Maybe there were others in the world like her.

A sketchbook and pencils. Appropriately lady-like. Smiling, she whirled down the stairs and out into the gardens.

The crunch of gravel behind her.

A rag, smelling sickly sweet...

Darkness.

Mary woke to a blinding headache and nausea that was not helped by a slight rocking motion. If she had slept last night, she wouldn't have been taken so easily!

She was laid out on a wooden floor, her morning dress still covering her trouser-clad legs. She moaned, licking dry lips.

Where was she? Who had taken her? Mrs. Medlock didn't have the strength.

A small sound to the right. Slowly, Mary turned her head—to see her nemesis tied up, with a gag. Tears streaked the older woman's face, and her eyes were wide. Her hair was askew, the bun landing on the side of her head.

Mary stretched, gratified that no one had thought to tie her up as well. She rolled over onto her hands and knees, panting as the world spun around her. As everything slowly settled, she reached over to Mrs. Medlock and removed the gag.

The woman pitched forward, crying onto Mary's shoulder. "I had no idea, miss. I thought...I thought..."

Mary patted her awkwardly on the shoulder. She preferred Mrs. Medlock full of fire. This gibbering heap would be of no use. "Hush, they'll hear us." *And I must think.*

This was a horrible situation. No two ways about it. Possibly Lord Archer knew she had been taken...but how far behind was he? Did he care enough to rescue a pouty, unnatural girl of a ward?

Yes.

He valued her mind, if nothing else. Still, it would be up to Mary and Mrs. Medlock to get themselves out of this.

"Your hair has fallen. Fix it," Mary commanded. The woman held up her bound hands, which the girl quickly untangled. As Mrs. Medlock fussed with putting herself to rights, Mary got busy.

They were in a small hold room. They had taken her sketchbook, but not the pocket full of tools under her dress. Careless. Tiny, they were built to work on jewelry or intricate mechanisms. Still—damage inflictors.

Mary looked quickly to Mrs. Medlock. Her hair was straightened again, her shoulders back, tears drying. *Good.* Apparently, having her hair set to rights made all the difference.

"We're going to have to rescue ourselves, Mrs. Medlock. Are you able to contribute?" Judging by the slap she had dealt Mary at the manor, she was more than able.

"That Ben—he came back different, treated me different. I thought...foolish thoughts for an old woman, I suppose."

"Well, you can slug it out with him. After we get ourselves out of this mess." Mary stood, wobbled briefly, and then nodded her head. The pain was still there, right behind her eye and exploding outward. At least she no longer felt like vomiting. "Do you know where we are and how many accompany us?"

The floor listed sharply, sending both women tumbling into the door. "Airship or water?"

"Air," Mrs. Medlock groaned, holding her ribs.

They could be anywhere. If they were hovering at the cloud line, there wasn't much they could do. Nothing for it, except to find out where they were and how far up. "Stay here," Mary whispered. "I'll be right back."

The door was unlocked, a piece of luck she wouldn't ask for twice. Creeping out into the corridor, she looked for the nearest porthole. Window? What *were* they called in an airship? There, down the hall.

Mary tiptoed, not even daring to breathe. Looking out, she saw a tree line close by—they'd be able to jump for it if they could find their way out. She turned to go back, and came face to face with Ben Weatherstaff. The gardener.

"What ho now, girl? Time to get back in your comfy cozy cabin. We'll have everything to rights here soon…"

Mary backed into the wall as he kept talking in her face. His breath was sour with whiskey, and drool kept flailing away from him

"Ben, why am I here?" She did her best to look confused. "You must help me return home!"

He leaned in, brows close together, head all wobbly.

With a grunt, Mary brought her knee up as hard as she could, then punched him directly in the chin. He blinked at her, once. Then landed face first on the floor.

The door behind him was partially open, voices coming from inside. "We know Lord Archer didn't come up with these plans. Who is the engineer?"

"I'm sure I have no idea what you're referring to." Mrs. Medlock's voice was hard, edged in steel.

"Who has come to the house lately? Have any of his friends suddenly paid a visit?"

Mary peeked around the door to see a man she didn't recognize holding Mrs. Medlock by the shoulders and shaking her with every word.

"No one has come to Misselthwaite Manor, except Lord Archer's ward. A nice, agreeable child, she is."

Mary smiled as she looked around the room. Creeping quietly, lest he turn and see her, she picked up a length of pipe. A percussive boom rent the air right as she prepared to swing, and the airship shuddered and squealed.

We've been hit.

Knocked off balance, Mary tumbled into Mrs. Medlock and her interrogator, landing all three of them on the floor.

The housekeeper was the first to recover, pummeling the man with her fists. Mary scrambled to find the pipe, but the pirate found it first.

With a wild yell, Mary leapt for his back, grabbing his forearm. Straining, she pulled on his arm, with all her strength, arching her spine for more leverage.

More cannon fire thundered in the distance while the ship lurched again, throwing her off. Boxes tumbled across the room, causing even more chaos.

When the ship righted itself, Mary stayed prone on the floor, panting. A slight tap—much softer than a slap on her cheek—startled her. Her eyes flew open, to look up into Mrs. Medlock's face. The other woman's hands were bruised and scraped up, but she was smiling.

"Shall we escape now?" the housekeeper said, winking at Mary.

Dumbfounded, the girl replied, "We'd better. They have no idea how to captain this ship!"

Hand in hand, they ran for it. Coming out into the main hold, they saw the crew jumping ship. Very low to the ground, then. They might get caught again...but at least they would hopefully be clear when the balloon blew.

"Ready, set...jump!"

Mary sat on the floor in her cottage, papers strewn about. The windows were flung open, letting in both light and the sound of birds chirping merrily in the garden. The first thing she had done to it was to install a fountain for the chirpers to play in. The second was to install a work table with a place for each and every tool she owned.

A shadow fell through her doorway, interrupting her lines. Frowning, she looked up to see Lord Archer. "You are in my light."

"Ah, I see. Or rather, you do not."

Chuckling, he stepped inside, swinging a picnic basket. "Mrs. Medlock says to tell you to eat at some point today."

Mary grinned, reached for the basket. Cheese and bread, a few apples. All things easy to eat while drawing. Oh yes, Mrs. Medlock had turned into a great friend. She plucked up an apple and took a bite out of it, savoring the crisp texture and sweet taste.

"I still find it hard to believe that the two of you saved yourselves. There was no need for the rescue at all."

Mary laughed at his crestfallen look. "We couldn't have done it without the bombing of the pirates. Or Mrs. Medlock's left hook."

"Yes, well. If you had followed instructions, we wouldn't have had to mount a rescue mission in the first place." He straightened himself up to look down his nose at her.

"You enjoyed it, don't bother denying it. You also were able to catch not only the spy in your household, but almost his full crew." Mary drew a few more lines before looking up at him. "When will I get Flit back?"

"Monday next. We should have all of the changes you made diagramed by then," he said.

"And you have the plans I made for the new airship, as well as the weapons..." She let her voice trail off.

"Yes, yes, thank you for that."

He looked uncomfortable, so out of his depth that finally she just asked him. "Why are you here?"

"Well, I am your guardian, and while you are on the grounds, it does...well... I wanted to make sure you were not overtaken by nerves or anything,"

Mary let out a bark of laughter. Nerves, indeed.

"What are you working on?" He moved so that he could sit beside her, looking at the plans correctly instead of upside down as he had been.

"It's silly." Mary splayed her hand over part of the drawing, hiding it from view.

"Pish, posh, give them a toss! I seriously doubt anything you came up with could ever be called silly."

"It isn't an airship, or a weapon, or even a design for a mechani-man."

"Tell me about it."

Mary bit her lip, considering. "I thought I might make a mechanical garden...and perhaps a menagerie of mechani-mals."

Grinning, he lifted her hand to see the drawing. "It's amazing. But I think I prefer the airship diagrams."

"Yes, well, some of these whirligigs could have applications to airships...in fact..."

She snatched a clean page and began sketching.

Lotus of Albion

Steve Ruskin

Captain Ian Vanson snapped his spyglass shut and handed it back to his first mate.

"Looks like a pleasure yacht, don't it, Captain?" said Olly, shivering in his thin, standard-issue deck coat. "Don't see many airships like that up here."

"Indeed," said Vanson. "And a posh one, too. But what the hell is it doing this high up in the Himalayas?"

"Lost, would be my guess," Olly said, rubbing his red nose. Even though it was almost noon and the sun was high, it was cold on the deck of the *Burma Maiden*, at an altitude of nearly seventeen thousand feet. Hard to breathe, too. But this was their last patrol of the year. Soon the winter storms would begin and all airships of the Royal Fleet would head to lower elevations.

Already the deck and railings of the *Maiden* were coated in a layer of frost, and small icicles hung from the rigging. His crew smacked the blue silk balloon envelope with poles at regular intervals to dislodge the crusting ice.

It was only September, and cold as hell already. So what was that fancy little airship doing way up here?

"Probably got blown north once she left the hill towns after vacation season," Olly mused. "Autumn winds can be rough. She might've been spun around in a storm, turned north when they thought they were heading back south to Delhi. Didn't realize their mistake until the peaks popped out in front of 'em. Then it was too late. Looks like she's lost her starboard balloon, and aft rudder."

"Hmm," said Vanson, watching the distant ship drifting in a slow circle, listing slightly to one side. "Surely they'd have a compass? Altimeter?"

"Maybe caught in a lightning storm. All that 'lectricity can wreck instruments real good. Seen it myself once. Rode though a nasty squall in a cargo dirigible over the Bay of Bengal. Fried all our navigation. We were adrift for days."

Vanson only nodded.

The airship ahead was an expensive yacht. Built to look like a swan, with carved wings, a curved neck and head at the prow, all floated by a purple silk envelope, now partially deflated. A real beauty, despite its obvious damage. And totally unsuited for flying at this altitude. But she was a British yacht, for sure—festooned with the insignia of Her Majesty's Empire. A tattered Union Jack snapped fitfully over the aft deck.

"Can you make out its name?" Olly asked.

"No," Vanson replied. "Too far."

Whatever the name, she was in dangerous territory. Vanson scanned the afternoon skies nervously. Himalayan peaks and even higher cumulous clouds provided lots of hiding places...

"She's adrift, Captain," said Olly, prodding. "The wind's got her. A few more leagues and she'll be over the Zanskar. That's the *Crow*'s territory. If we make a grab for her now, we could bring her back with us. Might be a Lord's yacht, perhaps there's a reward, or commendation even..."

"It looks deserted, though. No signs of life."

Vanson hated to risk his own ship and crew over a derelict ship, but it was his job to patrol this part of the border and provide assistance if necessary. So, as always, pride and duty overcame his practicality. "Fine, Olly. Let's do the honorable thing. The *Jade Crow*'ll not have her while she flies the Empire's flag, derelict or not. Engines full steam."

"Aye, Captain!"

Olly turned and barked down a brass speaking tube. "Ahead, twenty knots!" and the *Maiden* surged forward, Vanson taking the wheel.

Below, and just ahead, the wide Zanskar valley opened up, dropping twelve thousand feet to a river—little more than a thin ribbon of silver from their height—flowing far below. The damaged yacht was drifting close to a range of high peaks, the summits of which rose still another mile above them, topping out at twenty-three thousand feet.

Olly had his spyglass out again, scanning.

"Captain, ship ahead!" he said. Then, after a pause, "Looks like it's the *Crow*, sir."

There, coming upon the swan-yacht from behind one of the peaks of the Zanskar itself, chugged a huge dirigible. A frigate, with a black wooden hull and a blood-red balloon envelope. It bristled with cannon, a dozen per side.

The *Jade Crow*. A pirate airship if ever the term applied.

Vanson and his crew had seen the *Crow* before—sometimes alone, sometimes surrounded by its fleet—but always from a safe distance.

They never engaged it. That would have been suicide.

Today it was alone.

The front of the *Crow* was decorated with a large jade-green eye on either side of its prow. They gave the ship the effect of a great black bird swooping down on its prey, hence its name—at least among those who feared it. No one knew its real name, and the first time anyone heard of the *Crow* was when it reportedly downed a Royal Air Fleet freighter over Kabul, tossing the British marines overboard, and then disappearing—along with a flotilla of smaller ships—into the hidden valleys of the Himalayas.

It was a tale that spread outward to Russia, China and British India like a ripple, keeping those Empires' fleets on the fringes of the Himalayas, wary and cautious. Soon afterward British India lost contact with its territorial forts in Kashmir and the Punjab. All those subjects...imprisoned? Killed? Sold into slavery?

Sure, there had always been airship pirates over the Himalayas—but usually small tribal bands who protected their local areas. None of the other Himalayan pirates ever garnered the power or reputation the *Crow* and its fleet did.

No one had ever met the captain of the *Crow* either, at least no one who lived. He kept his mysterious airship hidden among the high peaks and low valleys of the Zanskar and surrounding areas. Actual confrontations with the *Crow* were legendary for their brutality—if the rumors were even half true, the *Crow*'s victims were tarred and feathered, set alight, and *then* tossed overboard. Or hurled down with stones around their necks, ensuring a head-first plunge, but only after their eyelids had been sliced off so the victims couldn't close them on the way down.

Nor was anyone sure just who these pirates were or how they had organized so quickly, coming to control the central Himalayas in just a few years. More immediately, one wanted to avoid getting captured by the *Crow* or its fleet if at all possible.

Vanson included.

But the damaged yacht was within reach now, and the *Maiden* was a small, but fast, patrol ship—much faster than the huge *Crow*. Vanson had speed on his side and felt the exhilarating rush of alpine wind on his face.

"More power, Olly. Full speed!"

The race was on.

The *Crow* was coming fast too, but the *Maiden* was closing the gap much more quickly. A few tense minutes later, Vanson knew they would reach the derelict yacht with time to spare. He grabbed a signal lantern and raised it in the direction of the *Crow*, warning it to turn back, that the salvage had been claimed.

The *Crow* did not turn back. Vanson didn't expect it to. But warning them was standard Fleet protocol.

"Pirates," he said derisively. "Olly! Ready the lines. We'll swing in and grab 'er with the hooks and pull her back with us away from the *Crow*'s territory."

"Aye!"

Olly yelled orders at the crew, who were assembled and waiting.

Gripping the wheel tightly, Vanson pressed foot pedals—slowing the engines, adjusting the rudders—swinging his ship first outward, then back inward in a tight arc. The deck swung like a pendulum beneath its helium-filled envelope, and the crew bowed their legs and swayed to compensate for the motion.

As they approached the yacht, Vanson slowed even further, just long enough for Olly to yell "Fire!" Then came the *zip zip zip* of cables launching from harpoon guns and the *thunk thunk thunk* as they punctured the wooden sides of the yacht.

He turned them away from the Zanskar, feeling the *Maiden* strain, slowed by the weight of the captured vessel. Springs in the cables' anchors absorbed the initial pull, and soon—the delay an eternity for Vanson—they were all moving again, slowly at first, then gaining speed.

He looked back. The *Crow* was still there, pursuing. Two nautical miles behind them, framed by towering peaks.

"Persistent, aren't they? Olly, take the wheel."

Vanson strode aft, where two deck-mounted cannon—smaller bore, for close range—had been primed.

"Last chance," he muttered, and signaled again for the *Crow* to retreat.

It didn't.

He turned one of the cannon toward their pursuers, aiming low.

"This one is a courtesy!" he yelled, and fired.

The shot arced like a comet, sizzling toward the *Crow* but then dropping—as intended—well below its hull.

The *Crow* turned aside.

As one, a cheer arose from Vanson's crew.

He held up his hands, approaching them with a wide grin on his face.

"Well done, boys! Let's drop down to the leeward side of a nice mountain and see what we've just rescued!"

More cheers, and two of his crew pointed their bare backsides in the direction of the *Jade Crow*, which was now making its ponderous way back toward the high peaks of the Zanskar.

It was late afternoon before they found a small, protected valley where they could float safely while boarding the abandoned yacht.

It was called the *Lotus of Albion*, no doubt some pretentious British noble's attempt to bridge Occident and Orient in three words or less. The little pleasure craft had been damaged, likely dashed against a cliffside or overhang. That she'd only lost one balloon and was still afloat at all was a miracle.

Once they were sure the yacht wouldn't sink while they were aboard, the first members of Vanson's crew swung across, Olly leading them. The team quickly surveyed the top deck before working their way below.

Kicking in doors, pistols at the ready, they carefully made their way throughout the vessel. Within five minutes—it wasn't a big airship—they were back on deck giving the *all-clear.*

Vanson swung across. "Report?"

"Not much, Captain," said Olly. "Looks like someone's already been through her."

"No sign of the owners? Bodies?"

"Nothing," said Olly. "Stripped of valuables as well. Pirates for sure. Not the *Crow* though, or they wouldn't have been so keen to get to her before us."

"Dammit," said Vanson, regretting the risk he had taken. "Well, I suppose we'll tow her down to Delhi and send word out. Find out which noble family is missing a yacht, let the Colonial Office investigate—"

Just then, they heard a noise coming from below decks. At first they thought it was the wind rocking the rigging, but then it came again.

Movement.

"I thought you went over every inch of her," Vanson said.

Olly stammered. "We did, Captain! Searched every room. Maybe it's animals—rats or something."

They drew their guns and Vanson led them quietly down the stairs. The interior of the yacht had been quite well appointed before it was looted: oak-paneled walls bore dusty square outlines where paintings had once hung; a plush velvet sofa, collapsed on a broken leg, rested atop a torn Turkish carpet. Hand-carved trim framed the entrances to a half-dozen private rooms, though each doorway was now splintered and broken, the result of his crew's overzealous explorations.

"The sound came from the back," Olly whispered.

Vanson nodded, pointing two of his marines—Jansen and Carter—in that direction.

From the aft end of the yacht, in what would probably have been the owner's stateroom, footsteps could be heard. The door had been kicked in, but had swung shut again, aslant on its top hinge.

Carter and Jansen stepped to either side of the doorway.

Vanson held up three fingers to mark a countdown. He slowly curled in one, then another. When his third finger touched his palm the two men rushed into the room.

There was a scream. A woman's.

His men yelled. The woman swore.

There was a gunshot. Then another. A bullet ripped out of the doorway. Vanson heard it whizz past his ear, followed by a *piff!* when a puff of feathers burst out of the broken sofa, marking the spot where the shot had ended its trajectory.

"Owww!" howled one of his men from inside the room.

"Report!" yelled Vanson. "What's going on?"

He and Olly ran in. Very little light filtered in through the portholes, frosted as they were by the frigid air outside. But he saw one of his men on a large bed, struggling with someone underneath him. The other was lying on the floor.

Olly lit a match. Carter had pinned a woman to the mattress. Or had pinned her as much as he could. She fought like a tiger, kicking one free leg violently. Her red hair was a thick, tangled mess, and her clothes were rags.

In one corner crouched a little boy, curled up and clearly terrified.

Then Olly's match went out.

"Ow!" yelled Carter in the dark.

Olly lit another match. Carter was doubled up on top of the woman, hands over his groin. To his credit, he still had her pinned.

The woman's eyes flicked frantically, clearly panicked. They were green and flashed defiantly. Her face was filthy, streaked with dirt.

And stunning.

"That'll show you damn devils!" she spat, in an accent as Irish as a shillelagh, and just as bludgeoning. And then, her eyes finally adjusting to the light, she got a look at the men around her, and their uniforms.

"Wha—are you, are you military? British?"

"Yes, we are," Vanson nodded, just as Olly's second match went out. "Oh hell, Olly, go get a lantern, will you?"

"Yes, sir!"

"Let her up, Carter," said Vanson.

Carter rolled off the woman and went over to Jansen who was moaning, his hand over his shoulder. Blood trickled down his shirt.

"The bitch shot me!" Jansen whined.

"'Cause you had your gun out!" the woman retorted. "I thought you were those, those... *brigands* come back for us!"

"Who are you?" Vanson asked.

"I'm Gweneth Doyle, daughter of the Earl of Meath," she said with raised chin. Then, indicating the boy in the corner, "that's Davey. Are you Royal Navy?"

"Yes, we are, Lady Doyle," said Vanson. A noble! The rescue had been worth the risk after all.

"So we're safe? Oh my god, they attacked! We got lost, heading back to Peshawar after a diplomatic conference in Simla. My father is—was—territorial governor...we...oh, god. Thank god." She started to weep, crumbing into a ball on the bed. Davey crept over and cuddled with her.

Just then Olly returned, lantern in hand.

Vanson went over to Gweneth and sat down. "How long have you been here?"

"On the *Lotus*? A week. There's a hidden compartment behind the bed, food and water in the galley. I was below decks when we were attacked. My father told me to stay here. He gave me his pistol. I'm a damn good shot." She inclined her head at Jansen. "Sorry about your man."

"What happened to the rest of the crew?"

"Killed. They were only a small crew, a pilot and five airshipmen. None of them soldiers, really. Also my father and our maid...oh, poor Sally. I heard her scream when they threw her over. After they had their way with...ah, poor Sally!"

She wept, leaning into Vanson's chest. He held her, unsure what else to do. She was warm and soft, and he was surprised how nice she felt next to him, especially on this cold airship.

"You're safe now. Let's get everyone back to our ship, especially my wounded marine. We have food. Warm stoves. We'll take you back down to Delhi with your yacht."

"Thank you," she whispered, squeezing his arm. She took the small boy's hand and followed Vanson up onto the deck.

Gweneth sat in front of the stove in Vanson's cabin, wrapped in thick blankets. She had been given a basin of warm water and clean, if oversized, clothes, and then left alone to wash up.

She was clutching a tumbler of Vanson's whiskey when he walked in. In the golden glow of the ceiling's swinging lantern he noticed she was draining her drink with a most unfeminine rapidity.

"What?" she giggled, seeing his raised eyebrows. "I am Irish, you know."

"Of course," Vanson smiled, adding, "Help yourself."

She really was beautiful. For propriety's sake he stood behind his desk, keeping both furniture and distance between them. She was gorgeous, but she was also an Earl's daughter. Even if that Earl was deceased.

"Davey's asleep in the room next door. He was my maid's little boy. Adopted, actually. An orphan, a dead soldier's son we think. Found him living on the streets of Calcutta, wearing an oversized coat of the Ninth Dragoons. Helped Sally with her chores. He's odd, but clever. I hid him with me during the attack. Thank you again for rescuing us," she said.

"Only doing our duty, Lady Doyle."

"Lady Doyle!" Her laugh was magical. "Please, it's Gwen. If I'm to be your passenger for the next few days, too much formality will just make us both uncomfortable."

"Ok, Miss....um, Gwen."

"As to duty, I know for a fact how little the Navy pays you and the rest of the Royal Air Fleet. It would have been far less dangerous to simply ignore our ship and sail on. So," she murmured, staring at him over the cut-glass tumbler, " thank you, Captain."

She told him of her childhood in County Wicklow, how her father, second-in-line to his family's title, chose to make his fortune in India rather than wait to see if his older brother simply died off. In a twist of fate, that brother did die young, making her father Earl. He went back to Ireland and married Gwen's mother; they had Gwen. But the Earl's heart remained in India, and so he returned to govern the northwestern frontier for the Empire. Gwen's mother stayed in Ireland, but Gwen eventually joined her father. She loved adventure.

She also explained how they got lost on their way out of Simla seven days ago. A storm blew them far off course and eventually into the side of a mountain. Pirates found them before they could make repairs. Gwen and Davey hid, and two days later—today—they were rescued by Vanson and the *Maiden*.

"I have some of my father's papers. Diplomatic documents concerning treaties with Russia against the pirates." She patted the coat she was wearing when they found her, now folded up next to her on the floor. "I tossed the rest of my clothes into your stove," she smiled. "Hope you don't mind. They smelled awful! Thank you for letting me wash up."

Vanson just smiled, secretly wondering how she smelled now.

There was a knock on the door.

"Come in," Vanson said.

It was Olly. "The starboard balloon on the *Lotus* is repaired, Captain. A smaller rip than we expected. It'll hold for now, but it'll need a new balloon before it's truly airworthy again. The rudder is beyond repair—at least the sort of repairs we could do while airborne. That'll require a good shipwright. All told, she won't steer, but she'll float, long enough for us to tow her down to Delhi. Shall we set course?"

"Aye," said Vanson, and Olly turned on his heels, shutting the door behind him.

"We've been up here too long," Vanson said, as much to himself as Gwen. "It'll be night soon, and I want to put some distance between us and the Zanskar. The *Crow* was coming after us pretty hot. Who knows what they might attempt under cover of darkness."

"The *Crow*?" Gwen asked, alarmed. "I heard one of our crew mention a *Jade Crow*. He said they were the worst pirates north of British India."

"He was right," said Vanson. "And you can thank the stars we got to you first. Your yacht was drifting into the *Crow*'s territory, and they spotted you soon after we did. Another ten minutes, and they would have had you."

Gwen shuddered. "I do owe you my life."

The *Burma Maiden*, which had been bobbing gently on cold Himalayan currents, began to move.

"Really, as I said, it was the very least—" He stopped when she stood up, facing him, with a look he was pretty sure he knew the meaning of.

She dropped the blanket from around her shoulders, revealing milky skin dotted with the freckles that Irish girls were famous for. She wasn't wearing the clothes she had been given after all.

Almost involuntarily, his eyes went to her two perfectly-shaped breasts. They were framed by cascades of red hair that spilled down from her head.

That hair. It draped around her high cheekbones, one or two curls stopping to point out her soft lips and dainty chin, while the rest tumbled over her shoulders and on down...to where his hands suddenly wanted to be.

But she was an Earl's daughter.

"Lady Doyle, I...I really can't. You're...I'm only..."

She moved casually around his desk, blanket still around her waist, her eyes holding his. When she reached his side of the table she hopped up on it—pushing aside some of the maps and charts as she did so—then she was sitting before him, reaching out and grabbing the lapels of his coat.

"I'm a big girl now, Captain. You saved me. I've been quite cold and lonely hiding on the *Lotus*. Hell, I've been

278

lonely anyway lately, living in that miserable frontier fort at Peshawar." She tilted her mouth upward.

"Um..." Vanson said. But he knew he couldn't come up with an excuse that either of them would accept.

"Please, Captain. Let me thank you properly."

She pulled him closer, spread her legs, and shrugged the blanket completely off her body. In the flickering glow from the lamp above, he saw the soft skin of her inner thigh and groaned, a noise she matched as she reached one hand around the back of his neck, lips parted. His tongue found hers while her other hand began to work its way down his chest, unbuttoning his coat.

Now he knew how she smelled. Of jasmine and balsam, vanilla and cinnamon—the most exotic scents of the Himalayas and the rest of Empire, made into perfume.

Intoxicating.

She grinned. "I keep a small bottle of it in my coat. A girl never knows..."

He grabbed her hips and pulled her across the desk toward him.

Just then, there was a frantic knock on the door.

"Damn." He pulled away. Gwen's mouth moved to his neck while her hands continued to work at his buttons.

"What?" Vanson yelled toward the door—more harshly than he intended.

"Captain!" shouted Olly. "We need you on deck immediately. We have visitors."

"What! Who?"

"It's dark, sir. We can only see their deck lights. A big ship, and some smaller ones. We're pretty sure it's the *Crow* again, back with her fleet. They must have waited for nightfall."

"But we aren't anywhere near their territory anymore! They must really want the *Lotus*."

He swore. "Gwen—"

"I know," she said, pulling the blanket back up around her shoulders.

"I will be back. Stay here." Then a thought occurred to him. "We may have to cut your ship free if we want to outrun them. I'm sorry, I know the *Lotus of Albion* is your family's yacht."

"I don't care, do what you have to do. Just keep us safe." She put her mouth to his and gave him one last jasmine-scented kiss.

Vanson ran up onto the deck, calling for all hands to follow.

The last of the sun's rays illuminated a large dark airship, its red-silk balloon envelope floating above it like another setting sun. It was still a ways out, but it was the *Crow*, he was sure of it. Other airships, smaller but similarly decorated, sailed alongside it.

They were about five nautical miles to port, flying at top speed, closing fast.

"They must have swung around that far ridge after we outran them earlier," Olly said, handing Vanson his spyglass.

He looked through the eyepiece.

"A clever ambush," Vanson said, the wind blowing the collar of his now-unbuttoned deck coat.

"Get us out of here. Full speed," he said. Below decks he heard the engines throb heavily as the noise from the propellers rose from a steady thrum to an angry whine.

"Captain," said Olly, "I don't know if we can stay ahead if we're towing the *Lotus*."

"I know. I already spoke to Gwen...I mean, Lady Doyle."

"But for now," Olly continued, diplomatically ignoring his Captain's sudden familiarity toward their female passenger, "We may be able to keep ahead of them. We're a faster ship."

"No," said Vanson, "The *Crow* is too close. I don't want to risk it. Let's cut the *Lotus* loose."

"Aye," said Olly. Then he yelled across the deck, "Prepare to cut the—"

Olly was interrupted by a great crack! from below decks and the *Burma Maiden* suddenly slowed, forcing its crew to grab madly at ropes and railings to steady themselves. The whine of the propellers was already diminishing.

"The engines!" Olly yelled. "Where's Dawes?"

Dawes, the engineer, didn't sound off.

"I'll check it out," Vanson said. "Olly, ready the cannon. Turn the *Maiden* broadside and let them see our guns." Then he leapt two levels down the main staircase to the engine room.

Bursting through the door, he saw a small figure hunched over the propeller shaft, its back to him. Vanson aimed his pistol.

"Stop what you are doing! Stand up!"

The figure stood and turned around, arms raised. In one hand was a wrench, in the other a handful of bolts. Important ones, Vanson saw immediately. The ones that kept the rapidly-rotating driveshaft in its housing.

It was the boy, Davey.

Now the shaft was spinning chaotically, free from the confines of its metal clamps, its power no longer transferring to the propellers but instead shredding the transmission to which it had recently been attached.

The uncontrolled force of the loose shaft was dangerous—it would tear the engine room apart. Indeed, Vanson already saw jagged pieces of metal and a thick cog embedded in the wooden ceiling of the chamber.

That explained the loud noises. The boy was lucky he hadn't been killed.

"What the hell are you doing?" Vanson yelled. "You've stalled my ship! Just as we're being pursued by pirates who'll not think twice about tossing us all overboard!"

Davey just stood there, expressionless. Gwen had said the boy was odd, but Vanson didn't have time to be sympathetic, especially after the damage he had done.

"What were you thinking?" He yelled again, running over and grabbing the bolts from Davey's hand. He bent down, careful to avoid the spinning shaft. There was nothing he could do. Both steam engines would have to be shut down before they could make any repairs.

Where was Dawes? Without his engineer, Vanson had to find and yank the lever that disengaged the engines from the driveshaft himself.

That's when he saw Dawes's legs, unmoving, sticking out from behind one of the giant cylindrical steam engines. Vanson turned and stared with growing unease at the boy called Davey.

The boy stood quietly, just staring up at him.

Vanson heard his men yelling. The *Crow* must be getting closer.

"Gwen!" he yelled, hoping she would hear him through the wooden floor of the ship. "I need you to come get this boy! And get Olly down here too—Dawes is hurt!"

He heard the soft click of a revolver's hammer behind his ear, and smelled jasmine and balsam, vanilla and cinnamon.

"I'm right here," she said from behind him, pressing the barrel of the gun into the base of his skull. "I told you Davey was a clever boy."

"Gwen, what are you doing?" Vanson turned his head just enough to see that she was fully dressed now, in the clothes he had given her, her tattered deck coat—and not the blanket—over her shoulders.

But Gwen, if that was her name, just laughed. She squeezed his behind with her free hand and purred into his ear. "Such a shame my ship arrived so quickly. I was looking forward to a little more time alone with you, Captain Vanson. Alas, some things aren't meant to be."

She pushed his head back around with the point of her gun.

"Now, back up on deck, please."

Night had fallen when Vanson stepped back onto the deck of the *Burma Maiden*, Gwen close behind. The sky was clear, its stars brilliant. The air tasted of ice and numbed the tongue.

His crew, manning the ship's half-dozen cannon, were tense, anticipating battle.

"Captain!" Olly turned to him, spyglass in hand. "It's the *Jade Crow* all right, and a half-dozen smaller ships.

They're staying just out of range of our guns. Did you find Dawes? What the bloody hell's wrong with the engines?"

Before Vanson could reply, Gwen spoke. She still had her gun against the back of his head and her other hand on his shoulder, keeping him where she wanted him. The boy stayed at her side like an impassive puppy.

"If I can have your attention please! I am assuming control of your airship. Anyone tries anything untoward, and your Captain gets a bullet through his skull."

The crew turned, and in the glow of the deck lanterns, Vanson thought they might laugh at what they thought was a joke, until they saw Gwen with her pistol.

"You ungrateful bitch!" yelled Olly. He rushed toward them, knife drawn. "We rescue you and this is how you repay—"

Her gun fired and Olly fell, his hot blood bouncing in droplets across the icy deck.

Vanson's ears rang, and inwardly he recoiled from the sight of Olly sprawled before him. But he did not budge. What a fool he had been! She wasn't hiding any diplomatic papers in her coat. Just her pistol. And a plan.

"As I said," she continued to the stunned crew, "I'll be taking this ship. Everyone move away from the cannon and drop your weapons."

The crew hesitated but Vanson, not wanted to see any more of them dead, said, "Do as she says."

They moved to the center of the deck, tossing pistols and knives away from them in a sad litany of thuds and clanks.

"Ok, Dahid," Gwen said to the boy she had been calling Davey, "Now."

The boy ran to the deck railing, where he took one of their lanterns and began signaling the large airship that had been circling them like a shark. Minutes later it pulled alongside the *Maiden*, its green eyes glinting in the low light of their deck lamps.

Those eyes—bright green and beautifully sinister—looked just like those of the woman holding the gun to his head.

Vanson noticed the *Crow* was nearly twice as long as the *Maiden*. And then, even though it was dark, he realized it was a repainted Royal Air Fleet frigate. No doubt one of the ones gone missing over the past few years, presumed lost or destroyed.

"Who are you?" Vanson growled.

"My name's Gwen alright, but not Doyle. I have no idea what my last name is. I grew up in a Dublin orphanage. My father was a soldier and my mother—who knows? A maid? A whore? Both? Either way, a girl has to fend for herself if she doesn't want to end up the same way. I found work in the household of a debauched Earl's son and moved with him when he became Territorial Governor in Kabul. He was a man of certain...appetites. Disgusting ones.

"Well, even I have my limits, you know. Dahid here was our errand boy. I took him with me once my little rebellion got going. And now, I've developed quite a following as you can see."

Figures on the deck of the *Crow* moved swiftly: hooks were flung over, biting into the deck of the *Maiden* with a series of thuds. A rope bridge followed, and suddenly they were surrounded by pirates of all sizes and races: Asians, Africans, Europeans, others he could not place.

Vanson looked at his own crew, shivering in their too-thin Air Fleet coats. They didn't get paid nearly enough for this sort of thing. And now they were terrified. He could see it on their faces.

"Let them go, Gwen. They're just doing their jobs."

"I don't kill wantonly, despite what you may have heard. That 'tarred and feathered, set alight and tossed overboard' stuff—that's all rubbish. Useful rubbish, I'll grant you. But your first mate there, he attacked me. I only want your ship. Let us have it, and we'll let you go in that old yacht you're towing. Lucky you didn't cut it loose. We spent a long time rigging that one just so."

The *Lotus of Albion* bobbed outside the glow of their lights. It had been a trap all along.

"But she can't be steered!"

"Exactly! So you can't come after us," she said, coming around to face him. "What did your mate say? 'She won't steer, but she'll float.' You're a good pilot, Captain Vanson. With a little luck, you can drop the *Lotus* down to the ground and walk to civilization."

"Why are you doing this, Gwen?"

"There are a lot of us, you know. More than the *Crown* would like to admit. Imperial outcasts. Orphans of empire. You can't dominate half of the globe and expect everyone to just stay in their places and be happy about it. We're making our own home, a little paradise up here in the Himalayas. And I'm building a fleet to help protect it."

She looked wistful and almost innocent, even with her gun still poking Vanson's neck. "There are valleys up there that Europeans have never seen, accessible only by air. Fertile soil, crystal-clear water, flowers, trees. Protected and pristine. Like paradise. There's no actual Shangri-La, of course. But we're doing our best to make the legend come true."

She remained beautiful in her defiance. Fiercely so—just like when he first saw her. Part of him wanted to—no, that would be treason. Still, her vision of freedom was...compelling.

She smiled at him—half mocking, half sincere, completely triumphant.

"Don't let me catch you up here again, Captain," she said. She leaned up and kissed him, nipping his lower lip with her teeth as she pulled away.

Then she sauntered, hips swaying, across the deck of the *Burma Maiden* toward the rope bridge. Pausing, she turned and looked back over her shoulder.

"Unless you come alone, that is."

An hour later Vanson was staring up from the deck of the *Lotus of Albion,* his crew slowly releasing helium from the yacht's balloons in a controlled descent. High above him he saw the dim silhouettes of the *Jade Crow* and the *Burma Maiden* heading toward the Zanskar valley, followed by the rest of Gwen's fleet, and he wondered how difficult it would be to hike back up into this area the following Spring.

Alone, of course.

And a Bottle of Rum

K.C. Shaw

Jo's new airship, *Dragonfly*, skimmed eight hundred feet above the ground. The trees below made a green carpet tufted with red and gold; the autumn sky was a blue of unmatched perfection. Jo grinned. All she needed now was a fat prize to take.

Her friend Lizzy surveyed the horizon with the spyglass. The two girls were almost nothing alike: Jo was short, curvy, elegant, and brown-skinned, while Lizzy was tall, skinny, and pale. But they were fast friends.

It was a pleasant change to have a third person aboard to take care of the boiler. Usually that was Lizzy's job, but they had rescued a young man named Dominic from a blimp explosion recently, and he was happy to shovel coal for them until he got home. He was handsome and didn't try to tell Jo how to pilot her ship, a good combination.

Lizzy said, "Nothing. No, wait, there's a big airship. South of us, headed inland."

Jo's pulse pounded with excitement—mixed, as always, with guilt that she took enjoyment from being wicked. "Time to see what the *Dragonfly* can do. Load the cannon."

Lizzy passed her the spyglass. The ship was a good ten miles away, barely more than a speck despite the magnification. Jo adjusted their course so as not to converge on the airship too quickly. No sense alarming her pilot.

"Standing by to fire, Captain," Lizzy said, with a twitch of a smile. She had hooked both of the forearm-length cannon to the rattan floor, one on either side of the small gondola. The *Dragonfly* had actual cannon ports.

Jo focused the glass on the airship again. They were a few miles closer already and she could make out more details. It resembled her old ship, the *Seagull*, in both size and conformation: twin balloon envelopes topped with a peaked wing, and twin propellers. The gondola was painted gray, with the Hulan flag snapping from its stern.

Jo started to say, "There's a small blimp on the other side of the ship," but stopped after "blimp." She went cold all over.

Lizzy said, "Oh, *shit.*"

Jo didn't even chide her for language.

"What?" Dominic asked.

Jo said, "The airship's an escort. She'll be heavily armed. Lizzy, watch closely. If you see a second escort we daren't engage."

She handed the spyglass over. She remembered the *Seagull*'s plummet, the terrible sense of helplessness.

No. She would not let that happen again. Neither would she give in to cowardice and flee.

Lizzy said, "No sign of a second airship. Jo, that blimp's carrying something valuable if they've got an escort."

Before Jo could reply, a man's voice crackled out of the radio. Jo jumped. " *Silver Two,* we've sighted an airship."

Lizzy, wide-eyed, whispered, "Can they hear us?"

"Not unless we press the red button and speak into the transmitter." Jo had almost forgotten the *Dragonfly* had a radio. Her old airship had not.

After a moment of silence, another man said, "Thank you, *Cirrus*. Does it look like a threat?"

"Hard to say, sir. She's not close enough yet to evaluate, but she's on a course to intercept."

The man from the *Silver Two*—Jo guessed that was the blimp—said, "Maintain present course for now. Keep an eye on it and let us know if you think it's aggressive."

"Yes, sir."

Jo exchanged a look with Lizzy. Her heart pounded; her hands were clammy in their gloves. But her emotion was mostly excitement, not fear.

"Here's what we'll do," she said, after she'd taken a deep breath. "We want to hole the blimp first. I'll take us in close so you can get a good shot or two. Then we go after the airship." She leaned over the gondola's side to look down. They were passing above patchwork farmland and stretches of forest. If the *Dragonfly* had to land, Jo thought she could do it without smashing into a tree.

Lizzy said, "I'm ready."

"So am I," Dominic said.

"Good. Give me plenty of steam, Dominic. There's obviously no use trying to sneak up on them, so we'll go full speed ahead."

She pushed the props to full. The *Dragonfly* kicked like a spirited horse, and then settled as she accelerated. Wind buffeted Jo and made the straps of her leather aviator's cap dance.

The radio said, " *Silver Two*, the airship has sped up and is approaching fast. Stand by for evasive maneuvers."

291

Jo bared her teeth. She could see the airship and blimp easily now even without the glass. The *Dragonfly*'s speed nearly took her breath.

"Fire at will, Lizzy."

"Aye, Captain."

Jo climbed fifty feet or so above the airship's altitude. They were closing fast, helped by a tailwind. Jo watched the other ship to get an idea of what she could do.

She came about neatly enough, climbing to meet the *Dragonfly* and steaming directly toward her. Jo suspected she would swing wide at the last second to fire.

Jo climbed another fifty feet, as though struggling to keep the high ground. The *Cirrus* matched her altitude. Then the ships were so close that Jo felt she ought to call encouragement to the other pilot.

Instead she said, "Lizzy, show them our colors," and opened the envelope vents.

The *Dragonfly* dropped so fast Jo felt weightless. She closed the vents again before they lost too much hot air.

The *Dragonfly* passed neatly under the *Cirrus*. Jo heard the snap of cloth and saw Lizzy holding out their Jolly Roger.

"Prepare to fire," Jo called over the roar of the props.

The blimp dropped ballast, the water resembling a solid block until the wind caught it, and shot upward—but not so quickly that the *Dragonfly* couldn't keep pace. Jo yanked her own ballast cord, emptying the two buckets that collected condensation from inside the envelope and dribbled it back into the boiler.

She slid beneath the blimp too, and then came up on its other side and slowed the props hard. For a moment the *Silver Two* shielded them from the *Cirrus*.

The cannon roared, and the *Dragonfly* kicked. "Got 'em," Lizzy said, already reloading.

Jo saw the hole, nicely placed near the top of the *Silver Two*'s gasbag. It would vent hydrogen fast despite the hole's small size—no bigger around than a saucer.

The *Dragonfly* slid past the blimp. The *Cirrus* came into view, broadside to them. Jo opened the vents again and dropped.

She heard the boom of the *Cirrus*'s cannon but felt no impact. It would take the gunner a few moments to reload. Jo closed the vents and pushed the props back to full.

Her stomach swooped with the *Dragonfly*. The airship rose again at Jo's direction, flying close to the *Cirrus*.

Lizzy fired as they passed, and then swore. "Missed the bastards."

"We need to draw them off anyway," Jo said. She sent the *Dragonfly* careening in a zig-zag course away from the blimp. "Are they following?"

"Yes," Lizzy said. "We're faster than they are. Don't pull too far ahead."

Jo risked a glance aft. The *Cirrus* was pursuing, but had already fallen nearly a quarter mile behind. The radio said, " *Silver Two*, what's your condition?"

"We've been holed and are losing altitude. Webber's climbing up to patch."

Jo wrenched the *Dragonfly* around and caught the same tailwind as before. It pushed them back to the *Cirrus* so quickly the other ship had no time to turn. Lizzy fired from the portside cannon as they came alongside. The *Cirrus*'s answering volley sounded at the same moment.

A cannonball shot through the gap between the top of the *Dragonfly*'s gondola and the lower curve of her envelope. Lizzy cursed so loudly Jo worried it had done some damage, although she hadn't felt anything. She turned again, jaw clenched with concentration, and presented the *Dragonfly*'s starboard side to the *Cirrus*'s port.

Lizzy fired again. The *Cirrus* did not—probably because her crew had not had time to reload. Jo brought them up a hundred feet to give Lizzy time to reload as well. "Did you hit at all?"

"I think so," Lizzy said. "Hard to see through all the smoke."

Jo took a moment to glance around. A mile to the south, the blimp hung just above the trees. The air smelled of gunpowder. And the *Cirrus* was rising to meet them.

"Here we go again," Jo said to Lizzy.

She turned the *Dragonfly* hard to port, to present a narrower target since the *Cirrus* was sidling toward them broadside, a tricky maneuver for an airship. She pulled the elevator stick back at the same time and shot over the *Cirrus*.

The whole ship jerked so hard that Jo thought she had misjudged their height and rammed the other ship. Then they were free.

"Damage?" Jo said, turning the *Dragonfly* again. She was momentarily disoriented: the sky empty, the *Cirrus* out of sight. She might be closing on them from any direction.

"None to us, I think," Lizzy said. "The *Cirrus* is a lost cause."

Lizzy was coiling one of the grappling hooks' ropes, which she hung in its place. Jo leaned out of the gondola to look for the *Cirrus*.

The airship fell toward a field, dwindling to meet its own shadow. Jo saw a long tear in the portside envelope, ending at a splintered spot on the *Cirrus*'s wing's edge.

Lizzy said, "I took a chance, hope that's all right."

"That was a big chance," Jo said.

"If we'd caught her wing instead of pulling through, I was going to cut the rope."

The *Cirrus* managed to land, but Jo knew she would be airborne again as soon as her envelope was repaired. The *Dragonfly* had no more than half an hour to loot the blimp and get away. She turned the ship back toward the blimp.

The radio crackled. " *Cirrus*, what happened? Are you all right? *Cirrus*! Come in, *Cirrus*!"

Jo held her breath, and let it out in a relieved whoosh when she heard the reply. " *Cirrus* here. We're grounded. What's your situation?"

"Webber repaired the hole but we're barely buoyant. The pirates are headed our way. We're prepared to bail out and blow the hydrogen."

Jo raised her eyebrows in surprise. Blowing up a blimp just to keep from being boarded seemed awfully drastic. The *Cirrus* responded, "What's your altitude?"

"Four hundred feet."

"The blast would slap you into the ground before your chutes opened. The pirates only have three crew that we saw; you may be able to take them out with the shotgun once they're close enough."

Jo said, "We daren't board. We'll have to hole them again." How long would it take the *Cirrus* to repair the tear in their envelope? Someone would have to climb up onto the wing to reach the tear, probably two people: one to glue a patch on, the other to hold the first one's ankles so he wouldn't fall. And even the most expensive silk glue took at least fifteen minutes to dry.

Lizzy said, "We could bottom their gondola and force them to bail out. Our cannon has a longer range than a shotgun."

"We'll try it," Jo said. "Tell me where to stop."

She slowed the props and spiraled above the blimp until the *Dragonfly* had lost most of her momentum. Then she brought the ship down cautiously, broadside to the blimp.

"This should be good. Can we hover at all?" Lizzy said.

"I'll try to compensate for the wind."

They were already nose into the wind, which was gusty this close to the ground. Occasionally an updraft tried to lift them, although—since the blimp bobbled too—that was less of a concern.

"I had a lesson doing this once," Jo said. "I did rather well, but no one was trying to shoot me at the time."

She flinched at the distant report of a gun. But Lizzy had guessed correctly at the safe distance, or perhaps the shooter wasn't much of a marksman. No bullet struck.

Lizzy said, "Why don't we hail them?"

Jo almost laughed. "Won't they be surprised?" She wanted to be the first to use their radio, but all her attention was taken up on keeping the *Dragonfly* hovering more or less in place. "Hail them and see what happens."

Lizzy picked up the transmitter, which hung on a hook beside the radio and was attached to the console with rubber-coated wires. "I press the red button?"

"Press and hold it down while you speak."

Lizzy said, " *Silver Two*, this is the *Dragonfly*. You have sixty seconds to jump ship before we put a cannonball into your gondola. No parley. The countdown begins now."

Jo admired how piratical she sounded.

Lizzy hung up the transmitter. "Suppose it'll work?"

"It already has. Look." Jo nodded at the blimp.

The gondola door opened and a man appeared. He hesitated, and then leaped into the air.

A parachute of white silk blossomed from his back. It barely had time to open before he reached the ground, but it caught the wind just in time. He stumbled then ran some distance away as though he expected the blimp to drop onto his head.

Two more men appeared in the doorway and jumped, one after the other. They both landed safely. Lizzy said, "How many crew in a blimp that size?"

"I have no idea. Four?"

"There's the fourth gone. They've all landed without splattering. I'll hail them again, just in case. It's been more than a minute."

Lizzy said into the transmitter, "Hope that's all of you. We're sending that cannonball through your gondola now."

Another man flung himself out the door, his parachute already opening. He hit the ground hard enough to fall, but was already up and limping toward his crewmates before they could reach him.

"Good enough. Let's board and see what they've got," Jo said. Lizzy drew her pistol.

The blimp's gondola was deserted, when Lizzy swung across and searched it. Jo knew immediately, because Lizzy's voice crackled through the radio to tell her. Jo laughed.

It wasn't long before Lizzy swung back, a wooden crate the size of a breadbox clutched to her stomach. From the way she carried it, it was heavy.

"What's in it?" Jo asked.

"We'll find out. There are more."

She and Dominic used the coal shovel and Lizzy's saber to lever the box's lid open. Lizzy whistled. Dominic said something in Tunnish that Jo couldn't understand.

The box was full of silver ingots, so bright that they almost didn't look real. "Foolish of them to advertise it in their blimp's name," Lizzy said. "There are five other boxes. I'm going to get them all."

"Hurry," Jo said. It had taken her five precious minutes to maneuver the *Dragonfly* against the blimp's lower curve, almost another five for Lizzy to snag the blimp's gondola with the grappling hook.

With no pilot, and without her engines running, the *Silver Two* drifted gently with the wind. Jo let it tow their airship along.

"Should I help her?" Dominic asked. "I can swing across too."

"It would take too long to move the other swing line to the starboard side," Jo said. "You can stow the boxes as Lizzy brings them over."

Dominic looked disappointed.

Lizzy was back in moments with the next box. The two gondolas were not very close together, but since they were moving with the wind instead of against it, the swing was much less dangerous than usual. Even so, Jo's heart banged with fear every time her friend launched herself into open air.

"That's all of them," Lizzy said at last, breathing hard from her exertions.

"Good. Let's get out of here."

Fast as Lizzy had been, the operation had taken another ten minutes or more. The *Cirrus* might be airworthy again at any moment, and the *Dragonfly* was vulnerable while lashed to the blimp.

"I want to take one more look," Lizzy said, and swung back before Jo could argue.

Dominic shoved the boxes of silver against the gondola's sides, spacing them evenly. The gondola rocked with each movement. Jo stayed at the controls and scanned the horizon.

As the minutes ticked by, Jo grew more and more anxious. "What's she taking so long about?"

"You could ask her with the radio," Dominic said.

"I don't want the *Cirrus* listening in." Suddenly, Jo gasped. "There she is!"

"Lizzy?"

"The *Cirrus*." Jo snatched the radio transmitter up and jammed her thumb on the red button. "Get back here now, Lizzy. The *Cirrus* is aloft."

Lizzy didn't reply. Neither did she swing back to the *Dragonfly*.

Jo watched the *Cirrus* lift above the trees and steam toward them. Her brain felt numb with terror, like a rabbit confronted by a dancing weasel.

Lizzy appeared in the blimp gondola's open doorway, unseated the grappling hook, and kicked it free. The *Dragonfly* drifted away from the blimp with Lizzy dangling from the swing line with one hand.

"Help her up, Dominic," Jo said—unnecessarily, since he had already rushed over to haul up the swing line. Jo started the propellers and pushed them to full.

Lizzy clambered aboard with Dominic's help. She had another wooden box under her arm, smaller than the others, and a bottle clutched in her fist.

As they veered away just ahead of the *Cirrus*, Lizzy waved the bottle at the other airship and blew its pilot a kiss. The *Cirrus* responded with a volley of cannon fire.

But the *Dragonfly* was already out of range, accelerating fast. Jo didn't care where they went as long as it was away. She had gotten turned around during the fight anyway. A quick glance at the compass told her she was headed toward the coast.

The radio shouted, "Stop in the name of the king!"

Lizzy finished replacing the swing line and grappling hook in their spots. "The king can kiss my arse," she said. "I bet it's gold in that last case. It was hidden well enough."

The radio shouted at them a few more times, promising dire consequences. Jo heard the splinter of a lock being forced, then silence.

"What is it?" she asked, imagining Lizzy lying dead of a poisoned dart or something equally improbable. She dared not turn around to look, not with the *Cirrus* still following.

"It's gold. I was right," Lizzy said.

Dominic added, "It's gold stamped with the Hulan royal seal. We just stole from the king of Hule."

Once they had left the *Cirrus* behind, Jo surveyed the crates full of silver bars and the small box of gold. "You know, I never understood why pirates were supposed to bury treasure. Now I know."

"We're going to bury it?" Dominic asked.

"Maybe. The trick is burying it where we can find it again when we want it."

Jo finally allowed herself to relax, and grinned at Lizzy. "This is our future. This is a lovely little house for both of us, somewhere quiet, after we've retired from piracy. Check the coast off Belleral for a likely-looking island. It can't be too small or we can't land safely, but make sure it isn't marked with any towns."

"We're going to bury our treasure on a deserted island?" Dominic sounded delighted.

"I think it would be safest. No one to see what we're doing and come along to dig it up after we leave, and an island is easier to find than a particular patch of coastline."

After consultation of the maps and considerable discussion, they settled on an island well off the coast called Hayforth. It was not a quick trip. The western sky blazed pink and gold as the sun went down; the first stars came out.

Jo's stomach growled. "How are we for coal?" she asked after a while.

"All right for now," Dominic said.

Lizzy said, "This new ship's got an efficient boiler, but I'd be happier if we stopped to top off the coal before long. We're over Belleral now. We needn't fear being arrested."

Jo was more worried about being robbed. She had her future to think of, hers and Lizzy's. "All right. Find us a town and we'll set down long enough to refuel and get some food. We can picnic on Hayforth and spend the night there."

"Good," Lizzy said. "Did you notice the bottle I found in the blimp? Black Hammerhead rum, the best you can get. It's got a shark on the label."

Jo patted the top of the radio. "I like this airship. I like her a lot."

Meet The Pirates

Stephen Blake — "Beneath the Brass" — Stephen Blake lives in Penzance, Cornwall in the UK. He's had a story previously published in the steampunk anthology *'Airship Shape & Bristol Fashion'* and numerous pieces within the e-magazine 'Far Horizons'. You can find him on twitter @UncannyBlake and he occasionally blogs on stephenblakeblog.wordpress.com, where you can follow his writing journey.

Jeffrey Cook & Katherine Perkins — "Maiden Voyage" —Katherine lives in Coralville, IA, with her husband and one skittish cat. Jeff is the author and Kate the editor of the Dawn of Steam series of alternate-history/emergent Steampunk epistolary novels. When not reading, researching, or writing, they enjoy role-playing games, in which the dice like Jeff a lot better.

Robert McGough — "Colonel Gurthwait and the Black Hydra" — Robert McGough was born and raised in south Alabama. An Eagle Scout and two-time graduate from Troy University, he pays the bills working at a warehouse. Writing in a number of genres, including steampunk, horror, fantasy, and southern gothic, he has been published in several anthologies and literary journals. He is a firm believer that puns are the highest form of humor.

Ogarita — "Captain Wexford's Dilemma" — Ogarita is an author, introvert, lapsed jogger, home-reno terror, ghost lover, watercolorist, retired military officer, and enthusiastic traveler. She possesses more academic degrees than necessary, imperfect Spanish, worse French, an old car, a Vitamix, and books. Her skills include cribbage, folding fitted sheets into neat squares, and surviving central Florida's mean streets on a cruiser bike. Although not yet a ghost, she haunts libraries, bookstores, museums, lighthouses, and Disney World. At present, she knows no pirates.

Lauren Marrero — "Her Majesty's Service" — When not creating romance novels, Lauren Marrero spends most of her time dreaming of heroes and steam-powered gadgets. After attending the University of California, Berkeley, where she studied English Literature, she traveled the world, slept in too many airports, and ate too much exotic street food. She is the author of Seducing the Laird, and has been published in *UnCONventional, Mirror Dance*, and *The Fifth Di...* magazines. You can find her online at www.laurenmarrero.com.

Andrew Knighton — "A Wind Will Rise" — Andrew is a freelance writer based in Stockport, England, where the grey skies provide a good motive to stay inside at the word processor. He's had over forty stories published in places such as Daily Science Fiction, Wily Writers and Ann

VanderMeer's Steampunk anthologies. His own steampunk anthology, Riding the Mainspring, is available now on Amazon. You can find out more about his writing at andrewknighton.com and follow him on Twitter @gibbondemon.

Rie Sheridan Rose — "Hooked" — Rie's short stories appear in numerous anthologies, including *Nightmare Stalkers and Dream Walkers Vols. 1 and 2, Come to My Window, Shifters, The Grotesquerie* and *In the Bloodstream* as well as Yard Dog Press' *A Bubba In Time Saves None.* Yard Dog Press is also home to humorous horror chapbooks *Tales from the Home for Wayward Spirits* and *Bar-B-Que Grill* and *Bruce and Roxanne Save the World...Again.* Mocha Memoirs has "Drink My Soul...Please," and "Bloody Rain" as e-downloads. Online, she has appeared in Cease, Cows, Lorelei Signal, and Four Star Stories. This is her first anthology edit.

Ross Baxter — "Go Green" — After thirty years at sea, Ross Baxter now concentrates on writing sci-fi and horror fiction. His varied work has been published in print and Kindle by a number of publishing houses in the US and the UK. He won the Horror Novel Reviews Creation Short Story Award in December 2014. Married to a Norwegian and with two Anglo-Viking kids, he now lives in Derby, England.

Amy Braun — "Lost Sky" — Amy is a Canadian urban fantasy and horror author. Her work revolves around monsters, magic, mythology, and mayhem. She started writing in her early teens, and never stopped. She loves building unique worlds filled with fun characters and intense action. She is the recipient of April Moon Books Editor Award for "author voice, world-building and general bad-assery." Amy's current work includes various short stories such as *"Hotel Hell"*, *"Call from the Grave,"* and the novella *Needfire.* She has short stories in various anthologies such as "Bring Back the Hound" in *Stomping Grounds*, "Charlatan Charade" in *Lost in the Witching Hour*, and her award winning short "Dark Intentions And Blood" in AMOK! Amy can be found online through her frequently updated blog, Literary Braun (literarybraun.blogspot.ca), as well as on Twitter (@amybraunauthor) and Facebook (facebook.com/amybraunauthor). Her upcoming work includes: "Secret Suicide" in That Hoodoo, Voodoo, That You Do anthology, as well as her first full length novel, Path of the Horseman.

Diana Parparita — "Miss Warlyss Meets the Black Buzzard" — Diana Parparita's stories have been published in *Allegory, Enchanted Conversation, Bards and Sages Quarterly,* and *Mad Scientist Journal.* A reprint of her first sci-fantasy set in a secondary world modeled after the Victorian age, Doctor Edmund Huntsfee's Perilous Expedition into the Heart of the Flood Plains, had been published as a stand-alone e-book.

Libby A. Smith — "Plunder in the Valley" — Libby A. Smith has a degree in English with an emphasis on creative writing from the University of Arkansas at Little Rock. She's previously had short stories and poetry published in *4StarStories.com, Caliber Comics, Hanthercraft Publications, The Little Rock Free Press*, and other small press publications. She also penned a version of "The Legend of the Rainbow Bridge" for counted cross stitch designer Sue Hillis. A sometimes actress, Libby lives in Little Rock, Arkansas with three fat and sassy cats.

Steve Cook — "The Clockwork Dragon" — Steve Cook is from London, United Kingdom. He is a part-time writer, part-time teacher, currently dialing down on the latter so he can focus on the former. He is married and lives with his wife and cat.

Jim Reader — "Adventures of a Would-Be Gentleman of the Skies"— Jim Reader was orphaned as a child, and raised by a pack of wild corny dogs. They taught him having a stick up the bu... well, it's a bad thing, and that the value of grease and mystery meat is incalculable. He's previously been published in *The Ladies of Trade Town* (Harphaven Publishing, 2011), *Zombiefied! An Anthology of All Things Zombie* (Sky Warrior Publishing, LLC, 2011), and *Coming Together Arm in Arm in Arm* (Coming Together, 2012), as well as in other publications. Jim has self-published a novel, and a novella, on Amazon. He lives in Central Texas with his wife and their five dogs... normal dogs, not corny dogs.

Steven R. Southard — "A Clouded Affair" — Steven R. Southard's short stories appear in nine different anthologies including *Dead Bait, Quest for Atlantis,* and *Cheer Up, Universe!* He's the author of the What Man Hath Wrought series, with twelve stories at last count. An engineer and former submariner, Steve takes readers on voyages to far-off places aboard amazing vehicles accompanied by engaging characters. He has tampered with several genres including steampunk, clockpunk, science fiction, fantasy, and horror...and seems to have gotten away with it. Set sail for stevenrsouthard.com to learn more about his fictional adventures.

D Chang — "The Climbers" — D Chang is one of the editors at spacesquid.com ("your puny planet's finest scifi, experimental, and fantasy"). His superpowers are killing flies, defending the Oxford comma, and inventing useless ultimate frisbee throws. He has a blog at videogamewriter.com.

Wynelda Ann Deaver — "The Steampunk Garden" — Wynelda Ann Deaver resides in Northern California with her merry band of misfits. When she is not out training dragons, commandeering pirate ships or finding stolen treasures, she can be found with a pen in hand, scribbling furiously.

Steve Ruskin — "Lotus of Albion" — Steve Ruskin is a native of Colorado, where he currently lives. He has also lived in Cambridge, England and Berlin, Germany. He is an historian of science and technology, focusing on the Victorian period with an emphasis on the British Empire and the American West. He has been a university professor, a mountain bike guide, and a number of things in between. In addition to fiction he has written for academic and popular audiences in publications ranging from the American Journal of Physics to the Rocky Mountain News. You can find him at www.steveruskin.com.

K.C. Shaw — "And a Bottle of Rum…" — K. C. Shaw lives in East Tennessee with her cat, Jekyll, and a lot of books. Visit her website at kcshaw.net, and visit the Lizzy and Jo site at lizzyandjo.com.

Other Books from
Mocha Memoirs Press

Subject 82-42 by Ronald T. Jones

The Portal Guards by Marcia Colette

The River God's Bride

Mocha Descent by Drea Riley